Praise for Supplemental Needs

This is a richly textured, moving novel about a mother's journey after her son, Jacob, is prenatally diagnosed with Klinefelter syndrome, also known as 47,XXY chromosomal variation. Through learning what this diagnosis means for Jacob, Rachel discovers more about herself and the world around her than she ever thought possible in a way that is sure to inspire. This story will resonate with anyone who has a loved one with Klinefelter's or who has a family.

—Liz Hills, D.O., Family Practice

If you have never heard of X and Y Chromosome variations, welcome to the world's most common unheard of medical condition that impacts 1 in 500 individuals. Life is never how you expect it, and Ginnie Cover shows us that the world does not end when things do not go as planned. Life challenges make you smarter and stronger in ways that you could never imagine. Cheers to Ginnie for recognizing that chromosomal variations exist, celebrating our uniqueness, and cherishing the things that matter most in life.

—Carrie R.

Ginnie Cover shines a light on modern parenting. With prenatal testing becoming widespread, a book featuring a family receiving a diagnosis of a chromosomal difference is long overdue. The journey does not end with the birth of a child, it is just beginning. From early intervention to supplemental needs trusts, you'll walk with the Gold family and be glad you did.

—Carol Meerschaert
Executive Director
AXYS (genetic.org)

VIRGINIA ISAACS COVER

I was very impressed by the way the author educated us about Klinefelter syndrome, while portraying a loving and supportive family and extended family dealing with real life issues. The description of the parents; emotions, decision-making, and their own education was especially good and - importantly - educates readers. The wrap-up at the end of the book was excellent. The workplace shenanigans were amusing and all too true to life. This was a fast read that kept me engaged all the way through.

—Marge Ort

Supplemental Needs

Supplemental Needs

a novel

Virginia Isaacs Cover

BOLD
STORY
PRESS

CHEVY CHASE, MD

Bold Story Press, Chevy Chase, MD 20815
www.boldstorypress.com

All proceeds from book sales of *Supplemental Needs* go to support
these resources benefiting individuals with X and Y chromosome
variations.

First edition published January 2024

Library of Congress Control Number: 2023911239

ISBN: 978-1-954805-52-1 (paperback)
ISBN: 978-1-954805-53-8 (e-book)

Cover design by designchik.net
Interior design by Sue Balcer
Author photo by Kimberly Beyer

Printed in the United States of America
10 9 8 7 6 5 4 3 2 1

To my boys: Al, Josh, John, and Cooper

Much as most people want to know what lies in the future, there are times when that future brings pain and uncertainty.

The morning starts the same as any other in the Gold household. Dave lets me luxuriate in bed for an extra fifteen minutes while he dresses and showers. I am lying on my back, holding my hand on my expanding belly to catch the tiniest movement of the baby, our unexpected good fortune.

The bedroom door slowly squeaks open. I close my eyes so that Adam, our six-year-old, will think that he is surprising Mommy when he climbs into the bed with me. Adam slides under the covers. Then he puts his hand on my tummy, remembering that we told him last week that he would become a big brother.

"Mommy," he asks. "When will the baby come out to see us?"

I open my eyes, grin at him, then pull him close to me. "Honey, babies come out when they're ready. Probably about when we get snow. Time to get up and get ready for school."

I toss off the covers and sit up on the side of the bed. Now that I'm in the second trimester, my pregnancy nausea is almost gone, but I still can't stomach coffee. Putting on a robe, I take Adam down to the kitchen.

"Tea, madam?" Dave asks. Dave doesn't drink coffee, only the occasional cup of strong Irish breakfast tea. He already has the tea brewing in our china teapot, a ritual that he instituted as soon as I discovered that I was pregnant again. I see that he has two slices of bread in the toaster. I sit down, and Dave pours my tea with a flourish, then lightly butters the toast for me. Monday is Dave's morning to get Adam off to school. He has cocoa and Cheerios ready for Adam. My only responsibility on Monday is to get myself into the office.

"Mommy, is the baby a boy or a girl?" asks Adam.

"We'll know soon," I tell him. Addressing Dave, I add, "Trudy tells me that results from amniocentesis usually take two to three weeks, so it could even be this week."

Prenatal testing was recommended because I'm forty. My obstetrician, Dr. Trudy Marshall, apologetically referred to me as an "elderly multigravida," a mom who becomes pregnant again after age thirty-five. But after two years of infertility treatment, including three failed rounds of in vitro fertilization, this pregnancy was a surprise.

This was such a wanted pregnancy, so unexpected. Although Adam was conceived within a few months after I stopped taking birth control pills, when we tried to have a second child, I simply didn't become pregnant. After a year of trying, we were given the diagnosis of secondary infertility. Another eighteen months of IVF treatment produced only miscarriages. We were emotionally and financially drained by the experience.

We finally decided that Adam, a terrific little boy, spirited, independent, and cuddly, provides us with a complete little family. Weeks after deciding to be a one-child family, we took a trip to Disney World. We all needed a break as well as some normalcy following the terrible attack the previous fall on the World Trade Center in Manhattan, only twenty-five miles south of White Plains. I began feeling nauseated while we were away and finally concluded that this might be pregnancy, not stress. On returning home, a pregnancy test showed a blue line, indicating that I was expecting.

Even though both Dave and I regard this as a miracle pregnancy, we agreed before having the testing that we would be unable to raise a child with a significant disability. But I can't bear to think there could be a problem, so I haven't. This morning, I'm anxious to get into the office to prepare for a meeting with the psychiatric emergency room staff. I am the director for administration and finance for the Department of Psychiatry at Hudson Valley Medical Center, a new hospital and medical school established in Westchester County, just north of New York. I want to look put together for this meeting, so I choose one of my new maternity dresses to wear. Nothing left from when I was pregnant with Adam is suitable. Six years ago, I was a research coordinator at the University of Michigan; maternity jeans and sandals were perfectly acceptable. I select a navy coat dress and add a colorful scarf.

Monday morning is routine: I read my email and work on my presentation for staffing the psychiatric ER. Mid-morning, I need the snack that I packed to satisfy my growing appetite and head to the lunchroom to get it from the refrigerator. Halfway down the hall, I hear my phone ring.

"Would you get that, Karen?" I call as I walk into the lunchroom. Karen is my assistant, a gem without whom the Psychiatry department would probably cease to function. New to this position four years ago, I hired her as she was finishing a business program at a nearby community college. She originally came to the department on a temporary appointment, answering phones at the reception desk. But she asked to take on other projects, and she showed so much initiative and organizational instinct that I tapped her to help me with personnel, budgeting, and all the other administrative tasks.

"I'll hold it for you," Karen tells me. "It's Dr. Marshall."

My amnio results, I assume. I hurry back to my office and pick up the call.

"Hi, Trudy. So, is it a boy or a girl?"

There is a slight pause before she replies, "It's a boy."

Another pause.

"Rachel, you remember seeing the genetic counselor before the amnio? She probably discussed a few other conditions that could be picked up on genetic testing. Having to do with extra X or Y chromosomes, and usually not as severe as something like Down syndrome. Your result shows a boy with an extra X chromosome. It's called Klinefelter syndrome."

I get up from my chair holding the receiver, walk around the desk, and close my door. My throat tightens.

"You still there?" asks Trudy. "Humans usually have two sex chromosomes, either an X and a Y for a male or two X's for a female. Any difference in that number, two, is referred to as sex chromosome aneuploidy."

I tell Trudy that I vaguely remember this, but I can't recall anything else that the counselor told me. I picture the woman. Her name was Heather. She wore a green corduroy peasant dress and Birkenstocks. I noticed a University of Vermont coffee mug on her desk. That fit. I think back to the karyotype, a photo of chromosomes, that Heather showed me. I remember vaguely the X and Y chromosomes, and a photo showing three chromosomes.

Trudy tells me that my baby boy has Klinefelter syndrome, also called 47, XXY, or forty-seven chromosomes instead of the usual forty-six for a human. She tells me that she is reading from a genetics text. It states that men with Klinefelter syndrome tend to be tall and that they are almost always infertile. They may have slightly reduced IQ's, about fifteen points lower on average, when compared with siblings, although mental retardation is rare.

Often, children with Klinefelter have delayed speech, as well as learning disabilities, low muscle tone, poor coordination, and, sometimes, emotional problems, gender dysphoria, and sexual insecurity.

I sit in my chair with a feeling of unreality, of time slowing down, of my happiness at being pregnant shattered by this sudden knowledge. This isn't the perfect baby we dreamed about. I can't think of anything to say or to ask; my mind is numb. I try to absorb this terrible new development.

A sudden lump in my throat makes it hard to speak. I take a deep breath and emit a strangled-sounding question, "What are my options, Trudy? What do I tell Dave?"

"Of course, you have the option of terminating the pregnancy," Trudy replies. "This would be a second trimester abortion that we would need to do in the hospital. But the range of functioning in Klinefelter syndrome has a great deal of variation. I think you and Dave need to speak with the genetic counselor as soon as possible. In fact, Soundview told me that they have an opening this morning. They can see you as soon as you're able to get to their office."

"Yes. I'll get hold of Dave," I tell her. I can feel my pulse beating in my ears. I feel a wave of nausea.

"There's no need for you to confirm the appointment, Rachel. We'll do that for you. I do need to tell you that given that you're in the second trimester, if you don't want to continue the pregnancy, we'd need to schedule the termination within a few days. I know that this is a terribly difficult situation, and I don't want to add to the pressure, but you will need to make your decision quickly. Let me know how the appointment goes. Call the office and tell them to find me. If you get the service, ask them to call me at home."

We hang up, and I call Dave. He's still at home after dropping Adam at school, finishing a load of laundry, and attending some conference calls for the law clinic that he supervises.

"Dave, I got a call from Trudy. The baby's a boy." My voice catches, but I force myself to continue. "Oh, Dave, he has an extra chromosome. Something called Klinefelter syndrome. We have an appointment this afternoon at Soundview to see the genetic counselor. Dave, I knew this was too good to be true."

Dave jumps in, "Wait. Wait. What do we know about this diagnosis? What did Trudy tell you?"

Very briefly I tell him—low muscle tone, speech delay, learning disabilities, infertility. The characteristics all jumble together, superimposed on a baby fluttering in my womb. My anxiety makes speaking difficult. It's taking over my breathing, my voice. I can't really continue.

"Honey, I'll stay home and wait for you. We should be finished at Soundview in time to pick up Adam. Rach, we'll get through this. I love you. See you at home." Dave sounds as shaken as I am.

"I don't know how," I reply. "I just don't know."

I hang up and try to think about what I will tell Karen. I need to have her cancel the meeting this afternoon.

My boss, Dr. Jim Costa, is the chair of Psychiatry. He will have to know why I can't make the meeting. I gather my briefcase and my coat and walk over to Karen's cubicle. Leaning down, I tell her that we have news from my OB that the baby has an extra chromosome. Not Down's, but another syndrome. I need to leave to talk with a genetic counselor. I ask her to keep this quiet, to talk confidentially with Jim. I write "Klinefelter syndrome" on a piece of paper and tell her to give this to Jim.

Karen slowly rises from her chair and comes around her desk to hug me.

"I'm so sorry, Rachel," Karen says quietly. "You have been through so much trying to get pregnant. I'll be praying for you and Dave."

We look at each other. I can't say anything. I feel tears coming on. I nod, turn, and leave the office.

The ride down the elevator and the walk through the parking structure pass in slow motion. I unlock my car, get in, and start the engine. I drive out through the exit, waving my magnetic card to lift the gate. My world has changed in minutes. I'm unable to cry.

I drive the four miles to our house, a modest brick Cape Cod on Church Street in White Plains, a close-in, suburban town north of New York City. For a minute, I sit in my car in the driveway, looking at Adam's swing set in the backyard. I wonder if we will be installing a baby swing next spring. The azaleas and rhododendrons in the yard are ablaze in reds and purples. I notice the new green leaves on the trees. Taking a deep breath, I exit the car.

Dave meets me as I enter through the side kitchen door. He already has on his jacket. We silently hug. I am not only overwhelmed, but am also green with nausea.

"Dave, I must get something into my stomach before we leave. Maybe some toast. No more tea. You could give me some of that seltzer in the fridge. I just can't believe this. I feel numb."

Dave reaches into the breadbox to make me toast. He gets me a glass of seltzer, butters the toast. We're both silent. I finish the toast, put my coat on, and give Dave the car keys because I'm not sure I am a competent driver at this point. It's as if I am looking at us from outside, observing this couple headed off to determine if we become a family of four or remain a family of three. We drive to Maternal-Fetal Medicine in a nondescript medical building attached to the hospital. Dave opens the door to the office suite for me. The waiting room is empty. We walk to the reception window. The receptionist looks up, a concerned expression on her face.

"Mr. and Mrs. Gold? The genetic counselor, Heather, will be right out for you. Please take a seat. Dr. Berggren is also here today, and he'll spend some time with you."

She smiles at us. I hang up my coat because my pregnancy makes me perpetually overheated. Dave shrugs that he would rather keep his leather jacket on. I look around the room: modern, blond oak furnishings. Mauve and gray upholstery and carpeting. Light-filtering blinds. Then I notice that there are photos of babies on the walls: singletons, twins, even a set of triplets. They are all smiling and looking totally normal. No apparent genetic defects. How unfortunate for expectant parents here to discuss their baby's genetic anomaly. I can't think of him as a mere fetus. He's a baby, his little kicks reminding me that he is there.

Heather opens the door to the waiting area and, indicating for us to follow her, says, "I am so glad that you could come right away. We're going to meet first with Dr. Berggren. Here, in the conference room."

Heather is as I remember her. This time she's wearing a jean skirt, a Fair Isle sweater, penny loafers instead of Birkenstocks, and a calm, competent manner. I now wish that I had paid closer attention to the "other" genetic conditions that amniocentesis might identify. We're here to discuss one of the "other." It doesn't seem real. I wish this excruciating experience would vanish.

She ushers us into a small room with the same mauve and gray color scheme, a conference table, and high-backed leather chairs. Fortunately, the paintings on the wall have a nautical theme. We don't have to have this discussion with adorable and presumably normal babies looking down at us. I sit down next to Dave. He reaches for my hand and squeezes. I find myself beginning to cry, silently. Heather reaches for a box of tissues and hands it to me.

Just then, Dr. Berggren enters the room from a side door, holding a file folder. He's a tall, gray-haired man. I notice that he has on an outfit identical to Dave's: khakis, light blue Oxford shirt, tie slightly askew. He acknowledges us and takes a seat as he begins speaking.

"I know that this must be very difficult for you, Mr. and Mrs. Gold. Please tell me what Dr. Marshall has told you about the amnio findings and what you understand about your baby's genetic condition."

I start, realizing that my voice is strained and sad. "Dr. Marshall called this morning and told me that we have a boy. He has an extra X chromosome. Something called Klinefelter syndrome. He's likely to be tall, possibly learning disabled, infertile. I don't believe that I've ever heard of this condition before, even though I have a master's in public health. It must be rare."

"Actually," responds Heather, "Klinefelter syndrome affects about one in six hundred live male births. Extra X and Y chromosome conditions are as common as Down syndrome."

Dr. Berggren pulls what I recognize as a karyotype from the folder.

"This is a photo of the fetus's chromosomes," he says, showing it to us. Using his pencil, he points to two chromosomes that looked like skewed X's. "These are the two X chromosomes where there should be only one."

He pulls several photocopies from the folder. "I have some summaries of information here from genetics textbooks. They all say much the same thing."

He shows us a page with a full-frontal photo of a naked man with his eyes blocked by a black box. Using his pencil again, Dr. Berggren points out the man's hips and his breasts.

"This morning, I spoke with a colleague who's an endocrinologist," he continues. "He has several patients with Klinefelter syndrome. His experience is that while they don't have mental retardation, as you see with Down syndrome, they don't do very well in school. Some of them have severe psychiatric problems, and few marry. In fact, because their levels of both testosterone and estrogen are aberrant, and because the hormone levels influence brain development, this is thought to contribute to homosexuality. In some cases, they have gender dysphoria or transsexual identity, although I don't know if this is simply speculation or if it's confirmed by research."

He stops and looks around the table, perhaps gauging whether this extraordinary information is registering with Dave and me. We say nothing, waiting for him to continue. I realize that I'm on emotion and information overload.

"My general impression is that these men can have challenging lives with not a lot of happiness. On the other hand, they are usually healthy. I understand that you had treatment for infertility, so I'd understand if you want to continue this pregnancy. But I consider it my duty to give you a realistic portrayal of Klinefelter syndrome. I will tell you that most of my patients with the education levels that you and your husband have attained decide to terminate their pregnancies."

Dave interrupts, "Aren't there articles with case studies or population studies that we can read? This is shattering news to us. I'd like to see clinical data. Are there any families we can talk to before making a decision to have an abortion?"

Heather has been looking increasingly uncomfortable. Now she jumps in, opening a folder containing legal-size copies, pulling them out to show us.

"There hasn't been a great deal of research on sex chromosome aneuploidy until recently," she tells us, handing a sheaf of photocopies to Dave, who begins paging through them. "I've copied a few recent studies for you. These are studies of forty thousand cases of newborn screenings carried out in the US, Canada, and Scotland. I think you'll see that there's significant variation in the levels of functioning of these kids. While two-thirds may have some special education needs, one-third have no learning disability. Some only discover the extra chromosome when having an infertility workup."

Dr. Berggren weighs in again, "Heather is admittedly more optimistic about the prospects for a child's future when we know that disability is a likely outcome. I'm more pragmatic about the impact on a family of having a child with a good probability of disability. Klinefelter boys have IQs that are about fifteen points lower than those of their siblings. They often can't succeed in the same sort of professions as the rest of their family members. On the other hand, you live in Westchester County where there are excellent schools. You can probably give this child all the benefits of special education and thera-py if he needs it. When he's ready to start puberty, you'll want to take him to a pediatric endocrinologist. Some boys go through puberty on their own. Others need help with extra testosterone. But, eventually, most men with Klinefelter syndrome need supplemental testosterone, al-though the treatment won't reverse infertility."

He pauses, and looks over his reading glasses, partic-ularly at me. Then I notice him checking his watch. Tap-ping his pencil. I wonder if he does this sort of prenatal counseling visit often. He doesn't seem especially com-fortable delivering this news.

"Unless you have additional questions for me, I'll leave you to discuss this in more detail with Heather. But I do want to warn you that there are many people who believe that men with Klinefelter syndrome tend to sexu-al deviance, even pedophilia or other criminal behavior. That may not be true, because the studies were based on inmate populations and were therefore biased. None-theless, if you decide to continue this pregnancy, I feel I should warn you never to tell anyone."

He stands, walks over to shake my hand and Dave's, and leaves the conference room, closing the door. I look at Dave. We'll probably have a discussion later in the car about Dr. Berggren's bedside manner or lack thereof. For now, I want to hear what Heather has to say. I want to look at the data. What are the real chances of a disability that we couldn't handle? And is this a shameful diagnosis that we will have to hide from everyone, including our families?

We wait for Heather to give us some good news, something to hang onto. Baby Boy Gold is turning his slow somersaults in my uterus, lightly kicking, as if he wants to make sure I understand who he is. Heather smiles at us. She starts speaking, calmly and softly, in contrast to Dr. Berggren, who was so direct.

"I know that it's difficult to have hopes and dreams for a perfect baby and then, suddenly, learn that there's a chance that baby may have some special needs. In your case, this is all the more difficult because you had prenatal testing to rule out a more significant disorder, such as Down syndrome or even more severe and fatal conditions like Edwards or Patau syndromes. Instead, you learn that your boy has something much milder that may or may not cause some disability—usually not intellectual disability, but perhaps slower development or perhaps a learning disability, perhaps not."

There are tears sliding down Dave's face. I reach for a tissue for him and take his hand. Heather pauses, giving us time to consider what she is saying, then adds, "We aren't talking here about Tay-Sachs, where the child will deteriorate and die after a few years. Or anencephaly, where the fetus develops with only a brain stem. We aren't talking about a child who can't grow up to become independent and self-supporting. But it appears that these boys do mature more slowly. They often take longer to graduate from college, if they do attend, and longer to establish themselves in careers."

My voice cracks with emotion as I ask, "If some men don't even know that they have this genetic disorder, then it must not be so terribly bad. What percentage, do you know, find out only because they experience infertility?"

Heather replies, "We don't know for sure. Maybe ten percent. Another ten percent find out due to prenatal testing. For the rest, there may be genetic testing for other reasons. This isn't a genetic disorder where children look syndrome-y. Just remember that some have significant learning disabilities, while others obtain graduate degrees."

I can't help but wonder if Heather has kids. She is wearing a wedding band and a simple diamond. I also see a multicolor, knotted cord bracelet peeking out from her sweater sleeve that looks like something a child would make at summer camp.

Dave looks at me and asks, "What do you think? I'm fine with a child who may have a mild disability. After all, does parenthood guarantee that we'll have a Supreme Court justice as opposed to an electrician or a cashier? Does it matter? Can he have a happy and satisfying life? Isn't that the question here?"

I am crying too much to respond. An event like this certainly does strip bare one's attitude toward parenthood. Choice isn't theoretical anymore. I have always been a feminist but how could I possibly abort this little baby floating in my uterus because he might have learning disabilities?

Dave, Heather, and I continue talking about parenthood and the prospects of having a child who may need early intervention or special education services, but as we talk, it no longer seems like the dreadful tragedy that I envisioned on first talking with Trudy. We look over the case studies from the March of Dimes, but I'm very bothered by Dr. Berggren's advice not to tell anyone. Why would this genetic condition be so stigmatized?

"Heather, why the emphasis on keeping the diagnosis quiet? What's so shameful about an extra chromosome?"

Heather is quiet, clearly deciding how to answer.

"I struggle with this myself, and with how candid I should be when counseling families," she says. "Many, especially fathers, equate fertility with masculinity. Particularly in some cultures, infertility brings into question a male's manhood. There's also some evidence that homosexuality may be somewhat more common in XXY than in the general population of men. We know it's a distinct minority, but no one seems to have studied this question, nor the question of what portion might have gender dysphoria, or live as women."

Dave asks, "Can you tell us what percentage of expectant parents terminate? And is it because of possible learning disability, or is it because of the sexual issues?"

"I can tell you that some studies indicate that as many as seventy-five percent of fetuses with XXY are terminated," Heather responds. "I can't tell you why."

"Infertility or the possibility of a gay son doesn't really bother me," answers Dave. "I'm much more concerned that we're able to handle learning disabilities."

"Same with me," I say.

We continue our discussion. Heather is a great listener. It's also clear that she can't make this decision for us. Only Dave and I can determine if this is a manageable disability, should there be any special needs. Heather also cautions us about information on the internet. She tells us that there's one small advocacy organization, Klinefelter Syndrome Association, or KSA, that has some resources including support groups, a listserv, and a newsletter. Otherwise, she warns us against looking at sensational pages that exploit myths about XXY. This information isn't scientifically vetted, she tells us. We continue to talk with Heather, taking down contact information for what few resources exist for expectant parents like Dave and me, thrown an unwelcome curve ball, a major diversion from the joy of pregnancy.

Then Dave looks at me and squeezes my hand. He's silent for a moment and then says, "Heather, thank you for all the time you've given us. And for these articles. I don't really have any more questions. Rachel?"

I shake my head that I don't. I know we're ready to leave and to make our decision. We push back our chairs, stand, and Heather follows us to the waiting room, where I get my coat. None of us speak. Heather hugs me, then Dave. And we leave the office.

CHAPTER TWO

APRIL 2002

We get into the car, both silent with our thoughts as we head back to White Plains.

After several miles, Dave asks me, "Do you think we should keep this to ourselves or tell our families?"

I respond, "I'd rather say nothing right now. If a problem develops with speech or anything else, we can always tell our families then. But why worry our parents if it's really nothing? Let's keep it quiet. But if he does have some issues, I can't imagine keeping it all to ourselves, as though he's some sort of freak."

I call Trudy's office as soon as we arrive home. She's on the line within minutes, and I tell her that Heather was knowledgeable and a good listener. We still haven't determined if we're going ahead with the pregnancy, but we do know now that any disability will be milder, and I feel more hopeful. Trudy tells me that she will support us either way. She also reminds me that we should not wait more than two or three days to give her our decision.

Dave is reheating some soup for our lunch. He has his legal clinic to supervise this afternoon and needs to leave in about fifteen minutes.

"I'm not going back to work," I tell him as I play with my soup spoon. "I can pick up Adam from after-school. I'm just not in any shape to go back into the office."

Dave stoops to give me a kiss. "Love you. We'll pick this up again this evening."

I decide that a walk in the neighborhood will be refreshing, if not head-clearing. I change into sweatpants, which now barely fit around my middle, and a maternity T-shirt that has an arrow pointed to my bump and the word "BABY." I reflect how this pregnancy is probably more constant to me than to Dave. I walk around with it, feeling the fetus kicking, knowing that there is a little being in there.

Before heading off to pick up Adam at school, I decide to check out the advocacy organization that Heather mentioned. The website is amateurish and doesn't seem to have been updated recently. There are a few newsletters to read and photos from a conference held a year ago in California. I dial the 800 number for the help line but get a recording telling me that the volunteer who answers is away for three weeks. The voice mailbox is full.

Dave and I continue our discussions that evening after Adam is in bed. Dave's main concern is the extent of learning disability we may encounter. While Dave falls into a sound sleep shortly after we get into bed, I do not get more than two hours' of rest. Even that is interrupted by my awakening, crying, at three in the morning, remembering what we are in the process of deciding. But I want to keep this baby more than anything. I know that I will not have another chance at pregnancy.

Quietly creeping downstairs, I make myself a cup of tea while paging through the photocopies of the multisite studies of children with extra X and Y chromosomes. Maybe Dave and I are putting too much faith in statistics, but it does appear that the chances of having a child with severe disability are small. Severe disability to this couple whose lives revolve around academics really means intellectual disability. I don't think that I view infertility due to XXY through the same lens as the parents who seem to focus on that as their greatest concern. The studies feature vignettes of the lives of over thirty children, some followed through age sixteen. Based on probability, which sounds devoid of emotion, our chances of having a child who can have a happy life are good, I think. I hear Dave coming downstairs. It's about four in the morning.

"Did you get any sleep?" Dave asks. "I see you're reading through the stats on these kids."

"Terrible. I may have slept from one to three. Then I woke up crying."

Dave kisses me, wrapping his arms around my shoulders.

"Rach, let's sit on the sofa. I'll get us both some more tea, and we can talk."

I move into the living room with the photocopies while Dave is putting water on. I also hear him making toast. He comes in with a tray for us complete with honey, sets it on the coffee table, and sits down next to me. He strokes my cheek, and we're silent for a few moments, holding hands. Then Dave starts looking at the March of Dimes studies.

I watch my husband. He's wearing faded plaid flannel pajama pants, and a worn looking Stanford basketball T-shirt. He's medium height with dark, curly hair in what we used to call a Jewish Afro. He keeps it shorter now than when we first met, probably because his hairline is beginning to recede. Dave's a law professor, with a specialty in land-use planning. He has always been a community activist, convinced that housing equality is key to providing economic development and educational achievement for underserved groups. He teaches property law, but his love is the school's legal clinic that he oversees. The clinic supports legal challenges to restrictive zoning throughout Westchester County and promotes affordable housing in one of the country's most expensive real estate markets. I know that he values academic achievement and that he wonders how a child with learning disabilities would do in a household like ours. Adam taught himself to read by age four. His kindergarten teacher has him doing second grade math to keep him engaged.

"What're your thoughts?" Dave asks. "In some ways, it's more your decision than mine. I also want this baby very much, but I don't want to put us in a position of possibly taking on severe learning disabilities and emotional problems. Is that fair to this child? Is that fair to Adam?"

While I had settled in over the past hour with the thought that we could give this child a pretty good life, I suddenly wonder if Dave is deciding the opposite—that it's too risky; that we should be content with one child. I decide to tell him exactly what I am thinking. Much of my thoughts are colored by revulsion at destroying the tiny being in my belly. He's somersaulting and occasionally kicking, fluttering away. I decide that I cannot have a termination.

"I simply can't have an abortion. I may have been a feminist since age eight, but this has nothing to do with feminism. I'm making this decision as a mom. My reading of the studies makes me optimistic about a reasonably normal life for this child. Learning disabilities are so common anyway. We could have a kid with completely normal chromosomes who might develop schizophrenia or childhood cancer. There are never any guarantees."

Dave takes a deep breath. "Then I'm in agreement. I appreciate that you, not I, are carrying this baby. I do have concerns about raising two brothers who may have very different abilities, but it seems that wildly different is not likely to be the case. And they'll be six years apart anyway. Intellectual disability is rare. I don't think we need to fear that. I'm a little concerned about the tendency to ADHD, to anxiety, to depression. That seems to affect lots of these kids, but I want to think that we could be fully supportive of a child with special needs."

I'm sipping my tea, nibbling on the toast, and looking out the window at the headlight of a cyclist passing the house. How different today is from yesterday morning when I didn't know any of this and didn't need to make a decision.

"You're comfortable with this?" I ask. "I don't think that I can live for another day with the uncertainty of what we're going to do. I want to decide. To tell Trudy we're continuing."

"Then I'm with you." Dave takes my hand and moves toward me for a kiss. I nestle against him. It's still very early, and I'm suddenly so sleepy that I curl up on one end of the sofa. When I awaken, I find that Dave has covered me with a blanket. He and Adam are coming down the stairs.

"Should we tell him?" Dave asks me.

I nod.

"Adam," says Dave. "You're going to have a little brother."

Later in the morning, I quietly tell Karen and my boss, Jim, about the diagnosis and explain that Klinefelter syndrome seems unlikely to cause significant disability and that we are continuing the pregnancy.

CHAPTER THREE

APRIL 2002

In the days following our prenatal diagnosis, Dave and I adjust to this new uncertainty. Although Heather advised us against looking at much of the information on Klinefelter syndrome that we find online, I find myself reading through some of the websites addressing XXY. There are postings that build on the myth of criminality, even pedophilia. I remind myself that these are based on old, discredited research using institutionalized populations. We find a raging debate among adult men with XXY—the term they seem to prefer over "Klinefelter syndrome"—about whether the syndrome makes them intersex. There are also posts describing gender dysphoria or uncertain sexual orientation. I wonder how widespread these issues are.

Through KSA, I find an online community of parents and join a listserv. Other parents warn us that we will see a variety of viewpoints online. Many parents seem focused on infertility as a major concern. Some are uncomfortable with the minority of adult XXY's who identify as intersex or transgender, or who are openly gay, but this usually isn't commented on openly—just brief posts to phone or message privately. And everywhere there seem to be concerns about disclosing the diagnosis, even to family members.

I feel lucky that we live in the New York metropolitan area, where there's greater acceptance of LGBTQ individuals, but it does bother me that we're advised not to tell anyone of this extra chromosome. Our families are likely to be accepting of learning disability, and I'm sure that possible differences in sexual orientation or identity wouldn't bother my liberal, barely religious family; I'm less sure about Dave's modern Orthodox extended family. We decide together, however, that because Klinefelter syndrome encompasses such a broad spectrum of functioning, we don't need to say anything at this point. If there is developmental delay later, then we'll tell our families about the extra chromosome.

We moved to White Plains from Ann Arbor, Michigan, four years ago. Dave failed to get tenure after six years at the University of Michigan, where he was an assistant professor in the Law School. The move from Michigan to New York was wrenching, but we made the best of it. We both landed positions at the newly established State University of New York–Hudson Valley. One could argue that by leaving the University of Michigan, with its ultra-competitive atmosphere, for younger and more innovative institutions, we both advanced our careers.

White Plains wasn't unfamiliar to me. My father grew up in White Plains, in an extended family of immigrants from Eastern Europe. They were Orthodox Jews who established themselves in the New York area, starting small businesses, such as tailoring, plumbing, and groceries. The men went to shul, and the women kept kosher kitchens. And no one except my father married outside of Judaism. When he brought home his war bride from Northern Ireland, the daughter of a conservative Presbyterian minister, his family members were not initially welcoming to the shiksa. But Dad's later success as a managing engineer, the birth of two granddaughters, and Mum's eventual conversion to Judaism redeemed Dad in their eyes. When I was a child, we visited New York each summer for a week. There are still a few relatives here who haven't relocated to Florida, or California, or Israel, including Dad's favorite sister, Aunt Toni. She dotes on Adam, and she is thrilled to be expecting another grandnephew.

This Monday, I'm headed into work for an early morning staff meeting. We have a guest presenter, the new associate dean for finance, Cameron Ellis. I already know a great deal about him, having sat on the committee that recruited him from Duke. I hope that New York State's micromanagement of all state universities doesn't cause him to run screaming back to the private sector. So far, however, he exhibits no undue impatience with the layers of decision making above him.

My position at the Hudson Valley Medical Center is a bit difficult to describe for those who are unfamiliar with American medical schools. Departments are established by discipline, such as internal medicine, surgery or radiology. Each department is responsible for teaching medical students, supervising residents and fellows, conducting research, and operating the inpatient and ambulatory services of the hospital. I serve as the administrator for finance and operations of the Department of Psychiatry, so I oversee budgets, personnel, policy, and procedure for a department with nearly two hundred employees. Yet, I trained to specialize in public health programs and research, and sometimes I miss being involved in the subject matter of my work. I also chafe a bit when it is implied that I am just "support staff." I usually chair administrative meetings, but today I've asked Alyce McCall to make up the agenda and run the meeting. Alyce is a new graduate of a health care management master's program. She did an internship at Hudson Valley, then was hired into the Department of Psychiatry in the position of residency coordinator. The chair of Psychiatry, Dr. James Costa, wanted someone familiar with SUNY. I deferred to him, although Alyce wasn't my first choice. Increasingly, I find myself irritated by her constant desire to impress everyone.

This meeting doesn't do anything to increase my comfort with Alyce. After an awkward introduction of the new dean, accompanied by an unneeded summary of her own qualifications, Alyce turns the floor over to Cameron. He gives a slide presentation of budget and administration priorities, concentrating on compliance with Medicare billing standards.

He does a good overview but is constantly interrupted by Alyce, who reiterates all of the measures she has taken to ensure compliance. I'm impatient with this performance. The other supervisors are unsuccessfully trying not to look bored. One examines the hem of her skirt; another doodles. Dr. Lynne Wexler, who oversees the residency program, sneaks glances at the clock.

There's a pause in the discussion. I decide to grab it to help move the meeting to a conclusion.

"Dean Ellis, thank you for taking time out of your busy schedule. Compliance is one of the things that we consider carefully in carrying out our clinical programs, as you've heard. Our Pleasantville site will be opening next month. We've taken advantage of video technology to allow attending physicians to supervise therapy sessions. You may want to visit to see it yourself."

Cameron rises to his feet, smiles and shakes hands with those sitting around him. He and Dr. Wexler exit the conference room into the hall. Alyce scurries to catch up with them as they walk toward the elevators. Two supervisors roll their eyes, and I give them a hint of a grin. Anything more would be unprofessional.

After the meeting, I turn to my inbox. All looks routine until I reach a memo from Alyce. I scan it quickly, determining that she seems to want a new title and a promotion for herself, even though she has only been in her current position for six months. Not only that, she is also proposing to report directly to the residency director with a dotted line to me. I take a deep breath. My gut instinct during her recruitment was that she wouldn't be happy for long in an operations role, aspiring to move as quickly as possible into a position as department administrator. She doesn't realize she needs more experience.

This memo is an example of her lack of experience—she has addressed it to me, copying Dr. Wexler but with no copy to Dr. Costa, the chair of the department.

I'll have to bring this situation up later today when I have my weekly meeting with my boss. The founding chair of the Department of Psychiatry at Hudson Valley Medical School, Jim is a masterful psychiatrist and administrator. He's also been a superb mentor. We've been a good team during our four years developing a new training program.

I think I've been supportive of Alyce, going out of my way to help her understand the arcane ways of academic medical centers and the state university system. Her current job as residency coordinator is a good stepping stone to another position in the future. She is not yet ready for a promotion, however, and I'm not sure she realizes she is pulling away a major area of my responsibility. In effect, she is proposing that we be co-administrators.

Just then, Karen enters my office doorway, arms crossed. "May I come in? I'd like to discuss something."

Karen is tall and slim. She keeps her hair tied back in a ponytail, probably because her day starts at the gym. She runs marathons and lifts weights competitively, but she's also an expert knitter. She's wearing one of the tunics she knit last fall with an owl pin. She loves owls. Glass and pottery owls decorate her cubicle.

Karen shuts the door, sits down in one of the guest chairs, and says, "I've been a little concerned over a number of things that Alyce has been saying, and then she put that memo on my desk. You've seen it? She's been pretty critical of things around here. I think that you should know. It almost seems that she thinks she could do your job better than you. She's told several people that she wants to report directly to Dr. Wexler, not you. And she also implies that given your pregnancy and the maternity leave you'll take, the office needs reorganization."

I'm silent for a moment before asking, "You've heard the other comments first-hand?"

"Yes," Karen replies. "She stops by frequently, and if she notices that you aren't in the office, she inquires about where you are. Sometimes it seems to me that she's checking up on you. She brought this memo to me late last Friday, when you left early, and said something about making a suggestion for reorganization so that your maternity leave would go smoothly. I couldn't help it. I read the memo. I think what she's proposing is outrageous."

"Well, thanks, Karen," I tell her. "If Alyce is questioning my commitment to my job, and being public about it, I may need you to speak with Dr. Costa about this. Do you feel comfortable telling him exactly what you have heard her say?"

"Absolutely," Karen replies. "I don't think this is good for the office. She hasn't made too many friends here. Most of us think she has a pretty high opinion of herself."

I tell her, "I'll speak with Dr. Costa at my one o'clock. If we need to have you come in, you'll be here? I hate stuff like this. Why can't she settle down and do her job?"

At one, I walk the short distance to the chair's office. His assistant nods at me to go in. I sit down in front of his expansive teak desk. He has a corner office with windows overlooking the medical center campus. There are the expected framed diplomas and certificates on the walls, textbooks filling the bookshelves. There's also an extensive collection of colorful folk art and sculpture that he collects on his annual medical missions to Central America.

As soon as he is off the phone, I tell him, "Dean Ellis did a nice job of giving a general overview of his budget priorities and of the compliance issue. He's going to be a valuable asset to the medical center. But I'm a bit concerned about a memo that I received today."

I hand him the memo.

"Did you have any notice that this was in the works?" I ask.

Jim scans through the memo, frowning as he reaches the section where Alyce requests a promotion, and a direct reporting line to Dr. Wexler.

"No, I know nothing of this," he answers. "It isn't going to happen. I can take care of this directly with Lynne. Why do you think someone who has been here for six months is proposing this out of the blue?"

I then tell him about Karen's visit to my office this morning, and about her revelations regarding Alyce's comments.

"Karen says that these statements are pretty public, and that Alyce seems to be suggesting that once I have the baby, the office will have to be reorganized because, for some reason, I won't be able to be effective anymore."

Jim looks at me, smiles, and says firmly and directly, "Alyce has a surprisingly dated take on working motherhood. Don't let this weigh you down. I'm going to make certain that she knows exactly how administrative decisions are made in Psychiatry. She's totally out of line. I'll speak with Karen and then with Dr. Wexler to determine if this has passed the point where we may have to ask her to leave, or whether her position here can be salvaged."

We then move on to other business. I'm relieved that Jim will make clear that Alyce's proposal is dead. In truth, this is a naive blunder on her part. Perhaps it's the result of wishful thinking that I will decide to stay home after my baby is born and that she can move into my position, having shown such initiative.

In the evening, after I've tucked Adam in and left him with Dave reading a story, the phone rings. It's my sister, Sarah, who's two years younger than I am. Sarah is the mother of three boys, sort of a fertility goddess, becoming pregnant each time she has her IUD removed. Sarah is an artist who continues to live in the counterculture of the seventies, well supported by her husband, an early success in Silicon Valley. Sarah's family lives on a plot of land in Menlo Park, California, where she raises organic produce, paints and sculpts, and serves as the brain center for a number of left-leaning political and social causes.

"So, how are you feeling?" Sarah asks.

"Great," I tell her, "now that I don't feel green for the better part of each day. The baby is getting active, doing the backstroke in there." Although Sarah and I are close, talking by phone at least weekly, Dave and I decided not to tell any of our relatives of the Klinefelter syndrome. We don't want to worry family members or send them looking online for information that may or may not be accurate.

"What's new in Menlo Park?" I ask.

"Oh, Rachel," Sarah sounds giddy. "I'm pregnant! Eight weeks. We'll have babies about ten weeks apart!"

I knew that she and Oren, her husband, were thinking of trying for a girl, but when I ask if she'll be having an ultrasound to determine the sex, Sarah tells me that the midwife practice she uses discourages the use of technology. At thirty-eight, Sarah is also of "advanced maternal age" and therefore at risk for genetic anomalies. I'm silent on that subject. I know she won't be having any prenatal testing unless it is an absolute medical necessity. We compare notes on pregnancies and update each other on our kids. Sarah tells me that she's about to call Mum and Dad to let them know. I hang up as Dave comes downstairs from Adam's room.

"You knew that Sarah and Oren were trying for a girl?" I ask. "Well, she's pregnant. Eight weeks."

"Be fruitful and multiply," Dave says. "Fill the Peninsula School with little left-wing geeks—who are also, by the way, astounding consumers of all the latest in technology and child enrichment materials."

Dave can be sarcastic about Sarah's and Oren's politically correct life and about the progressive private school where they send their kids, catering to Silicon Valley executives who can pay the astronomical tuition. With the help of a midwife, Sarah gave birth to her third son at home. She intends to do the same with this baby. I wish that I could have her absolute faith that everything will be fine.

This week is Passover, or Pesach. I was raised in the Midwest, where my family was part of the Jewish community in Beloit, a small industrial city in Wisconsin. We always invited my mother's sister, Margaret, and her large Italian/Irish family, plus other non-Jewish friends to provide a crowd at our Seder table. Now surrounded by Dad's extended family in White Plains and within a three-hour drive of Dave's family in Boston, we have started a dance of scheduling several months ahead. If my parents are flying out to join us, we negotiate whether to visit Dave's family in Boston for the first or the second night.

The issue here is that my mother is a convert to Judaism and my own family is casually observant, as many Reform Jews are. My father grew up as an Orthodox Jew, as did Dave in Boston. Both Dad and Dave, however, now identify as Reform. We might host family and friends who are either relaxed about keeping kosher or non-Jewish, or we might attend a Seder at the home of one of the relatives who not only keep kosher but also maintain special Passover dishes and cookware, preparing the kitchen and house in an elaborate ritual to rid it of chametz, or any leavened bread.

Dave's family typically doesn't come to us during Passover because we neither keep kosher nor prepare the kitchen. This year is an easy negotiation. My parents won't be here for Passover, and Passover occurs on the weekend, so we will have both Seders in Boston.

Dave and I take Thursday afternoon off. While he runs out for the kosher wine, our only contribution to the Seder, I finish packing clothes. Adam is working on filling a duffel bag with his favorite stuffed animals, books, puzzles, and cars. It's overflowing at twice capacity.

"Sweetie," I tell him. "We need to be able to zip it up. Besides, Nana always has new toys and books for you. You'll also get to play with all of Daddy's and Uncle Ben's toys from when they were little."

Adam pleads as always, "But Mommy, I like my home toys, so I don't feel lonely. And I need my blankie."

Adam's blankie is a frayed red and white scrap quilt that I threw together to keep myself occupied when I went two weeks past my due date. On one visit to Brookline, when I neglected to bring it along, Adam refused to nap and would only succumb to exhaustion if I slept with him in the guest room, leaving Dave to occupy his childhood bunk bed.

We load our little Volkswagen station wagon, buckle Adam into his booster seat, and head out onto the interstate that will take us up to the Mass Pike, getting into Brookline by dinnertime. Once in the car, Adam dozes.

He no longer naps, but sleeping in the car will be good for him, because evenings at Nana's tend to go longer than at home, and he winds up getting into bed late. Ellen, Dave's mother, loves spoiling Adam, sometimes reading six books to him before bed, in contrast to our limit of two or three.

"I wonder what additional developments will have taken place in Ben's observant life," I ask Dave. "It must be difficult for your mother, having to accommodate his increasingly religious life. She's only a little past the first anniversary of your dad's death."

"I know. Mom does try, but I know that she finds it stressful when he imposes some new standard on her. Like the remodel of the kitchen to include two sinks and two dishwashers. And the special hot plate settings on the stove so she won't turn a knob on Shabbat. Or should I say Shabbos? His disapproval of her wearing pants inside the house."

Neither Ben, Dave's older brother, nor Ellen has seen me yet in maternity clothes. I'm hoping that having her grandson at Passover, and the prospect of another grandchild to be born this year, will help to take some of the gloom from the home on Naples Road. Jacob, Dave's father, died suddenly of a massive stroke at his desk. He was seventy but still worked in his law practice full-time. Perhaps we shouldn't have been so surprised because he had suffered several silent strokes in his late sixties. He had migraines that occurred with increasing frequency, but he had still played tennis twice a week and enjoyed working out at an old fashioned YMHA. It has also been harder for the family to recover from Jacob's death because of the unexplained events that changed Ben's life so markedly.

Ben moved back to Boston two years ago. He was always the more religious one, while Dave was decidedly secular, even though both graduated from Brookline Jewish Day School. While Ben attended Brandeis and adopted an increasingly Orthodox lifestyle, Dave went to Stanford and described himself as agnostic. They both followed their father into the law, with Ben attending Harvard, while Dave went to Columbia.

Ben was married to Resa, a Jewish Education teacher. They met when both were undergraduates at Brandeis. Resa was raised in a modern Orthodox family, and while she didn't cover her hair with a wig or a turban, as ultra-orthodox women do, she dressed modestly, with high necklines, calf-length skirts, and sleeves that covered her elbows. Ben and Resa appeared to be a perfect couple, with satisfying professional lives and a home life that revolved around Jewish law and custom. Ben completed clerking for a Supreme Court justice and became an associate with one of the top law firms in Washington.

Then, suddenly, they separated. Resa and Ben both refused to state the reason for their separation or to blame each other. They denied that either one had had an affair. In any event, that seemed unlikely. They concluded a no-fault divorce as quickly as possible. Ben granted Resa a get, the religious document that allows a Jewish divorcée to be married again. In less than six months, she remarried.

Shortly after, Ben resigned from the law firm and moved back to Brookline. Dave's parents still lived in the old, three-story frame house that they'd occupied for forty years. The third story is a separate apartment that had always housed graduate students or faculty members from Boston's numerous colleges. The apartment happened to be vacant, and Ben moved himself and his few possessions in. He also joined my father-in-law in his one-man law office, giving up his high-flying corporate law practice for trusts and estates, small business, and real estate law in suburban Boston. After Jacob's death, Ben continued the practice.

Ben refuses to discuss anything about his marital breakup and divorce, immersing himself in attending shul, regular prayer, and Torah study. The family continues to feel sad about what derailed Ben's personal life, and that, combined with Ellen's grief following Jacob's death, has given visits to Brookline a somber character.

I feel the drowsiness of pregnancy, and I drop off to sleep. I don't wake up until we are approaching our exit from the Mass Pike. Dave hands Adam a juice box and graham crackers. Soon there is a fine dusting of crumbs surrounding his booster seat. The streetlights come on as we turn onto Harvard Street and wind toward Brookline. The Boston area uses yellowish sodium lights, so different from those in Westchester County. I love driving through Boston neighborhoods, with their signature triple-decker houses. As we near the neighborhood surrounding Dave's family home, I recognize the kosher food stores and Judaica shops that remain. White Plains once had a street of such shops, but those storefronts are now largely gone. We turn onto Naples Road and then into the driveway of the familiar clapboard house with the full front porch.

"I see Nana!" exclaims Adam. He and Nana have a close relationship. He's her only grandchild. Ellen was an elementary school teacher until her retirement four years ago. Since her retirement, and especially since being widowed, she's been a frequent visitor to White Plains.

She comes down the steps toward our car as Ben opens the front door and steps out onto the porch. Ellen hugs me, and then pats my pregnant belly. "My next little grandson is right here."

Dave lets Adam out of the car, and he runs to Ellen, throws his arms around her legs and buries his face in her skirt. Ben descends the steps, extends his hand to Dave.

I smile at Ben. "So good to see you, Ben." But I don't touch him. Ben's observance level of Orthodox Judaism dictates that a man never touches a woman who is not his wife, lest the woman be "unclean." I admit that the concept that a woman is unclean for two weeks after the start of her menstrual period is somewhat offensive to me. I respect this religious belief, but the emphasis in Orthodox Judaism on women as a distraction to men, as well as relegating them to home and non-leadership religious positions, collide with my feminist philosophy. Since my last period was over five months ago, I should be able to give Ben a big hug, but I won't.

"I have a dairy meal ready," Ellen says. "With Adam's favorite egg salad." She tousles his hair. "You can wait to bring in everything until after we eat if you want."

There is a lazy Susan on the table, each individual dish filled with deli and fish salads and cut vegetables, surrounding a center dish with dill–sour cream dip. I follow Ellen into the kitchen. She has borscht on the stove. The aromas are always so luscious in her kitchen.

"What can I take into the dining room?" I ask.

"If you'd take our final loaf of bread in," Ellen responds, "I'll serve up the soup and you can help me carry the bowls. I know Adam thinks purple soup is yucky, so I have a bowl of buttered noodles for him. Might as well cook up as much chametz as possible today."

I deliver the bread on the cutting board to Ben. Since my father-in-law died, Ben has taken the chair at the head of the dining table, seated opposite his mother. I bring Adam's noodles and carrots out to him, and Ellen and I follow with the steaming bowls of borscht. We sit down, and Ben rises to bless the bread.

"But it isn't Friday!" Adam exclaims. On Fridays, we light Sabbath candles, and I say the Hebrew blessing over the candles. It's one of our few Jewish rituals. I had to talk Dave into it once Adam was eating meals with us. That and putting our loose change in the tzadakah box each week to introduce Adam to the concept of charity.

Ben says, "We want to thank God for this good food each time we eat. First, I say the blessing for our bread. Baruch atah adonoi . . ."

Ben hands out pieces of bread to each person. Then he continues his mini-lesson for Adam.

"Take a bite. And now we will thank God for these vegetables, our beet soup and your carrots. Baruch . . ."

Adam repeats the Hebrew after his uncle, struggling over the pronunciation.

"Adam starts religious school next fall," I tell Ben and Ellen. "We're about a year late. Starting in pre-K or kindergarten is recommended, but the temple dues and building fund were a bit much for the budget until recently." We chose White Plains' Reform synagogue, Temple Isaiah, the only one that wouldn't question our children's lineage, given that my mother went through a Reform conversion.

Ben smiles. "Judaism light, I say. Dave and I have never been quite on the same page with respect to halakhah."

Ellen shoots a warning look at Ben and adds, "Well, I'm glad that Adam and his little brother will grow up with an appreciation of Jewish heritage and values. Adam, tomorrow we get ready for Passover, where we tell the story of the Jews' escape from Egypt. We'll use feathers to sweep away all of the crumbs of bread. Can you say pesach?"

Adam responds, "Pay sock?"

"Yes, that's Hebrew for 'Passover.' We use the Hebrew language for some of our prayers and to talk about holidays," explains Ellen.

"Adam's learned the four questions," interjects Dave.

Even I'm surprised. I had no idea that Dave, who has shunned organized religion, had been teaching him. The four questions are part of the Passover Seder, where the youngest child begins by asking, "What makes this night different from every other night?" Or in Hebrew, "Ma nishtanah halailah hazeh mikol haleilot?"

Adam proceeds hesitantly, but he makes it all the way through, with Dave and Ben's assistance. Then he smiles broadly at us.

> "Ma nishtanah halailah hazeh mikol haleilot?
>
> Sheb'khol haleilot anu okhlin hametz umatzah; halailah hazeh, kuloh matzah.
>
> Sheb'khol haleilot anu okhlin sh'ar y'rakot; halailah hazeh, maror.
>
> Sheb'khol haleilot ein anu matbilin afilu pa'am ehat; halailah hazeh, shtei f'amim.
>
> Sheb'khol haleilot anu okhlin bein yoshvin uvein m'subin; halailah hazeh, kulanu m'subin."

In translation:

> Why is this night different from all other nights?
>
> On all other nights we eat leavened products and matzah, and on this night only matzah.
>
> On all other nights we eat all vegetables, and on this night only bitter herbs.
>
> On all other nights, we don't dip our food even once, and on this night we dip twice.

On all other nights we eat sitting or reclining, and
on this night we only recline.

"Adam, I'm so proud of you! And Dave, that's marvelous.
I certainly didn't expect this," says Ellen.

"Not to wonder, Mom. I'm a cultural Jew; I respect the
rituals as a teaching tool. I want Adam to have a good
grounding in Judaism's values, but I don't now and never
believed that strict observance of Jewish law would make
me a better person. Ben and I will never agree on this
subject, but this works for me as an agnostic."

Dave and his brother have diverged on religious views
since childhood. Their parents were Orthodox, although
not as strictly observant as many families, and Judaism
was central to their lives. They wanted the boys to have a
Jewish education and they wanted the rigorous, competitive academic setting that Brookline Day provides. The
school sends many of its graduates to top colleges and
into demanding professions.

After dinner, Ben and Dave leave to visit a favorite
teacher, now retired, who lives in the next block. Ellen
and I clear the table and load the dairy dishwasher, one
of Ben's upgrades to the vintage forties-era kitchen. In
addition to the meat and dairy dishwashers, the island
Ben had built in the spacious kitchen also contains two
stainless steel sinks, to help ensure separation between
meat and dairy dishes—as if Ellen needs any assistance in
keeping kosher. I ask Ellen about Ben. He's seemed so iso-
lated since moving back to Brookline. His world revolves

around daily attendance at shul, his law practice, and religious study groups in the evenings.

"Ellen, does Ben have any opportunities to meet wom-
en? It's been almost two years, and I expected that he
would have started dating by now."

Ellen looks out the window for a moment. She seems
to be considering her words before responding. Then she
takes a deep breath.

"Rachel, at first, I thought that Ben appeared to be
clinically depressed, traumatized by whatever ended his
marriage. I did try to get him to tell me, not in any detail, but a broad outline of what might have happened.
It had all been so perfect. He and Resa were so in love,
so committed to each other. But he declines to discuss it.
I suppose their attorneys and the rabbis who issued the
get were told. The only clue we have is the fact that Resa
remarried within a year. So, while he tells me that there
was no affair, I have trouble believing that."

Dave told me that Resa is the only girl Ben ever dated.
They were engaged by their senior year in college, marrying the week after they graduated. Ben started law school
that fall, while Resa studied for her masters in Jewish
education.

I first met Ben and Resa after moving to Washington
for an internship. Dave and I were introduced at a Michigan football game viewing party. Dave had taken a year's
leave as a faculty member at the University of Michigan
for a fellowship in Washington. We quickly knew we'd be
spending lots of time together, and Dave felt comfortable

inviting me to a Yom Kippur "break the fast" dinner at Ben and Resa's apartment. Although we didn't share their observant lifestyle, Dave and I spent more time with them than with any other people during our year in DC. If there were potential marital troubles, we never saw them coming.

Passover weekend in Brookline is filled with visits to numerous Gold family relatives, in varying states of aging. We have our second Seder at the Jewish Home for the Aged, with Ellen's sister, whose Parkinson's disease has advanced to the point that she requires round-the-clock care. She was a soprano and sang professionally but now struggles to feed herself or walk. Adam provides entertainment for the dining room with his recitation, with assistance, of the Four Questions.

I expect that Ben will eventually talk to Dave about the reason for the end of his marriage, for leaving his law firm position. But Dave tells me that Ben shut him off immediately when he once broached the subject, and he's reluctant to try to talk with Ben about it again. Although we have a nice, family-centered Passover weekend in Boston, we leave feeling as though there's something missing. No doubt Ellen feels this way constantly, seeing Ben daily but knowing that his divorce is a subject closed to her.

CHAPTER FOUR

NOVEMBER 2002

As spring moves into summer, and summer into fall, the trauma of learning that the baby has an extra chromosome fades. The events of day-to-day living take over much of the worry over whether our baby will have developmental issues.

Adam begins first grade. Dave starts the fall semester teaching and overseeing his legal clinic; in addition, he undertakes writing a land-use law textbook. In Psychiatry, I make detailed plans with my staff to cover my two-month maternity leave. Alyce is subdued. She continues to be effective, but she acts as though her wings were clipped since Dr. Costa and Wexler met with her and made it clear that her proposal to reorganize the office was inappropriate.

On my due date in November, I awaken early with contractions that steadily become more frequent and stronger. By ten in the morning, we know this is labor for real. I call Aunt Toni, who has a key and will let herself in to stay with Adam after school. An hour later, the contractions are five minutes apart. Trudy tells us to head for the hospital. She will meet us there. I go into the bathroom for one last pee, as has been my habit for the past month. As I waddle through the door, I feel a gush of water.

"My water just broke!" I gasp, as a sudden, strong contraction hits my middle, an unbearable pressure building around to the small of my back. I double over, hanging onto the sink and yell to Dave, "I need some dry clothes."

"No, Rachel. Let's get to the hospital."

But I convince him that I do need a dry pair of my stretched-out maternity undies and jeans. I dress in between strong contractions, and we set off for the hospital. Fortunately, I chose the birthing center at our community hospital, not some hospital in New York City. I find myself panting to cope during the short drive.

"Dave, let's use the Emergency Room entrance."

Dave pulls in under the ER entrance and runs inside. He and an orderly reappear with a wheelchair. With Dave's assistance, I hoist myself out of the car and get into the wheelchair. The orderly pushes me down a long corridor toward an elevator. Dave, I am told, will be joining us after he gets the car parked. I lose track of time, closing in on myself to manage contractions knocking the breath out of me. As we approach the labor and delivery suite, I feel an urge to push.

A nurse with blond hair caught up messily on her head greets me. "We need to get you registered, Mrs. Gold. Dr. Marshall is on her way. I'm Nessa, and I'll be your nurse."

I shake my head. "There isn't time. I have to push. I need the delivery room now!"

She tells the other staff around the desk, "We may have a stat delivery here. Let's get into Room Two. Jeannette, bring a standard tray. And we need a warming bed."

Dave still isn't here. I'm surrounded by efficient staff, helping me out of my clothes and into a hospital gown, lifting me onto a narrow, gurney-type bed. I remember labor with Adam, where anyone who came near me could stick a gloved hand inside for a quick exam, as two staff members lift my legs.

Nessa declares, "She's crowning. Rachel, go ahead. Take a deep breath and then push."

I respond with a long, forceful, groaning effort. And with that, I feel a slippery body emerge. I can see in the mirror above me that Nessa has him firmly in her grip. A few seconds of silence are met with a newborn's wail. Then I see Dave making his way over to me, beaming.

"Mr. Gold," says Nessa, "You've got a boy and you're here just in time cut the cord."

Nessa gives Dave a pair of scissors and, tying off the cord, shows Dave where to cut. Then my protesting baby boy is placed on my chest.

"So, I almost missed my own baby's birth," exclaims Dave. "I had no idea it could happen so fast. Rachel pushed for three hours with Adam. He was almost a C-section. Wow, good job!"

"I've heard of one-push babies," I say breathlessly. "But I never dreamed I'd have one. All I can say is that I am very surprised at how easy it was. After the past few hours of labor, that is."

Nessa takes him away briefly to put him on the baby scale.

"Seven pounds, twelve ounces," she announces. "Twenty-one inches. Time of birth eleven forty a.m. Apgar's ten and ten."

Nessa clamps little ID bracelets on both of his ankles and then puts matching bands on my wrist and Dave's. She wraps our baby in a blanket and gives him to Dave.

Trudy appears, tying on her mask, and exclaiming, "This lady is all business! Couldn't even wait for her doctor."

Trudy quickly takes charge of my lower regions, pronouncing, "No tearing. We have hemostasis. Dr. Vanessa Harris," she says, referring to Nessa, "another masterful delivery. What's his weight?"

"Seven, twelve," answers Nessa. "When mom says there isn't time for registration and she needs the delivery room now, she's usually right."

The nurses change my gown and help me get freshened up. We announce that Baby Boy Gold is Jacob, and one of the nurses writes his name on the card in his bassinet. I have an automated blood pressure cuff on my arm that startles me when it inflates. I realize that I'm hungry.

"Is there any chance of some lunch?" I ask Nessa, who is gathering my belongings in a plastic bag.

"Actually," she replies, "we have a room for you on the mother-baby unit. I'll get you moved before shift change.

We have sandwiches to hold you until dinner, which usually gets up to the floor by five. Baby can stay with you for a little while. Then they'll want to take him to the nursery for a bath and a newborn exam. But you'll get him back after dinner so he can start nursing."

She leaves, returning with a wheelchair. I sit in the chair, and Nessa directs Dave to follow her, pushing the bassinet. I'm anxious to spend some time with our baby after the activity of labor and delivery. We settle into my room. Dave hands Jacob to me. I unwrap the blanket enough to hold his tiny hand, and he grasps my finger. He looks into my eyes, even though I know that a newborn can't focus. It's hard to believe that we were so worried, so devastated when we learned of his extra chromosome. He's beautiful. With his quick birth, his head is rounded instead of bruised and molded into a pointy shape as Adam's was. I nuzzle him. Kiss his forehead. Inhale his baby smell.

I just can't imagine now how we could have thought about terminating the pregnancy. Maybe it's the hormones associated with labor and delivery, but I feel fiercely protective of my little baby. I am surprised that I have strong feelings about how wrong the geneticist, Dr. Berggren, was in suggesting that most parents in his practice who have the education levels that Dave and I do would choose abortion. I am a firm believer in the right of all women to control their own bodies, but what he said to us was essentially that children, adults, anyone with a disability, detracts from a family. Detracts from what? What does that say about our society, that families are better off without someone with special needs, even the relatively mild special needs that a child with Klinefelter syndrome may have? I'm surprised at my anger.

Looking down at Jacob, wrapped in his blue- and pink-striped blanket, I'm overwhelmed with what must be motherlove. I'll give him every opportunity for happiness and for a fulfilling childhood and adult life even if we must call in some special services. I don't see how that detracts from our family. Jacobs eyes flutter open. He yawns and looks around. I open his blanket just enough to take his tiny hand again. I give him my pinkie finger, and he grips it.

Later that afternoon, I finally eat an early dinner, and the nurse returns Jacob after his bath. Dave and Adam arrive, both wearing yellow paper gowns over their clothes. Adam is more interested in the hospital bed controls than his new brother. He sits close to me in the bed, and I show him how to cradle Jacob.

"Why's he wearing a hat, Mommy?" asks Adam.

"Because it takes a while for a newborn to be able to keep himself warm. So, we keep him in a blanket and let him wear a cap," I explain.

"My mother expects to get to our house about seven thirty," Dave tells me. "She'll sleep in the study. Your mom will be taking a taxi from White Plains Airport to Aunt Toni's apartment tomorrow and staying overnight there. Once my mom goes back to Boston, we can have your mom in the study."

Our house on the edge of the downtown area is small. Dave uses a little bedroom on the first floor as a study that doubles as a guest room with a sofa bed. On the second floor, there are two more bedrooms as well as a tiny sewing room. The sewing room has been furnished and decorated as a nursery, but I think that our days in this cozy little house are limited. Adam and Jacob could share a bedroom, but their age difference of six years could complicate that. Other than the study, the first floor has a living room, a dining room, and a small kitchen. The living room is full of toys that overflow into the dining room because the basement, with its moisture patches and spider webs, isn't fit to be a playroom. Soon, baby equipment will add to the clutter.

Adam asks a few more questions about the baby and then announces that he and Daddy are going to get ice cream. We kiss and hug each other. I make Adam promise to see me tomorrow after school. Then Jacob and I are alone again. He's rooting against my breast, so I pull my gown away, and he latches on as if he's been doing this for weeks.

I try to remember if I had the same feelings for Adam after he was born, when he was engaged in the ultra-intimate activity of nursing. I know that I'm calmer now because I am experienced at this. When Adam was born, Dave and I were green at parenting, and somehow in awe of this tiny being, fearful that we might be doing something terribly wrong. I let Jacob nurse until he drops off to sleep, listening to his tiny baby breaths.

Two days later, I'm dressing to go home. Dave drops my mother off to help me with readying the baby while he picks up groceries. We agree to be downstairs at the front entrance by eleven, where Dave will meet us with the car. My mother has put Jacob into his newborn "going home" outfit when he begins to fuss. I suspect hunger so give him my breast and look at my watch.

"The nurses asked me to record his feeding time in the chart on his bassinet," I tell my mother. "Could you write '10:30 a.m.' on the chart?"

Mum picks up the chart and looks through it. Then she takes on a look of puzzlement.

"It says here 'Klinefelter syndrome.' What do you suppose that is?" she asks. "Did you know about this?"

I'm silent for a few seconds. We hadn't planned to tell our parents unless problems developed later, but it's probably best to let her know about the diagnosis now.

"Mum, we knew this from the amniocentesis. He has an extra X chromosome. But it isn't like Down syndrome. He may have mild learning disabilities, or some speech delay. Or he may experience nothing. It's highly variable, and after everything we went through with infertility treatment, we weren't prepared to have an abortion just because he might have some special needs. We thought that we wouldn't say anything unless a problem developed. That's why we didn't tell anyone."

"Wasn't that somewhat traumatic to learn? I wish I'd known. So, you'll have the pediatrician watch him for milestones?" She looks down at Jacob, nursing with his eyes closed. "He looks so perfect. Sometimes I wonder if some of this new testing doesn't give us more information than we really want to know."

I tell her, "We had a wonderful, supportive genetic counselor who researched Klinefelter syndrome—it's also called XXY—at a medical library. She brought copies of what little research has been done. I'll give them to you to read once we get home. She told us that the disabilities tend to be mild and that many with this extra chromosome don't even know it. Many never find out. The doctor who started out the counseling session essentially told us that if it were his pregnancy, he'd have an abortion."

I find myself suddenly needing to stop because I'm feeling emotions that make my voice quiver. I swallow, look at Mum, and take a few seconds to resume.

"Fortunately, he couldn't wait to leave our meeting, so we spent most of our time with the genetic counselor. She was much more optimistic and supported our decision to continue the pregnancy. I couldn't have done anything at that point. Jacob was kicking inside me. I couldn't have terminated."

"I know you'll do fine, whatever happens," Mum says, her voice catching. I can tell she is on the verge of tears, so I give her hand a squeeze.

Later that evening, Dave calls his mother to tell her about Jacob's extra chromosome and explain why we aren't terribly concerned about it. He also calls his brother to tell him the same thing. I'll let Sarah in on the news but probably not until after her baby arrives.

When Jacob is eight days old, we hold a brit milah, his ritual circumcision. In Ann Arbor, my obstetrician did the circumcision before we left the hospital. In White Plains, suddenly surrounded by my Dad's Jewish relatives and within driving distance for Dave's family, we observe the ritual that marks a Jewish male. Ellen and Ben arrange nearly everything, from bringing with them from Boston a mohel, who is also a pediatric urologist, to ordering the kosher catered lunch for the guests. Ellen tells me that the mohel who will perform the circumcision is a friend of Ben's. They met through one of Ben's religious activities and learn or study together each week.

Our family, including my parents and Ben, Ellen, and the mohel, all arrive at the small synagogue at the same time. We exit the cars and greet one another. Ben introduces us to Dr. Eli Rubin, who is wearing a black velvet yarmulke, a black suit, white shirt, and slightly visible tzitzit, tassels that observant men wear at the bottom corners of their shirts. Dave, cradling Jacob, approaches Dr. Rubin. Jacob is swaddled in a white blanket and wears a tiny blue knit yarmulke.

Dr. Rubin takes Jacob and addresses us. "I'm absolutely honored that you entrust your little boy to me for his bris. Such a handsome little guy."

We walk toward the entrance. Dr. Rubin leans over toward me and says quietly, "Ben told me that you learned of Jacob's extra chromosome prenatally. I'm so glad that you continued the pregnancy. So often, parents get dreadful counseling, and they terminate because of fear, even though the impact of XXY on development is generally quite mild. I'm only telling you this because I see a number of patients in my practice who have Klinefelter syndrome. Most of them do pretty well, not at all like the horror stories parents can be given when the fetus is found to have 47, XXY."

"Dr. Rubin, thanks so much for telling us this." What a warm, supportive doctor this man is. And so reassuring to us, the parents of this newborn.

I continue, "We really have stopped worrying about it. Right now, we're concentrating on being good parents to a newborn who doesn't sleep too much!" I'm a bit surprised that Ben told the mohel that Jacob has Klinefelter syndrome, but he's a physician and that information seems to be medically relevant.

We're almost at the door of the little synagogue, a large, older former residence in the leafy Prospect Park neighborhood. Another car with two women pulls into the parking area. One waves at Ben and Eli. As soon as the car stops, she exits and strides over to Eli, beaming.

"The baby! He's gorgeous," she exclaims. "These are the parents?" She smiles at me warmly and reaches for my hand.

Dave and Dad both smile and quickly assess her appearance. She's clearly frum, or Orthodox, and observant. Long skirt, dark stockings, elbows covered by her cardigan. While she shakes my mother's hand, welcoming her, the men merely nod and smile to acknowledge her.

"Dr. Shira Goodman, another pediatrician," says the mohel, introducing her. "And Aviva Weiss. Aviva's a law professor at NYU. A friend of Eli's from law school." He indicates the woman who drove the car.

Dr. Goodman stoops down to greet Adam, who is wearing a navy-blue blazer and khakis purchased specifically for this occasion.

"And you're the big brother?" she asks. "I'm a friend of your Uncle Ben's. And this is another friend, Ms. Weiss. This is a very special day for your family. What grade are you in school?" Dr. Goodman is clearly a pediatrician comfortable with little kids. Adam launches into a conversation about first grade at the Church Street School, helicopters, and his continuing requests for a dog, which have accelerated with Jacob's arrival.

Ben holds the door for us as we enter the synagogue. We are motioned into a room by several women setting up the lunch, where Ben deposits what must be the doctor's "mohel kit," a sports bag packed with plastic wrapped towels, sponges, instruments, and a few tubes of medication. Dr. Rubin gently places Jacob on a table covered with a changing pad.

"I want to do a brief exam to make sure we have no surprises before the circumcision. Would you undress him enough to remove his diaper?" He motions me over. I unwrap his blanket, unsnap his little white sleeper, and unfasten his diaper while holding my cupped hand over his penis, just in case he pees. The doctor briefly looks at his testicles and penis. Then he applies some topical anesthetic, which gives me great relief.

"We sometimes see micropenis with these boys, but that's clearly not a problem," Dr. Rubin says. "You can put a fresh diaper on him. Now, who's designated the sendak?"

Dave tells him that we discussed this at some length. My father thought that he might be too squeamish for this honor, so Ben has volunteered for this role, although Dad will carry Jacob into the room. I can hear people arriving. My parents and Ellen greet them. Most are my relatives, but Ellen has two cousins who have traveled up from Manhattan. I look out into the room, which appears to be a multi-purpose synagogue and social hall with dark wood paneling. A mechitza divides the women's section from the men's, but it appears to be symbolic only: a white plastic planter topped by a small artificial ivy "hedge." This will not be an egalitarian service, with both parents participating. But for a bris, I'm more than happy to sit on the women's side. I take my place, seated between Ellen and Mum, while the men don their prayer shawls.

Dave and I are too sleep-deprived from Jacob's feedings every two hours to object to the Orthodox overtones of the ritual, which Ben arranged in this small synagogue. Ben knows members of the congregation from his Harvard days. All my father's relatives, regardless of how observant, should feel free to eat and drink wine with us because everything is kosher. Dad holds forth as the proud grandfather. I appreciate how comfortable the setting is in contrast with years ago when he arrived back in White Plains with his new non-Jewish bride, and they were shunned.

Following the mercifully short bris, during which Jacob furiously sucks a pacifier but makes not a peep, we gather in an adjoining room for wine, bagels, and various dairy salads. I look over at Ben. He seems transformed, hanging out with his group of observant friends. Relaxed, laughing, clearly very comfortable in this setting. Baby Jacob is passed among all the relatives, overseen by both grandmothers. I know that Ellen and Mum are being protective, making certain that whichever relative has him is holding him securely, supporting his head.

No one other than the grandparents, his uncle, and the mohel is aware of his extra chromosome and our questions about whether he will meet his developmental milestones and have a normal early childhood or meet challenges. What would they think if they knew that we were told we should never tell anyone about his extra chromosome? That one medical professional implied that we should terminate the pregnancy? Instead, they see the perfect little infant that Dave and I do. And I'm being congratulated as the mother of a beautiful baby boy. It's a wonderful feeling being supported by the extended family and many friends. In this little synagogue, with this ritual, those worries about an extra chromosome are far away.

In about two months, Mum and Dad will travel to California to meet their new grandchild after Sarah gives birth. Sarah has everything prepared for her home birth, which the three boys are invited to watch. If the experience of labor and birth is too intense for the boys, some of her women's group members will be attending and entertain the boys, who are ages seven, five, and four. If the baby is a boy, instead of the hoped-for girl, he will not be circumcised because Sarah and Oren reject circumcision as an unnecessary mutilation of a male child, although they seem to accept it as a legitimate religious ritual.

Before my maternity leave of two months ends, Dave and I conclude that sending Jacob out to daycare plus paying for the after-school program for Adam doesn't make financial sense. My boss agrees to let me work from home one day a week. We interview four women for a live-out nanny position and choose Sandra Cantrell, a warm and delightful woman from the Dominican Republic. Dave insists, wisely, on limiting hires to citizens or Green Card holders and on paying Social Security and other mandated payroll taxes. More than half my income now goes to paying the nanny and a weekly cleaning woman, but we don't have much choice if I'm to maintain my career.

CHAPTER FIVE

MARCH 2004

J acob is a beautiful baby. After the first six weeks, during which he engages in what we call the "witching hour," screaming inconsolably every afternoon for an hour, he adopts a quiet, smiling presence, coos and babbles but doesn't insist on being held or entertained. He has a far more patient attitude toward hunger than his brother. Adam rocketed awake in his crib each morning at six. He was crying with hunger by the time I got into his room to nurse him. Jacob, by contrast, awakens and is content to watch his mobile while I head downstairs to start the coffee before I feed him. While Adam resisted my attempts to wean him from breastfeeding at a year, Jacob seems happy drinking milk from his sippy cup.

During Jacob's first year, he hit every milestone on time, a great relief to Dave and me. The boys' pediatricians not only were aware of his extra chromosome, they read up on its possible impact on early development and assured us that he showed no sign of developmental delay other than slightly low muscle tone, which we expected.

I'm a little uneasy, however, because Jacob, now sixteen months old, is still not walking, whereas Adam walked at a year. At our last visit, his pediatrician assured us that Jacob is within normal limits on everything, but on the slower side. He didn't sit by himself until eight months. He didn't crawl until eleven months or pull himself up to stand until thirteen months. In fact, my assessment is that Jacob doesn't move much unless he needs to. I can leave him in one corner of the living room looking at a board book and return twenty minutes later to find him in the same place. The pediatrician tells me very clearly that I shouldn't compare the development rates of my two sons. But still I wonder.

Jacob and I are on a plane to visit my parents in Minneapolis. My sister will be there with her fourth son, Noam, born three months after Jacob. Adam is staying at home because he has school, as do Sarah's three older boys. This visit is just the sisters and their babies, meeting midway across the country.

Although Minneapolis is the current home of our parents, Sarah and I didn't do much of our growing up in Minnesota. For the first sixteen years of my life, fourteen of Sarah's, we were firmly ensconced in the small industrial city of Beloit, a few miles north of Wisconsin's border with Illinois. We attended Beloit public schools. Our father worked as chief engineer of a small manufacturing company located along the river. The story of how the Zimmerman family became Midwesterners is complicated, centering on religious conflicts within families.

My mother, Caroline, and her sister, Margaret, came to the United States as post-war brides in 1947. Born in Northern Ireland, the daughters of Ian Rainey, a stern Presbyterian minister, they volunteered for war duty in England as a way of escaping their repressive home. When Margaret became engaged to an American GI who was Roman Catholic, she was disowned by my grandparents. She and Uncle Bud settled in Rockford, Illinois, and became part of my Uncle Bud's Italian-American family.

Mum met my father near Manchester, England, where he was assigned by the Army to use his engineering skills in a top-secret radar project. Until Dad enlisted, he had never eaten non-kosher food, he put on tefillin daily for morning prayers, and he had never contemplated marrying a gentile girl.

Mum was a handsome woman and a great dancer. Dad also loved to dance. She worked as a secretary for the research unit developing radar applications when she and Dad noticed each other and began spending time together. On their one day off each week, Mum and Dad took to the countryside on bicycles and then attended dances held for servicemen stationed in the area. Six months later, he presented her with a modest diamond ring and asked her to marry him.

When Mum and Dad visited Belfast to get the blessing of my grandfather, he said that he would not give it until Dad agreed to convert to Christianity, but he and my grandmother also did not disown Mum. In their Irish Unionist value system, marrying a Jew was not as despicable as marrying a Catholic, as Margaret had done. But there was no conversion, at least not to Christianity. Mum and Dad were married in a Registry Office in Manchester after obtaining the Army's approval. Two months later, they sailed for New York.

Initially, Mum was not accepted by Dad's family because she wasn't Jewish. Soon, Dad and Mum took the train to Illinois to visit Margaret and Bud, where they were enveloped in the warm hospitality of Bud's family. Dad discovered that his GI Bill and the savings from his four years in the Army would support them well while he finished his engineering degree at the University of Illinois. When he took his first job, he and my mother settled in Beloit, less than a thirty-minute drive from Aunt Margaret in Rockford.

Small city life provided a great sense of community for our family. Mum was active on the school board and in various charities. Dad was a social action leader in the synagogue and in a variety of liberal political organizations. Sarah and I both had comfortable niches in the local high school. Sarah excelled in art and volleyball, and I in orchestra and track. We had a large, comfortable home in an upscale neighborhood. And then when I was a high school junior and Sarah, a freshman, it all disappeared.

One morning, Dad was called in by the owner of the company and informed that the business had been sold to a competitor in Alabama. At the age of fifty-two, Dad no longer had employment. There was no severance package. To make matters worse, Dad also found that he had no claim on a pension that he had counted on for retirement fifteen years away. In addition, Dad learned that the patent for an engineering process he had developed was held exclusively by the company owner, who had originally agreed to share ownership.

These events occurred during an economic slowdown. It took our father more than eight months to find another job. He and my mother were forced to use retirement savings to pay living expenses. Dad finally found another job, at a much lower salary, in Minneapolis. The proceeds of the sale of our large home in Beloit paid for a more modest home, a three-bedroom rambler in a close-in suburb of Minneapolis.

So, Minneapolis isn't truly home for Sarah and me. Despite having started a new high school during my senior year, I continued to get good grades and quickly became active again in extracurricular activities. I returned to Wisconsin for an undergraduate degree at University of Wisconsin-Madison. Sarah had three years to adjust, and she attended the Twin Cities campus of the University of Minnesota.

I can truly say that my parents are now very happy. They have friends through their progressive political groups and Mum's charities. They're active in a small Reform synagogue. And Dad was on a mission, successfully it turns out, to develop a light rail transit system for the Twin Cities, engaging in public speaking and lobbying to promote smart development. He and Dave always have lots to talk about on land-use planning and smart growth, and often exchange phone calls and emails.

The plane is beginning to descend when Jacob awakens and looks distressed, pulling at his ears. He hasn't had a baby bottle for three months, but I have one filled with juice in case he needs to swallow to open his ear tubes. Jacob sucks intently at the bottle and eyes me a bit nervously as the plane makes its approach to the airport. I look out the window and notice gray military transport planes on the Fort Snelling side of the airport, parked next to pallets of supplies, reminding me of the war in Iraq that has been grinding on now for months since the invasion last year. Not the quick war we were promised. And then we are on the ground.

I pull the folding stroller and diaper tote from the overhead bin and make my way down the aisle to the jetway. Unfolding the stroller and popping in Jacob, I hurry toward baggage claim where we planned to meet. Soon, I see Mum, Dad, and my sister and her baby. Sarah and Noam arrived from California about half an hour before.

Sarah and I haven't seen each other for three years. We hug, rocking back and forth, and hug more, while Mum entertains Noam, and Dad takes Jacob. Jacob fusses as I embrace first Mum and then Dad, so I pick him up. Then I notice that Noam, who is three months younger than Jacob, is walking.

"When did he start walking?" I ask. "Jacob's still cruising around tables but won't let go."

"He's been walking since eleven months," replies Sarah. "Earlier than my other boys. And he can run now, but he doesn't have any sense, so I'm always scrambling after him."

"Well, maybe Jacob will be inspired by Noam," I tell her. "I asked the pediatrician last week if he was late at walking. But the doctor said that anything up to sixteen months is considered within normal limits. He needs to start walking this month, or I'll start to worry!"

We check the signs for my baggage claim area. It turns out that we're standing next to it. The carousel starts, and the second bag off the conveyor belt is mine. I point it out, and Dad lifts it off the carrousel.

"We borrowed a friend's minivan for the week," Dad tells us as he guides the stroller and luggage caravan toward the exit. "We also borrowed and installed two child seats for the babies. You two will get to sit in the back."

We walk through automatic doors out into the massive parking structure. The Minneapolis-St. Paul Airport has added concourses and parking every time I visit. We troop along with the boys and their strollers and luggage. Of course, Dad has selected the economy lot that one might use a shuttle bus to reach, but it's easier to walk than to wait for the bus and board with babies and all their equipment. Dad believes that saving money is a moral obligation. Using the economy lot will save him two dollars.

We approach a dusty maroon Dodge Caravan, festooned with left-leaning political and social action bumper stickers. My guess that the minivan is the friend's loaner is correct. Dad slides open the side door. I lift Jacob into the van, and settle him into his car seat, adjusting straps and buckles to fit. Sarah is doing the same with Noam.

"You did a superb job of installing these seats," I call to Mum and Dad, who fit the luggage, strollers, and diaper bags into the cargo area at the rear of the van.

"Well, this is Betty McNamara's van," Mom tells us. "She bought it to ferry around her five grandchildren. I did her a favor taking her food collection route for Twin Cities Harvest after she was laid up with a hip replacement. When she told me how grateful she was and offered to help in any way if I ever needed it, I let her know that allowing us to borrow the van would be great."

Although Mum retired as soon as she turned sixty-five, she has a full schedule of volunteer duties, including the awesome job of coordinating leftover food pickups from over thirty restaurants. In addition to stocking food pantries, Mum is a volunteer literacy instructor, and a docent at the folk art center and museum. She's determined to leave her mark on society. And in her spare time, she pieces and hand-quilts full-sized coverlets.

I marvel at how little traffic there is during non-rush hours here, at how little time it takes to drive from the airport to their house, right outside the city limits, compared with the drive from LaGuardia to White Plains, which takes from one to three hours, depending on traffic. There is something so soothing and simple in the grid pattern of the city and the prairie architecture of the bungalows and older homes that we pass. There are few hills to speak of except for the bluffs along the Mississippi River.

Dad turns into our street of little clapboard ranches. I can remember how disappointed Sarah and I felt when we first arrived here from Wisconsin. This modest neighborhood and the small, tidy house were such a contrast with the large home in the country club area of Beloit that our family sold to relocate here. Sarah and I did not dare disappoint our parents by complaining. Dad had suffered enough humiliation from the sudden loss of his management position at the engineering firm, the difficult time he had in finding any position at all, even one at barely half the salary, and the betrayal of the man whose business he helped to build.

The babies are both sleeping by the time that Dad pulls the minivan into the driveway. Mum and Dad take the bags into the house while Sarah and I wait for a few minutes to see if Noam and Jacob wake on their own. It's still very chilly in Minnesota in March, so we can't stay in the van for long.

"It's so, so good to see you, Rach." I notice then that Sarah looks tired. "I'm so looking forward to catching up. What's new?"

"The usual," I tell her. "We both struggle for any time for ourselves between work and kids. Work is more like eighty hours a week for Dave, who's on the umpteenth draft of a land-use law textbook. I was looking forward to coasting for a bit, having gotten a new department up and running. But a week ago, my boss informed us that he's been appointed section chief at the National Institute of Mental Health. He'll be leaving for the new position in less than three months. That means adjusting to a new chair, a new management style, and all sorts of time-consuming initiatives. And I'll probably have to give up the one day that I work from home."

I hear Jacob making little waking up sounds and sucking his fingers. I quickly pull myself around the middle van seat so that he can see me once he opens his eyes. He quiets and settles again into his nap, although probably not for more than a few minutes.

"I also feel overwhelmed at this point because we've decided that it's time to sell our starter house and look for more space. One full bathroom and only two bedrooms are not enough. When am I going to do this? What about you?"

Sarah looks away. She doesn't answer immediately. As Sarah continues, I notice uncharacteristic frown lines. She's always been the lighter spirited of the two of us.

"Noam is easy. They say that going from two kids to three is the game changer, but when we went from two kids to three, the second and third were eleven months apart. So, the fourth child is so much easier than having two babies in diapers at the same time. But I . . . we need to talk once we have some private time. Maybe after the babies are in bed we can get out for a bit, if Mum agrees to babysit."

Jacob's eyes open at that moment, and he slowly smiles, that gorgeous two-toothed grin that he gives me on awakening. I unbuckle him, contemplating what concerning news Sarah wants to share with me. I hope that it isn't a relapse. Oren was treated for alcoholism early in their marriage.

Perhaps sensing this, Sarah assures me that this has nothing to do with a return to drinking. Oren remains sober, although Sarah enjoys wine periodically outside of the house. She tells me that she even has a California red in her luggage for us. Our parents have moved on from drinking only Manishevitz, cloyingly sweet Jewish household wine, to Reislings and rosés. But their taste in wine is still too sweet for either of us, so we make a point of bringing our own wine when visiting.

We bring the babies inside. Mum has set up each of our childhood bedrooms with a porta-crib and borrowed two highchairs for the kitchen. She has a late lunch ready for us. First, diaper changes for each boy and then we all meet in the kitchen. I am amused and warmed by this sixties kitchen painted in harvest gold that retains all its Coppertone appliances. The speckled linoleum of my teen years is still on the floor, and Mum's cross-stitched Irish prayer and quilted peace banners are on the walls. The picture windows still look out on mountains of snow covering the lawn and the pine trees.

Mum says, "Now we're on a very casual schedule here, knowing that both Jacob and Noam are out of their native time zones. All the meals I've planned can be delayed if you are busy with your kids. Feel free to eat anytime you would like. In fact, this evening Dad and I have an anti-war organizing potluck, so we'll be leaving you alone with deli fixings for sandwiches. There's news today that the Commission found no weapons of mass destruction in Iraq. Just an excuse for Bush, or more likely Cheney, to go to war."

Sarah and I look at each other, smiling.

"Great, Mum. I brought a bottle of wine, so we'll catch up while you and Dad are out."

Privacy problem solved.

As soon as we have the babies tucked in and settled for the night, Sarah takes down two goblets and pours us each a glass. We carry them into the living room and sit in the worn but comfortable recliners. I notice a new quilt hung above the fireplace, but the room still holds a record changer and LPs. Dad has yet to adapt to CDs. I look at Sarah to start.

"We've had some difficulty. I debated telling you about it. Hope I don't get so emotional I can't tell you, but Oren had a fling with a young, hot engineer. This started while I was in full cow mode with a breastfed newborn. That and my extra fifteen pounds. I think that somehow my earth mother persona couldn't compete with this sexy young thing."

She looks into her wine glass, takes a deep breath, and continues. "There was a software developer's convention up at Lake Tahoe. Oren was leading a group of their sales staff there to introduce this new line of products. He'd planned to spend three days there, which morphed into five. And then there were late nights and sudden overnight trips. All arranged at the last minute. Investments in upgraded clothing. He even started using cologne. I never questioned anything; attributed it all to his need to roll out this product that he spent three years developing."

She stops, takes a sip of wine, and closes her eyes. I wait.

"At some point, Oren realized that the fling had turned into something serious for her. She began putting more demands on him for time, for a commitment that would mean leaving his family. Oren said that it needed to end. That they were both competent and consenting adults, but that he had made a huge mistake. He couldn't jeopardize his family's life to continue this relationship. That's when she became crazy vindictive. Sent him hundreds of messages that she would tell me; ruin him. She was making, in writing, extortion demands for a commitment or for money. Like half a million."

"Oh, God, Sarah. I am so sorry. I had no idea, but maybe I should have known, when you didn't return calls, when we didn't talk by phone for weeks at a time." I pause. "I should have asked if you were okay. I just assumed that you were as super busy as me. How did you find out?"

"Oren came clean to me, but not until this girl, Jessica, sent me a letter, four pages, telling me the history of their relationship and explaining why Oren needed to leave me because I was holding him back from a fulfilling life. I can't believe I'm telling you this. I haven't talked to anyone about this since her letter. When I confronted him, he broke down and begged me to forgive him."

Sarah begins to cry. I leave my chair and kneel next to her, wrapping my arms around her and holding her while she sobs. We're silent for several minutes. Then I head out to the kitchen for some Kleenex.

"I banished him to the study for a month. We found a marriage counselor and have gone weekly. I know that Oren is truly sorry; he's genuinely guilt-ridden, but I've lost my trust. I don't know when I can regain it. And I felt so angry, so furious that I was physically repugnant enough that he would be tempted. Oren says it isn't my fault, that I had no role at all in this stupid caper."

"She isn't still working in his company, is she?" I ask.

"No. Oren showed her written demands for hush money to his attorney, who told him that it constituted extortion. In exchange for her agreement to leave the company, and to have no further contact with him or with me, he agreed not to press criminal charges. But Oren needed to tell his board what happened. It's been beyond sordid.

"I can't let Mum and Dad know about this. My own therapist tells me that this is a long-term process. The hurt will diminish. I'll learn to trust again, eventually. I don't think I've forgiven Oren yet. My anger bubbles up, and I am so resentful. But I think I'm getting there."

During our four days together, I let Sarah talk out her anguish. She needs to do this. I find myself angered, infuriated at my brother-in-law for putting my sister through this.

Oren is a charmer, a brilliant computer scientist. He's had career success with developing blockbuster computer products. He was with the right startup when it went public, and his shares became worth millions of dollars. He's good looking, tall, and athletic.

Oren's mother, Pearl, is Taiwanese. She met Oren's father, Joseph, when he was on his Mormon mission to Taiwan, the two years overseas that Mormon men are obligated to do following high school. His mother was one of Joseph's "baptisms." Dating is not allowed during a mission, but they carried on a correspondence courtship. Eventually, Joseph brought her to the United States as his fiancée. Oren is one of six children raised in a strict Mormon home, and the only one of his siblings to leave The Church of Jesus Christ of Latter-day Saints.

He chose to attend Caltech immediately after high school, informing his parents that a mission was impossible given his lack of faith. His parents were devastated. After Caltech, Oren went to graduate school in computer engineering at the University of Minnesota, where he met Sarah. Sarah and Oren were not married in the church but rather by a justice of the peace, but Joseph and Pearl have never lost hope that one day Oren will return to the church and have his wife and children baptized, as well. So, non-traditional religious practice, at least with respect to marriage, continues with my sister.

I admit to having felt envious of my sister and what appeared to be their worry-free family life in contrast to ours. Her family has plenty of money. Oren has job security that academics seeking tenure don't have. Add to that Sarah's ability to get pregnant whenever she wants. But now I wonder if this is the first time Oren has been unfaithful? Now Sarah will always have reason to distrust whether her marriage is secure.

Sarah seems to relax during our time in Minnesota. She visibly unwinds. There are some sunny and almost warm days that allow us to bundle the babies up and take long walks. We visit childhood friends and eat the comfort food for which Mum is famous.

I also have an opportunity to talk with Sarah in detail about the trauma of learning, prenatally, that Jacob has an extra chromosome. I have mostly buried that experience. In White Plains, I don't yet have any friends close enough to have shared my concerns with them. Sarah is a great listener, but I'm not sure that anyone can truly understand the mixture of fear and anger that I have felt at times, having been given this news about my infant son and knowing he has a genetic condition that could affect his development. The worst is knowing that Klinefelter's seems to be shameful enough, possibly associated with what some people believe to be sexual deviance, that some physicians tell parents not to discuss it with anyone, not even family.

Then, the last evening of our visit, Jacob stands up, grins at all of us, and walks across the room as if he had been doing this for weeks.

CHAPTER SIX

MAY 2004

I hear jumping. It's five thirty in the morning. Jacob is engaged in his favorite early morning activity. Standing in his crib, holding onto the rail, and jumping vigorously. Of course, the fact that his "bedroom" is a tiny sewing room off his parents' room, with a pocket door that doesn't quite close anymore, makes it impossible to sleep through. The noise doesn't disturb Dave, but if I don't take Jacob downstairs, he will also succeed in waking his brother. Saturday is my morning in charge of any early-waking kids. I hop out of bed, pick up Jacob, grab a diaper, and head downstairs.

Surveying the living room, I know that I need to step carefully. Adam's wooden train tracks snake around the furniture. His play tent is set up in one corner. LEGO pieces are strewn about. Dave's book chapters cover the dining table and extend to several of the dining chairs. Looking for a free surface on which to change Jacob's diaper, I conclude that the floor is the best bet.

Yes, we badly need a larger house with a playroom and a real bedroom for Jacob. My goal of getting the house ready to put on the market keeps getting put off. I've already missed the opportunity to have it listed at the beginning of the spring buying season. I need a week off work to sort through and discard excess stuff and have the walls painted and the oak floors refinished. But life intrudes. Dave is trying to meet a publishing deadline of June 15. And the recruitment of the new chair for Psychiatry is in high gear, the committee having identified two finalists who will arrive for repeat interviews this month.

On Jim's departure, Lynne Wexler was appointed acting chair. She and I have a good relationship. Lynne keeps me informed of the recruitment committee's progress. I meet most of the candidates to give them administrative overviews of the department. Now, Lynne asks me to prepare detailed notebooks summarizing the teaching, research, and clinical programs, along with snapshot presentations of our very complicated funding scheme, a mix of public and private funds within a state university system. A week that I might have spent preparing our house to show potential real estate agents has disappeared.

Dave and I have another concern weighing on us. We were so relieved when Jacob took his first steps in Minnesota, meeting his walking milestone a week before the age of seventeen months. But at his well-child visit two months later, when Dr. Patel reviewed my answers to the Ages and Stages screening questions, she told me that Jacob should have at least six words by eighteen months. Jacob has none, not even "Mama" or "Dada." She questioned me about other forms of communication, such as pointing and general sounds, and confirmed that Jacob is now behind in speech.

While I know that two siblings shouldn't be compared, I think constantly about how Jacob's development has been slower than his brother's. Different in ways that I can't quite put my finger on. Dr. Patel gave us a referral to Early Intervention for an evaluation. We now have an appointment at a local child development agency, Building Blocks. I should feel guilty for not taking the earlier appointment that was offered to us, but both Dave and I are so busy with work that we can't take off a day on short notice. Also, I know that I am putting off the evaluation because I fear the results.

On Monday, I walk into the medical center from the parking structure and hear someone behind me calling, "Rachel. Rachel. A word?"

I recognize the voice as that of Rebecca Kahn, the executive director of Faculty Practice Associates. FPA, as it is known, is a strange beast, a for-profit organization created within a state university so that medical school professors can bill insurance companies without that income becoming state revenue. It also allows the medical school to pay salaries that approach, but by no means match, what our professors could earn in private practice. But it is a strange duck. And even stranger because Rebecca sees herself as a sophisticated emissary to this provincial suburban institution, sent to guide us into the world of high-powered academic medicine.

I turn and see Rebecca, carefully coifed, try to hurry toward me. She's a bit awkward in four-inch heels, a designer suit, and pearls. She is always dressed as her version of a Manhattan female executive. I wait for her to catch up, knowing that I will get the once-over assessment of my outfit. My guess is that everything will meet with Rebecca's approval except for my flats—heels are not optional in her view.

"Rachel, I was wondering if we could schedule some time to coordinate our presentations to the chair finalist candidates. I'm sure that you'll be fully occupied explaining the research and graduate medical education programs."

For all of Rebecca's pretentions, she delivers her pronouncements with a Queens accent. Rumor has it that she takes elocution lessons to erase the origins of her speech.

I'm careful with my words. I've learned that Rebecca takes very poorly to any disagreement from a department administrator. There is no supervisory relationship between her and me, but she acts as though there is, often ordering me to perform one task or another and giving me deadlines. It's nothing personal; she does it to every department administrator.

"Dr. Wexler and I will be working on the agendas for the two candidates," I tell her. "We're in the process of assembling binders. I'll be happy to send you the table of contents and our proposed schedule."

Rebecca raises her chin and responds, "Well, I am particularly concerned that we present the clinical practice in the right manner. My concern, Rachel, is your use of the term 'clinic.' It may be acceptable in the Midwest to refer to the Mayo Clinic or the Cleveland Clinic, but on the East Coast, the term 'clinic' connotes a facility for Medicaid or non-insured patients. We've put great effort into establishing a private practice here, and I want to make certain that the candidates understand that we are not primarily engaged in charity care."

"Rebecca, I don't think you need to worry about that. I've lived here now for four years, and I'm aware of the meaning of the term. We use the term 'teaching clinic' only to refer to our supervised resident settings, where we do have a sliding payment scale. I think that you know that."

Rebecca gives me a patronizing nod. "I'll have Barbara give you a call. I think we need to coordinate." She straightens her scarf, almost smiles, and heads in the direction of her office.

I can't help but mouth, "Good grief!" I turn to take the elevator up to the sixteenth floor. When the doors open, I see my counterpart in the department of medicine. Entering, I tell her about my encounter with Rebecca. We roll our eyes and laugh. Rebecca has no idea how she is perceived. Or if she does, she doesn't care.

Later that day I'm summoned by phone for a meeting on Friday with "Ms. Kahn," as her assistant always refers to Rebecca. I know the issue well by now. Rebecca has been trying since arriving at Hudson Valley to have FPA oversee all clinical operations rather than their being managed by individual clinical department practice administration. Several departments, including radiology and pathology, contract with FPA for this service, but the rest of the clinical services have no desire to give up control to Rebecca. She keeps trying, however. My guess is that she wants to establish a relationship with the incoming chair and to convince him or her that she is better qualified to take on responsibility for medical practice management than the department staff.

Leaving the elevator, I enter my office, drop my bag, and walk over to see if Lynne is already in. She looks as though she is deep in paperwork, so I indicate that I would like a word if it's convenient. She motions that I should come in, so I settle myself in one of the chairs facing her desk and begin explaining the issue.

"Rebecca Kahn stopped me on the way in. She wants to quote, 'coordinate,' unquote our presentation to the candidates next week, which means she doesn't want me to talk about clinical operations at all. When I tried to assure her that we have already prepared our briefing books, she let me know that she would be scheduling a meeting so that she can lean on me. My approach would be to yes her to death but go ahead and present whatever we planned. I've never found it useful to take her on directly and say no to anything."

Lynne replies, "Well, we're all aware of this. She's good at billing and accounting, but none of us believes that she has either the heart or the expertise to be responsible for running patient-centered practices. I trust you to meet with her, choose your words carefully, and then we'll make a skillful presentation to the chair candidates about the benefits of exercising operational control over our clinical programs."

She smiles. "I'm not much of a politician. You can't imagine how much I am looking forward to giving up the acting chair position! I want to return to teaching and taking care of my patients."

"Any thoughts on the two finalists?" I ask.

"Well, my preference," responds Lynne, "and you need to keep this in confidence, is Dr. Martin, but I don't think she has a serious chance. While she would bring two NIH grants with her, she's a child psychiatrist. Child psychiatry almost never plays a leadership role in departments nationally. That's especially true here, with Children's Hospital completely off the main campus.

"I didn't feel the same sense of connection with Dr. Katsaros," she continues. "He'd bring a research power-house with him—expertise not only in imaging research but also in psychopharmacology. He's currently over-seeing almost thirty clinical trials. If I had to guess, his rather slick operation is his draw. Teaching and graduate medical education are probably secondary to him. He'll do enough to keep our ranking up, but the dean seems already to favor him over Dr. Martin—at least that's my impression. Mentioning child psychiatry reminds me, how is your little guy?"

I've spoken several times with Lynne, sharing my concerns about Jacob's slow progress—actually, lack of progress—toward speech. One of her sons was born at twenty-nine weeks, and he has struggled with learning disabilities and mild cerebral palsy. Lynne has been a supportive sounding board.

"Jacob's scheduled for an EI evaluation at Building Blocks in three weeks. I have to tell you that I'm distracted with worry over it. I was also trying to get the house ready to put on the market. That little Cape Cod is too small for us now. Would you mind if I took the week of the twentieth off?"

"Of course not. The resident appointments are all under control, so yes, take off. July 1 is when the craziness descends. You need to be well rested for it!" Lynne smiles at me then turns back to the papers on her desk.

On Friday, when I walk into Rebecca's outer office, Barbara hears me and calls out that they are just finishing and that I should come in. Barbara is standing on one side of the desk and another staff member seems to be occupied on Rebecca's other side. As far as I can tell, Barbara is directing Rebecca in signing a folder of documents. The role of the other person is only to turn the pages as Rebecca signs. Extraordinary.

The other memorable part of my meeting is that I notice that Rebecca isn't wearing her wedding ring—her ring with a very large diamond of several carats. Her personal life is something else that she likes to flaunt to us. Not only does she live in a Park Avenue co-op on the Upper East Side of Manhattan, but she lives there with her husband, plastic surgeon to the stars. She likes to remind us of both her address and of her husband's position in society medicine. While the meeting is exactly what I thought it would be, and my response to Rebecca exactly what Lynne and I planned, I can barely wait to get back upstairs to query my staff. They have their counterparts in FPA who can be relied on discreetly to provide information about Rebecca. I know that I shouldn't stoop to medical center gossip, but in the case of someone as focused on status as Rebecca, it somehow seems justified. Indeed, when I ask about the absence of the ring, one of my staff confirms that Rebecca's husband has left her.

The next week, we host Dr. Elizabeth Martin, a child and adolescent psychiatrist from UC San Diego. She's a truly solid candidate with a strong triple-threat (clinical, teaching, and research) background, as well as having a steady track record of NIH funding. I like her instantly. Dr. Martin spends half a day with me, including time driving to the Children's Hospital and to one of our community mental health satellites.

Immediately following her visit, Dr. Michael Katsaros arrives. In contrast to Dr. Martin, he has little interest in off-site locations. He's brusque with me, firing questions primarily focused on finances. Tall and patrician, wearing an expensively tailored suit and jeweled cufflinks, he lived in his native Greece until his graduate studies at Harvard. Central Florida Medical School has been his academic home for the past ten years.

My gut instinct is that the search committee will recommend him. Our dean will follow that recommendation, because he's interested in attracting research stars who can propel this new medical school into at least the second, if not the first, tier. Although Dr. Martin's research and publishing history is stronger, Dr. Katsaros's research centers on neuroimaging, far sexier than Dr. Martin's projects in areas such as school phobia and ADHD. While clinical trials don't really count as research, I'm sure that his impressive list of pharmaceutical sponsors is attractive to the medical school.

CHAPTER SEVEN

JUNE 2004

Dave meets his publisher's June 15 deadline. The next day, he loads the notes and draft copies of the textbook littering the dining room into boxes and takes them to his office. He even dusts and polishes the dining room table, vacuums, and declares that we're now ready to host dinner parties!

My week of vacation promises to be busy. We have Jacob's evaluation on Monday; It is Adam's last week of school; Dave volunteers to attend Field Day while I start decluttering the house.

Monday morning dawns overcast and threatening. Sandra arrives as usual at 8:30 a.m.

She greets Adam, "Honey, we have a special treat. I'll walk you to school today because baby Jacob's going to the doctor this morning with Mommy and Daddy. Let's get your raincoat in case it rains later."

Adam adores Sandra. Although he can procrastinate forever when I want to get him ready to leave for school each morning, he wastes not one minute getting on his yellow raincoat and heading out the door with her.

We are due at Building Blocks at nine thirty. I dress Jacob in his striped Oshkosh overalls and struggle to put on shoes and socks before he runs over to pick up his current favorite toy, a little school bus, which now accompanies him everywhere. He won't go to sleep unless it's in bed with him.

Dave packs a diaper bag with a snack and some of Jacob's toys and favorite books. I also select several Klinefelter syndrome articles given to us by Heather, copy them, and have them in a folder for the evaluator. We are both quiet as we go out the door. I buckle Jacob into his car seat and sit down in the passenger seat. Dave takes a deep breath and starts the car.

"Is this as hard for you as it is for me?" he asks. "We suspect that our baby is behind in speech and now we're headed to an EI evaluation. Somehow, I thought he would be immune to the effects of the extra chromosome. I don't know why I assumed that we would escape any developmental issues."

I wait a minute to answer because I feel that I may start to cry. "Seems difficult to believe that this is where we're heading. He was such a perfect baby. I have to believe that what they find, if it's anything, will be mild and easily corrected."

We're quiet for the rest of the ride to Building Blocks, a brightly colored building with giant alphabet blocks framing the entrance. Dave pulls into the parking lot. I unbuckle Jacob and resist the urge to carry him in. I want them to see that he walks, holding my hand, like any other little boy.

Inside the front entrance, we give our names and tell the receptionist that we are here for an EI eval. She makes up name tags and escorts us to an alcove waiting area. We see toddlers and preschoolers in the hall, accompanied by therapists. Some have physical disabilities and ride in wheelchairs or walk with difficulty, using tiny walkers or crutches. With others, the developmental problems are not so obvious. One little boy lying on his tummy is being pulled on a low cart by his therapist. He has a blank look to his eyes and periodically waves his arms, making unintelligible sounds.

I feel suddenly overwhelmed by the sight of all these small children with disabilities. And the fact that we're here to have our toddler tested. Could he be one of them? My stomach churns. Dave is reading Jacob one of his favorite books, *The Very Hungry Caterpillar*. My eyes pool with tears. I'm panicky that I may start crying. Just then, I see two staff members, a man and a woman, walk toward us. When I meet the woman's gaze, she smiles. I try to keep myself together and seem to succeed. They approach and the man introduces himself.

"Good morning. I see that you are Mr. and Mrs. Gold. I'm Dr. Stevens, the child psychologist. This is Lois Seigel, the speech pathologist." He holds out his hand. I stand up and shake his hand, then Lois's.

"I'm Rachel Gold. This is my husband, Dave. And Jacob, being shy."

Jacob has buried his face in Dave's shoulder, turning his head every few seconds to peek out, scowl, and quickly look away.

"Glad to meet you," says Dave, rising while clutching Jacob, who refuses to look at the strangers.

"We'll do most of the evaluation in my office." Dr. Stevens indicates the door on the left of the hall. He ushers us into a large room that accommodates not only his desk but also a seating area as well as a play space with shelves of toys and puzzles. We sit down in chairs around a low coffee table. Jacob sees the toys, slides off Dave's lap, and runs to the play area. He looks them over and takes vehicles off the shelves, lining them up on the carpet as he does at home.

"He's fine over there." Dr. Stevens continues, "We've both reviewed the questionnaire and the pediatric records that you sent us. It does seem as though Jacob may be showing some delays. As you probably know, the research into the developmental profile of these boys is limited, given that this is a fairly common genetic disorder, one in about six hundred. I've seen a few boys with Klinefelter syndrome, and the phenotype is marked by great individual variation in symptoms. I also obtained a March of Dimes publication on sex chromosome aneuploidy that includes large-scale longitudinal studies."

I'm impressed that the psychologist has taken the effort to obtain this book, which Heather loaned us after our prenatal testing result.

"We read the same publication," says Dave. "Until we began to fear that Jacob wasn't making any progress toward speech, we didn't see any signs of delay, nor did our pediatrician. The thing that alerted us was that he had

no words as of eighteen months. He does seem to understand everything that we say, however. He can point
to pictures as we say them and follow simple directions,
such as 'get into your car seat' or 'give me the toothbrush.'
He just doesn't seem to say anything."

The speech pathologist tells us that they will be assess-
ing expressive language delay. She will look for nonverbal
communication skills, such as pointing or looking at an
object to get our attention. She will also test the muscle
tone and strength around his mouth to determine if motor skill deficits are inhibiting speech.

Dr. Stevens has walked over and is observing Jacob
play. Jacob has found every single vehicle among the toys
and lined them up.

"Do you notice how he's sitting?" he asks. "We call this
W-sitting. It often indicates low muscle tone in the legs as
well as poor balance due to truncal weakness."

"Yes, he always seems to sit like that," I answer. I realize that Adam never sat with his legs in a "W," but it never
occurred to me that Jacob's way of sitting was unusual.

Again, the psychologist asks, "And does he typically
line up toys like this?"

Dave answers, "Yes, we've wondered if he's turning
into a little order freak."

Dr. Stevens kneels next to Jacob and moves the cars
and trucks out of order. Jacob looks back at me and then
protests, trying to swat the psychologist's hand away and
grab the cars so that he can return them to the line. The
psychologist continues to interfere. Jacob screams and

lies face-down on the carpet. I'm briefly alarmed. Then I realize that Dr. Stevens is deliberately frustrating him to see how he reacts.

"I should have warned you," Dave says. "Jacob doesn't like anyone messing with his stuff when he's arranged it like that. In fact, he likes his routine, and, increasingly, he throws a tantrum if something isn't the way he wants it. But that seems typical for a toddler."

Next, the psychologist and speech pathologist proceed to conduct a very structured evaluation using toys, chimes, blinking lights, and other items to engage Jacob and elicit reactions. Jacob likes the attention and is cooperative. When he tires, the speech pathologist suggests that he take a break for a snack. She uses the opportunity to observe how he drinks, takes a bite of cracker, and chews. They also have Dave read a book to him, observing how Jacob copies actions that Dave does. On their instruction, Jacob and I use items in a play kitchen while they take notes. Then Dave and Lois take Jacob for a hearing test and a series of motor skill tasks, such as walking up and down stairs.

Dr. Stevens and I stay in his office while he discusses with me the questionnaire that I completed. He seems focused not only on communication skills but also on Jacob's behavior, particularly his insistence on routine and ability to tolerate frustration. He also questions whether Jacob attempts to play with Adam, which he seems delighted to do. I ask for a preliminary judgement about his development.

"Dr. Stevens, in your opinion, is Jacob showing significant delay?"

The psychologist looks at me, silent for a few seconds, and then tells me, "I'd rather cover that once I can meet with my colleagues, score our session, and get a multi-disciplinary perspective. We can generally do this over the lunch hour. When Jacob and your husband return, you can decide if you'd like to take a lunch break of about ninety minutes and return for a wrap-up and our recommendations. Or if Jacob needs to get home for a nap, we can give you our findings at an appointment in a few days."

That isn't a choice. I'm so anxious to hear what they have to say that I tell him we can take Jacob to a nearby restaurant for lunch, play a bit in the park, and meet back at Building Blocks at one thirty.

During lunch, Jacob is most interested in the French fries. He dips them in ketchup before shoving them inexpertly into his mouth, coating his face and hands. Dave eats a grilled cheese sandwich while I pick at a salad. After cleaning up our child, we drive to a nearby playground and distract ourselves by pushing him on the swing and exploring the play equipment. I slide down the spiral slide with Jacob, getting dust all over my jean skirt. He is clearly having a wonderful time, enjoying the full attention of both parents for the day. So unusual for a second child. The rain starts just as we are getting ready to leave. We drive back to Building Blocks. Dave and I are both silent in the car, contemplating what the child development experts will tell us. It's pouring, so all of us manage to fit under a golf umbrella to run into the center.

I let the receptionist know that we're meeting again with the evaluation team. She motions us to proceed down the hall to Dr. Steven's office. As we approach the door, I see that there are several staff members in the office. Jacob scampers into the office and over to the play area. He immediately takes vehicles off the shelves and out of bins, lining them up again on the floor.

"Hello, Mister Jacob! Welcome back! He certainly doesn't have any difficulty occupying himself, does he?" says Lois. "We've finished our assessment, so why don't we begin?"

Dr. Stevens closes the office door and takes a seat. He and the other staff compare notes and assemble some scoring sheets. Dave and I look at each other, then around the room. I take in the bright, primary colors, the children's artwork tacked up on the walls, the bookcase filled with child psychology books. The cheerful, child-centered atmosphere does nothing to reduce my anxiety at being here for a serious and sobering purpose.

Lois begins, "We're showing a substantial delay in Jacob's communication skills. On the basis of the other domains that we tested, Jacob also has additional delays in social skills, adaptive behavior, and fine and gross motor development. We say that he's globally delayed in multiple areas. Although his chronological age is nineteen months, he's functioning at the level of a typically developing thirteen-month-old."

I'm stunned by what I am hearing. I listen in silent disbelief. Neither Dave nor I say much while they present specific examples of Jacob's verbal and non-verbal deficits, followed by the findings of the physical therapy assessment and the psychological testing. Dr. Stevens then provides us with an outline of the recommended EI services. He conveys more optimism about Jacob's ability to progress than the speech pathologist's rather stark diagnostic summary.

"We're making a recommendation that Jacob receive intensive services at home focused on building speech and motor skills." Dr. Stevens makes careful eye contact with both Dave and me and continues. "His receptive language is strong, which is what we typically see in sex chromosome aneuploidy. He has secure attachments to his parents and is very affectionate. And he can be engaged and occupy himself with play. So, we have quite a bit to build on. Whenever possible, we bring the services to the child at home rather than delivering them in the center, particularly when the child is so young.

"I would plan on Jacob having three speech therapy sessions each week, and a session each of OT and PT. In addition to the therapy sessions, an infant teacher will be providing stimulation and skill building. This amounts to approximately eight hours of services per week."

Dr. Stevens pauses to let us absorb the information. Dave and I are both silent. I realize that it's easier for me to discuss logistics than my terror at this assessment of Jacob's developmental delays dropped into our laps. It is easier to consider scheduling than to glimpse a future where he may have special needs, one where he may or may not be able to work and live independently.

He then adds, "An important element of the program is having a parent available at least weekly for training because regular practice and repetition has to occur outside of the sessions."

"That isn't a problem," I answer. I'm aware that I can only barely speak, that my fear of the future makes this feel like an experience happening to someone else, not to me or my family. "My husband and I have enough flexibility in our jobs that we'll be able to do this. I work from home on Fridays, and his nanny is terrific. She'll be vigilant about following through on any therapies."

"I'm sure that you have questions." The young occupational therapist talks now. "It's quite a bit to absorb. We will write up our findings and prepare a services plan. It must be approved by the Westchester County office that oversees Early Intervention. Before we can submit it, a parent will need to sign off that you're in agreement. It should be available by Friday, if you'd like to make an appointment with our social worker. You'll have an additional opportunity then to discuss the report and the services that we recommend."

Dave asks, "Will the therapy be covered by our insurance? I mean, of course we will pay for it if it isn't covered, but . . ."

"Oh, no," interjects Dr. Stevens, "EI services are completely funded by a combination of state and federal funds. There's no charge for the services or for this evaluation. Some parents choose to supplement with private services, but we're recommending a rather intensive eight-hour program each week. I don't think that you would gain anything by adding services."

During all of this quiet drama, Jacob has played happily with the vehicles. He occasionally will bring one over to show to Dave or me. He's oblivious to the implications for his future. Now, he walks over to us with his school bus in one hand and a plastic giraffe in the other. He stops and beams at the group of us, then giggles and hands the school bus to the speech therapist before doing a little dance and plopping his head in my lap.

Dave stands up and picks up Jacob's diaper bag. He needs to negotiate some with Jacob to get him to give up the giraffe. When Dave picks him up, Jacob relaxes over his shoulder, and closes his eyes. It's been a long day for all of us. Dave addresses me, "Why don't you set up the appointment on Friday? I'll get Jacob settled in the car."

I follow Dr. Stevens to reception, where I'm given an appointment. I leave the building and join Dave and Jacob in the car. Jacob is already sleeping. During the ride home we are again quiet, this time because I'm weeping.

For the next four days, I distract myself by decluttering the house. I am ruthless about discarding things, beginning with wedding presents that we have never used: sandwich scissors, ugly blown-glass vases, two fondue sets. We have no intention of having another baby, so I collect the playpen, infant swing, maternity clothes, and other baby stuff for Dave to take to Goodwill.

I get an estimate from our handyman for painting and select a neutral shade for the walls. He promises to bring in colleagues to refinish the floors with water-based refinishing materials so that we don't have to vacate the house overnight while fumes dissipate.

Dave and I decide to postpone speaking with our parents or siblings about Jacob's delays until we've seen the full report. Ellen would want to see the report, given her background in special education. I am not at all certain when, if ever, I will be ready to talk about Jacob's delays.

On Friday, my last day off, I drive to Building Blocks. The social worker, Fiona McGuinn, is originally from Northern Ireland, so we chat about our common heritage. Then she gives me a copy of the report. I read through its pages. The language is clinical, of course; the report provides a comprehensive assessment of Jacob's early progress through milestones and a discussion of the impact of Klinefelter syndrome in placing him at risk of significant developmental delay. The report states that by age two, seventy percent of children with XXY display the types of deficits found in Jacob. It contains detailed observations of behavior, communication, and physical "domains." The evaluation puts words to my hunch about how Jacob's development had been slower than Adam's, things I'd detected but been unable to describe in concrete terms. I read over raw, percentile, and composite scores in various tables. The score that gives me greatest pause is an estimate of IQ: a range of 65 to 75. Even I know that means borderline mental retardation, now called intellectual disability. My stomach drops. I have the familiar sensation of this being some other child, not mine. How could this be happening to us? I have the feeling that when we decided to continue the pregnancy, we gambled that our child would not have any significant disabilities. My initial reaction is that it appears we've lost.

Somehow, I get through the meeting with the social worker, signing the forms that I agree with the recommendations. I'd planned to be off for the afternoon, fortunately. Once home, I barely remember the meeting or the drive to and from Building Blocks. In the driveway, before I go into the house where my darling baby is probably napping, I tell myself that I've got to snap out of this, that my distress can't be apparent to my kids. I've got to find a way to accept sobering news. If only I were religious and could lean on prayer or meditation and somehow accept the situation. I used to run and have been working up to jogging for two miles. Maybe a run will help with this psychic pain.

Entering the house, I tell Sandra, "I'm going out for a bit of exercise before picking up Adam."

I change into exercise clothes, put on my sneakers, and leave the house, running toward a park.

CHAPTER EIGHT

AUGUST 2004

We spend the summer adjusting to the new reality of a toddler who needs intensive developmental therapy and hoping, praying that he'll make substantial progress. Our greatest hope is that his future won't be greatly limited.

Members of the therapy team arrive four mornings per week to put Jacob through a series of exercises designed to engage him in play and exploration while developing skills in small steps, reinforced by repetition and lots of positive feedback. There are notebooks filled with "homework" for us to complete with Jacob to augment his therapy sessions. All the while, we try to maintain a normal family life for seven-year-old Adam and keep up with the demands of our jobs.

Adam attends day camp, with some unscheduled weeks at home with Sandra and Jacob. He discovers soccer and rocketry and meets twin brothers who become his best friends. Suddenly, he is far more grown up, having sleepovers, and even spending a long weekend with the twins' family at a lake cottage in the Berkshires.

Dave's textbook is released to excellent reviews. It will probably take a year for royalties to provide even a modest source of income, but Dave is proud that he now is the author of a book. In addition, when the dean of admissions of the law school takes a position on the West Coast, Dave is asked to take on this role in an acting capacity, with a small increase in salary.

In Psychiatry, negotiations with Dr. K, as we have taken to calling him, stretch over two months before he finally agrees to all the terms of his recruitment package. Neither Lynne nor I believe that the medical school needs to go to these lengths to fill the position. But no one asks us, of course. I receive a phone call from the human resource director's office to meet with her and Cameron Ellis to prepare for the new chair's arrival. I'm told that he will bring a research coordinator, three PhDs, and a research assistant. My job will be to get these people on staff and transfer research grants and clinical trials from Central Florida to Hudson Valley.

The next week, I enter the office of Dorothy O'Connor, the HR director. It's utilitarian, all business, with gray industrial carpeting and Dorothy's walnut desk and hutch. I take a seat at the small conference table, and she hands me a folder. Cameron Ellis joins us.

"So, how's your summer been?" asks Dorothy.

"Busy and too short," I answer. "My only vacation was a week at home getting the house decluttered and painted so that we can put it on the market and find something with a bit more room now that we have two kids. We're hoping to take off for a long weekend before school starts. And you?"

"I've completely stopped taking summer vacations," she says. "It isn't relaxing for me with faculty and residents coming on and off the payroll all summer. I have two weeks planned for after Labor Day. We'll be in Virginia this year."

Dorothy's been hiking the Appalachian Trail in segments each year with her partner, a medical librarian who is also at Hudson Valley. A bit of silence. We wait for Cameron to add something about his summer. Or to begin. He's not much for small talk.

"Dr. Katsaros has five people who he plans to bring with him," says Cameron. "He negotiated salary funds for them for a five-year period as well as about three thousand square feet of dedicated clinical trial space in downtown White Plains."

Cameron gives me a summary table of the budget provided as part of Dr. K's recruitment package. Positions, moving expenses, lots of equipment, and substantial rent for this off-site facility.

"He insisted on offsite space for his pharmaceutical trials, although I can't see that this is the most efficient use of dollars. The people he's bringing are all routine appointments. He originally requested that the research coordinator, a woman with an MPH, be hired in at your level but have no reporting relationship to you, Rachel. I told him that I couldn't approve this, even though it's true that Elizabeth Brown's qualifications and experience resemble yours. Department administrators are responsible for research within our departments, and his support team needs to be accountable to you. He's agreed, although I don't think he or Libby—that's what she goes by—are happy about it."

Dorothy slides a folder over to me and opens it to show me the job descriptions and résumés for the five positions. I'm curious to see Libby's résumé. I'm not sure that I'm enthusiastic about having someone as a subordinate if she doesn't want to be. Her paperwork is first in the folder.

"Has there been any discussion of her relationship to Carol Russo?" I ask. "Carol works half time as our research nurse and half time as the department's research specialist, helping faculty with grant paperwork."

"I think that Dr. Katsaros anticipates retaining Carol in that capacity because he views her work as largely clerical," Cameron answers. "Libby plans to be up here to look for housing and to begin setting up their research facilities within the next two weeks. I have her card here. Perhaps you can show her around and introduce her to the offices she'll need to get to know. I believe that she intends to move here as quickly as possible."

"Anticipated arrival time for the chair?" I ask. "And is there a wife or a significant other?"

Cameron smiles. "He's not terribly forthcoming about his personal life. Apparently, there is a Mrs. K, but she's not planning to relocate at this time. She's a high school principal and wants to explore her options in the New

York area before making a move. There are also two children, both college students. I believe he plans to be here October first."

Dorothy excuses herself to attend another meeting. Cameron asks me if I would stay for a moment to discuss something else. He looks uncomfortable.

"This is a bit awkward, but I know that you arranged to work from home on Fridays after your son was born."

"I'd anticipated going back to the office every day as soon as the new chair arrives," I answer. "I'll start back on Fridays right after Labor Day."

Returning to my office, I decide that I will have Karen phone Libby to see what her travel plans are. I know that things always change substantially when a new chair arrives. From the discussion today, I am somewhat apprehensive about how radically the working atmosphere will be altered.

The next day, however, I forget about my fears about the new chair. When I enter Jacob's room in the morning after hearing him babbling, he gives me a big smile, and says, "Mama! Mama!"

I sweep him out of his crib and hug him.

"Dave!" I shout, bringing him over to the bed. "Dave, he just said 'Mama.'"

We cuddle him. Dave kisses me, then Jacob. And Jacob, with all the reinforcement, repeats "Mama" all day.

The therapists take a break over the last two weeks of August. Before the break, Dave and I meet with them for a progress report. The infant teacher, Cheryl, is a middle-aged woman with a warm manner who oversees Jacob's program. She's been providing EI services for over twenty years. Her recommendation when Jacob started therapy was that we keep a notebook for daily communication. I see the therapists only on Friday when I am home. Reading through the notebook over the eight weeks that Jacob's been in the program, I thought I had seen evidence that he was picking up new skills. Now she confirms this.

"Jacob's doing beautifully," she tells us. "When I first was assigned the case, I thought that he was going to present as quite low functioning. The assessment indicated global delays, which usually means more challenges than children with, say, speech deficit alone. It took him a week to warm up to us so that we could begin engaging him in therapeutic exercises. But once he started, we've been amazed at how responsive he is. His receptive language skills are perhaps several months beyond what we would expect for this age. What's your impression?"

"Well, we all know now that he's saying 'Mama,'" Dave responds. "I'm waiting now for 'Daddy.'"

Cheryl, the speech therapist, tells us that he's doing an excellent job of imitating sounds, as well as performing the mouth exercises that they do with him.

Barbara adds, "Jacob has overall difficulties with motor planning, both in terms of the muscles that he needs for speech as well as more gross motor skills, like raising his arm and pointing at something when he wants to get your attention. Since this movement was so difficult, he didn't even attempt it, which is why you told us that it seemed he didn't move around very much. He didn't appear to you to be as animated as he should be. So, overall communication, not just speech, is impaired. At this point, he's rapidly making up all those milestones. I feel quite confident that he'll develop functional speech and that you'll start seeing progression to multiple words soon. It's probably too early to be concerned with IQ, but none of us thinks he is in the MR range, as his evaluation estimated."

I reach over and grab Dave's hand. We smile at each other, so relieved that we're probably not facing intellectual disability. I listen while Cheryl praises the way that Sandra incorporates exercises into daily play with Jacob. But all I can think of is that Jacob probably has fewer challenges than we had feared.

CHAPTER NINE

SEPTEMBER 2004

Over Labor Day weekend, we visit the Bronx Zoo with the family of the twin boys, Luke and Nathan Carlson, who became Adam's best friends through soccer camp. The Carlson family lives in Scarsdale, a few miles south of White Plains.

Dave and I have spent weekends visiting open houses in White Plains as well as nearby suburbs, including Chappaqua and Scarsdale. We like White Plains but have decided that we want to live in a village where the traffic is less heavy, with neighborhoods where our kids can have some independence. I suspect that we both think of our childhoods in Wisconsin and Massachusetts, imagining our boys walking around town with their friends or riding their bikes safely. White Plains has become too urbanized for that. We still want to be on the Metro North commuter train line for easy access to Manhattan. Scarsdale is a short train ride from New York City. The other communities that we look at north of White Plains add time to any train ride. With Dave's interest in land-use planning and smart development, I know he's leaning toward Scarsdale. Although it's known for its mansions, there are many smaller, modest homes there that we can afford, particularly those near the small shopping area.

The Carlsons tell us that a four-bedroom Tudor has just gone on the market in their neighborhood, walking distance to the train station and village center. It's in our price range, which means that many things need updating, including the kitchen and baths and probably also the windows and heating system. Then the realtor who originally sold us our Cape Cod phones to tell us she has a cash buyer for our White Plains house. Within two weeks, we're in contract on both properties. Our move-in date will be in November. It means a mid-year change of schools for Adam, but he seems unfazed by this, particularly because he'll be at the school the twins attend.

Meanwhile, in my work life, the immediate concern for me is Libby's visit. Dorothy assures me that the organization chart clearly shows her reporting to me, but I know that the new chair is still not happy about Libby reporting directly to anyone other than him. I wonder what her attitude is toward having me as her boss.

My goal for her visit is to introduce her to the group in sponsored programs, the office that administers grant funds for the university. I'll go over personnel matters for the employees transferring here, as well as renovations and equipment purchases for the clinical trial space. I'll also introduce her to people she'll be working with in facilities. Karen arranges for Libby to meet me first thing on a Monday morning.

When I arrive at work on Monday, Libby is walking around the administrative offices, peering into the various rooms. At first, her back is turned to me. She's about my age, wearing a dark blazer, gabardine pants, and loafers—very business-like. She turns, and I see large glasses and a face framed by a blond pageboy. She looks at me, unsmiling.

I feel a bit awkward, but quickly say, "Welcome, Libby. I'm Rachel Gold. Let me get some coffee on and then we can meet in my office. Did Karen fax you the tentative schedule?"

"Yes, I got it." Libby replies, still without smiling. "Thank you for arranging the meetings. But I like to introduce myself, so I think I'll go on my own to sponsored programs. I'll also speak with the facilities manager. I'm sure you have other things to do."

I'm momentarily dumbfounded. I realize that she doesn't intend to accept that I am her supervisor. I know I'd better assert myself immediately, or I will lose any chance to oversee her work.

"I appreciate that, but both the research dean and the facilities manager made it clear they want me in on the first few meetings. Why don't you come with me to the break room while I get coffee?" I indicate the short hallway off the waiting area. Frowning, Libby follows.

Busying myself with switching on the coffeemaker and getting filters and bags of coffee out of the cupboard, I decide that it's up to me to keep conversation going.

"It's quite an impressive group of clinical trials you're bringing. Also, how many years do you have left on the NIH-funded imaging study?"

"We're finishing up a four-year award," she says stiffly. "We have a second four-year award to continue the work with four additional sites. Hudson Valley's equipment and your ease of recruiting subjects were two of the attractions of coming here," she says. Libby looks around the room, avoiding my eyes. "I've added a visit to Radiology while I'm here."

I ask her if she likes coffee or tea, but she shakes her head, purses her lips, and says, "Never. I never drink caffeine."

"Oh, we have decaffeinated everything," I tell her. Opening the cupboard, I take out some of the herbal teas to show her. "If you like herbal tea, we have that."

Libby smiles, a somewhat tight smile, but nonetheless a smile. "Oh, yes, I like peppermint."

I show her how to get hot water out of a heated reservoir on the coffee brewing machine. Then I pour my coffee and show her the way to my office. Karen has arrived for work and is just sitting down in her cubicle. I introduce the two, although they have spoken by phone, and seeing several other staff come in, also make those introductions. Libby is no friendlier with these staff than she was with me. I wonder what's with this woman. She seems to have no social skills and no interest in creating any sort of relationship with us.

Inviting her into my office, I ask her to tell me about herself. I can tell that Libby isn't comfortable with small talk, but she seems perfectly comfortable talking about her own career, and she adds a bit about her personal life. We talk about our master's degrees in public health and our career interests. I learn that she's not married and that she currently lives with her mother in Florida. Moving into her own apartment in White Plains will be a new experience. She chose a building one block from the clinical trial space. She also tells me that she'll have her office there.

Libby is animated and conversational as long as we're discussing her. But when I move to the subject of her duties as research coordinator, her face becomes what I can only describe as sour. I point out in the job description where three quarters of her effort will be devoted to Dr. Katsaros' project and one quarter to general research administration for the Psychiatry faculty. Jobs evolve, she tells me, and she then adds that Carol, the current research associate, doesn't seem to need any help.

At sponsored programs, Libby is considerably more forthcoming with information, appearing to want to make as good an impression as possible. Her standoffish manner may be largely directed toward me and the unwelcome fact that I'm her supervisor. Or maybe not. Perhaps she's uncomfortable in new environments and takes a while to warm up. We return to Psychiatry before lunch. I show her an empty office that she should feel free to use now and until the renovations to the offsite space are complete.

The schedule that I made includes lunch with me at noon. I planned to take her to a café across from the Medical Center, but when I mention leaving for lunch, she tells me, "Oh no, I'd rather not. I'm vegetarian and gluten free. Until I know the places in White Plains that I can trust, I always bring my own food. Besides, I have the appointment at Radiology this afternoon." She then turns away from me, picks up the phone, and dials a number. This is not starting well.

After Libby leaves for her meeting at Radiology, we don't see her again, even though her visit was to last three days. It's always possible that it's taking two full days to arrange her apartment lease, even though she already knows where she will be renting. Karen and I make some phone calls to determine whether she is in any likely place in the center, but she hasn't been seen in facilities, sponsored programs, or any other location that would make sense. Our only contact with her is an envelope that arrives the next week with her trip expenses, requesting reimbursement.

CHAPTER TEN

∽

OCTOBER 2004

The next two months are filled with our family's moving plans. We also celebrate the High Holy Days, attending services at the Reform synagogue where we are now members. Ellen and Ben visit for Rosh Hashanah, although Ben leaves early to return to Boston for more traditional services for the second day.

Ellen stays in White Plains to give her an opportunity to meet with Jacob's therapists. As an elementary school teacher, she also has expertise in communication disorders in children. Now we ask her to give us her opinion of the program. After Jacob's evaluation, we told our families that Jacob would begin early intervention. We didn't reveal the full extent of our fears for his future, however, including the findings of a six-month delay in development and the estimate of borderline mental retardation. I'm glad that we held off. Jacob now has ten words that we can understand clearly and numerous others that are "under construction."

This morning, Ellen joins Jacob, his speech therapist, and his infant teacher for his morning session. I make a point of not participating so that Ellen can observe and ask questions on her own. After the therapists leave, I let her read Jacob's evaluation.

Ellen finishes reading and is silent for a few moments. Then she looks up at me and says softly, "I really had no idea that you and Dave were confronting this level of delay. The first thing that they told me was how very delayed Jacob was when they first worked with him. But they also told me how quickly he has progressed. It must have been hellish to believe right after his EI eval that you might have a son with intellectual disability.

"As far as I can tell, they're using really sound, evidence-based methods. And Jacob is progressing daily. I must tell you that while Massachusetts has very good services, the supports you're being provided by Westchester County are probably superior."

At Building Blocks after lunch, Ellen and I meet with his social worker, Fiona. She's very pleased with his progress and tells us they estimate that Jacob, who is twenty-one months, is now functioning at the level of a seventeen-month-old child. He's made up about half of his delay.

Fiona hands me a newsletter that I recognize from the Klinefelter advocacy organization, KSA, telling me, "The mother of one of our Pre-K students gave me this. I told her that we have another little boy with Klinefelter syndrome. Of course, I didn't identify you. She asked me to give this to you. If you're willing, she'd like to exchange phone numbers."

"I'm on a listserv with other parents of kids with XXY. I'd love to speak with another mom in person."

I note that the mother has written her name, Star Esposito, and her phone number on the newsletter. I hand it to Ellen who scans it.

"Oh, look," she says. "This group, KSA, has family conferences. There's one that was held this summer in California. But next year they plan to meet in Boston. I'm sure we can go."

"We also have a monthly support group where you can meet other parents," Fiona adds. "It's a good opportunity to share resources. Also, your feelings about having a child with delays."

She hands me a flier about the group with the schedule of meetings. But I'm not sure that I want to incorporate "special needs" into my life yet. I'm still hopeful that Jacob will continue to make up his delay so that we can eventually put this behind us. I'm intrigued, however, to meet another family with an XXY boy. Of course, if he attends Building Blocks preschool, then he most surely experienced developmental delays.

That evening, after the boys are in bed, I make a phone call to Star. She answers and I introduce myself.

"My name's Rachel Gold. Your name and number were given to me by the social worker at Building Blocks today. I have a little boy who's almost two who has Klinefelter syndrome."

"Oh, yes," Star exclaims. "Fiona phoned to tell me that you'd be calling. My Donny is four. I had hoped that I could meet another family, and I was so happy when she told me that the school has another boy with KS. After Donny didn't walk until eighteen months or talk by two, we took him to Developmental Peds at the medical center. They did all sorts of testing, including a blood test that turned out to be a karyotype. I was so relieved that there was an explanation. We were referred to Building Blocks. They've been great. He seemed so timid and lost before he could talk. He cried constantly and threw terrible tantrums. Believe me, life has been much better since Donny started being able to communicate with us."

We talk for a while on the phone. The Espositos' home is in a school district west of White Plains. Star tells me that after the age of three, children are no longer authorized for services by the county but rather by the local school district. She also tells me that Donny progressed so well in making up his milestones that by age three, her school district told her he no longer qualified for services. She had to get an advocate to help her fight for continued services. She succeeded because Donny still has delays in multiple areas.

Again, I'm reluctant to acknowledge that Klinefelter syndrome may be a continued presence in Jacob's development—or in our lives. I tell Star that I'm busy with the move but will keep her number for later in the fall. Star, hearing that we are moving to Scarsdale, tells me that she's envious. Scarsdale is an affluent district with a generous special education program. And while Dave and I didn't discuss special education services specifically, the well-funded programs of Scarsdale figured into focusing our housing search.

After we hang up, I realize that this must be the process of adjustment to special needs: Hope for the best but plan for a continuing need for support. It's true that Jacob's development is always in the back of my mind now, a constant presence.

CHAPTER ELEVEN

∽

OCTOBER 2004

Since Libby's visit, I'm surprised that I haven't heard anything more from her or from Dr. K. I know that Libby is working with facilities on the clinical trial office and with sponsored programs on transferring grants. But I know this only because those offices phone me when they need purchase orders or forms signed. She seems to prefer acting independently.

Karen and I complete the appointments for the staff who are moving here. We schedule orientation. Dr. K will have a private session with Dorothy to complete his enrollment as well as the all-important disclosure forms of any possible financial conflicts of interest. Faculty and professional staff in the SUNY system obtain permission for any outside consulting income or employment. They also agree to share royalties from patents for drugs or medical equipment developed while working at SUNY. I'll be interested to see what he reports.

The second week in October, Karen tells me that she just saw Dr. K go into his office. I think that I'll welcome him, so I walk over to his assistant, Susan. His door is shut, so I can't just pop in.

"Susan, has Dr. K put anything on his calendar for this afternoon? I'd like to have a word with him."

She looks a little uncertain and says, "Well, I have several meetings on his calendar that others have asked for: Lynne and the chief resident, the hospital CEO, the chairs' lunch on Friday. I penciled in all the standing meetings, but he's barely spoken with me. He took the calendar, without a word to me, went in the office, and closed the door. When he comes out, I'll ask him if he can see you. I'll tell him that you usually had an hour update each week with the previous chair."

I return to my office. As I pass Karen, she gets up and indicates that she wants to come in. She follows me and closes the door.

"Rachel, Libby arrived while you were downstairs. She asked me where the personnel files are. When I told her that we keep them locked in the file room, she asked for the key. I felt that I had to give it to her. I'm sorry. I guess this change in administration is making me nervous. She's been in her office with a stack of faculty files. I don't see how her job description gives her any right to rifle through confidential files."

I was afraid of this. It probably isn't wise to confront her immediately. But from now on, I'll keep the keys in my office, and she'll have to ask me for them. I can then explain that personnel files have to be reviewed at the table in my office. I tell Karen that we're all a bit apprehensive with this change at the top and that the best way to handle this would be for me to keep them in my office key box where I hold masters and off-site keys. Anyone, except the chair, will have to review files in my office.

My phone rings. It's Susan. She tells me that I can see Dr. K now. I'm frankly rather uncertain about this new regime, but I know that I'm a strong manager and that I'm well regarded in the medical center. We have healthy finances and growing research activity. Our teaching program has good ratings. I've summarized this information in the various reports that we prepared for his recruitment. I bring another copy with me to his office.

The door is open. Susan indicates that I should go in. When I enter, Dr. K doesn't raise his head or acknowledge me. He's reading something at his desk. I stay standing, expecting him to greet me or at least invite me to sit down. Finally, he looks up. Without smiling, he says, motioning to his conference table, "We can sit over here."

I take one of the chairs and open the notebook.

"Welcome, Dr. Katsaros. How did your orientation meeting go this morning? Do you have any questions that I might be able to answer?

He looks at me. I may detect the start of a smile. I don't know. He isn't a warm person. Aloof, I think—my impression of him when he interviewed.

"Well, you might be able to help me with a referral," he says. "I understand that your husband is a professor at the law school. Perhaps he could direct me to someone familiar with New York State labor law?"

This wasn't at all a question that I expected. I tell him that Dave can probably recommend some names, even though Dave's area of expertise is land-use planning law. Then, to bring the subject back to Psychiatry, I tell him, "I want to show you the indicators that I track monthly. I usually have this summary prepared in the second week, provided the reports that I need have arrived. Although we're supposed to be the paperless medical center, they haven't quite figured out how to transmit much of the data without dropping it to paper, so I'm still getting reams of printouts by interoffice delivery. And then I need to transcribe them to spreadsheets."

Dr. K leafs through the notebook. He says nothing for a few minutes. I take it that silence is just his style. I go on.

"Generally, I had a weekly meeting with Dr. Costa. About an hour, no more. I updated him on any operating or financial issues in the department, and outlined what I was currently working on. He gave me projects for the week. We prepared once a month for the division heads' lunch. Would you like to continue with a similar arrangement?"

He appears to be considering this. Then he tells me, "I'm not a fan of frequent meetings. I would like a written memo from you each week on Monday morning. It helps to shorten or even eliminate meetings. We can meet monthly before the division chiefs' lunch, and you can set the agenda with me and prepare materials I want to circulate. Also, I am not one for lots of chit-chat. I understand that there is a computer messaging system available within the medical center, and I would like to make use of it, rather than wasting time with face-to-face meetings.

I see that some of the secretaries are still using dedicated medical billing terminals and typewriters, rather than PCs. Some of my negotiated funding is to be used to modernize the department, starting with the administrative offices. What do you know about PCs and networking?"

"I know a fair amount about PCs," I reply. "I've had PCs in my office and at home for at least ten years. I'm afraid the only thing I know about networking is that we managed to share printers and some software by networking six of us. The center's been slow to adopt a common networking design and vendor for the academic departments. Susan, Karen, and three other assistants are on PCs. Beth and the clerks in the billing department use terminals for the dedicated billing network. We keep a few Selectrics around because there's no other way to do some of the required state and federal forms."

We talk for a while about modernizing systems and about the drawbacks of the current software. Then he tells me that I can give him my thoughts in a memo, written on the messaging system, next week. He gets up from the table, sits down again at the desk, and makes a phone call. I detect that I am dismissed.

That evening, while making dinner, I tell Dave about my meeting with Dr. K, including his inquiry about a labor attorney. We both speculate that it has something to do with the disclosure forms. Dave agrees to get some names of attorneys with labor expertise. I also tell him about Libby's demand to see the faculty personnel files and of my fears that Libby has no intention of either working within her job description or taking any direction from me.

"Dave, I never actually thought before about how my union contract benefits me. The professional union at SUNY is pretty toothless, but we do have some limited job protection. Having completed four years, I'd be guaranteed six months of employment beyond the end of my current appointment, ending in May. I can't tell if Dr. K's aloofness is that he doesn't intend to keep me and intends instead to move Libby into my job, but at least we'd have some income stability if he decides to terminate my contract.

"I can't read him. I think I need to see how this plays out. He doesn't seem hostile, but he doesn't seem very interested in having a close working relationship with me as his administrator. It can't hurt for me to look around at what else might be available. I'm glad that the new house is walking distance to the station. Gives me lots of options."

Dave adds, "You know, that might not be a bad idea, although a commute into the city would probably add about two hours to your day. You probably want to make a point of staying long enough to vest in the retirement system. That's quite a chunk of change you'd be leaving on the table if you jumped before your five-year anniversary."

I agree. And we'll have the additional expenses associated with a bigger mortgage and higher property taxes, along with having an older house that needs lots of updating: replacing the pink-tiled bathroom with its flamingo wallpaper, updating the harvest gold appliances and red Formica countertops in the kitchen, replacing the ancient boiler and water heater.

The first few weeks of the new chair's tenure are routine. I provide lots of data and reports to him. He indicates that they're all very useful in getting a picture of the department. I know that he has a steady stream of faculty meeting with him. With Dr. Costa, I would have been included in these meetings. Dr. K prefers to have them one on one. I decide that this is okay. It's his style. He asks for clinical productivity statistics, and for published articles and research for each faculty member. That's easy to provide because I always inventoried these things for our annual reports. But what he does with it gives me pause, or more specifically, a sickening feeling.

One morning, Susan pops her head into my office to ask when I am free today to meet with Dr. K and Libby. Any time after eleven, I tell her.

Later, when I enter the office, Dr. K and Libby are already looking at charts and spreadsheets that are unfamiliar to me. Dr. K, without any greeting to me, starts in immediately. "We've been reviewing the productivity of the faculty and comparing it to salary, a return-on-investment perspective. It's my conclusion that while the emphasis on clinical growth and teaching was appropriate for the early days of Psychiatry, we need to change the focus of the faculty. I've identified fourteen faculty who should clearly move on. Your job, Rachel, is to draw up a strategy and a timeline for doing this according to what we can manage in this union-driven environment. Only New York State would allow unionized physician faculty members. It's absurd, but I suppose that you approve of unions, protected as you are by your union contract?" He focuses on me and raises his eyebrows.

The HR director had warned me that one of Libby's issues is that her position is on "soft" money, while my position is on the medical center's state budget. Soft money–funded positions are all temporary and thus not unionized. I have some protection from arbitrary layoff, while Libby does not. In truth, the protection is minimal, since layoffs can occur for cause, during reorganizations, or during budget crises, which seem to occur every few years. But soft-funded and temporary positions, such as Libby's, have no protections.

I look at the list. It includes almost a quarter of the faculty, some of whom are tenured, including three pillars of the medical school, one a former dean nearing retirement. Lynne is on the list, with the notation ("poor clinical productivity, no research") next to her name. The list also includes half the child psychiatrists. A wave of panic washes over me. This is a hit list. But I'll have to react in a business-like manner, not showing any emotion.

Trying to think on my feet, I tell them, "What I can do is advise you of the term dates for the faculty if they are not tenured. No one here is on a temporary appointment, so all of them would need six to twelve months' notice from the term date that they will not be renewed. For those who are tenured, you'll have to speak to the dean. Terminating someone who is tenured is above my pay grade."

Libby adds, "There's far too much emphasis on these teaching clinics, which are just Medicaid mills, in our opinion. And Child Psych doesn't earn its keep, so we've decided that the faculty needs to be downsized considerably. They have fellows over there who can handle most of the clinical work."

I find it interesting that Libby uses "we" in terms of department strategic planning. Clearly, she doesn't know any of the regulations regarding supervision of residents by attending physicians. Although I've explained the different funding streams that support Psychiatry to both Dr. K and Libby, they don't show any evidence that they understand. They haven't factored in hospital and county contracts, in addition to clinic revenue.

"We do have extensive contracts with the children's hospital to provide services there," I tell them, "as well as with the county community mental health facilities, group homes, and school districts. They provide substantial revenue that's not reflected in the fee-for-service data from Faculty Practice Associates. That's the data that appears under the Contracts tab."

Libby and Dr. K look at each other. They seem to have missed this in the cost-benefit analysis that went into making up their list. Libby leafs through the pages and nods. They seem to have a discussion that doesn't include me. I busy myself and look around the office. The teak bookshelves that held textbooks and Jim's collection of folk art are empty. Nothing on the walls except for some framed diplomas and certificates. A largely empty desktop. No photos or personal items. The setting is cold, and so is the fact that their discussion excludes me.

"Well, I think you'd better sharpen your pencil, Lib," advises Dr. K. "We'll rerun these numbers to see if it saves any of these dinosaurs.

"Oh, there is one more thing before you leave, Rachel. I've had numerous faculty members explain to me how proud Psychiatry is to be a pharm-free program. You don't allow pharmaceutical representatives in the teaching clinics, nor do you permit them to provide meals for the residents or refreshments for grand rounds. No pens, paper, mugs, or anything. I'm about to change this. We need to see the pharmaceutical companies as our partners, not as enemies. I'm opening access to the residents and faculty during clinic hours. I've also provided the chief resident with a list of consultants that I want incorporated in grand rounds and resident lunches during the year. I'm giving you a heads up because we're getting quite a bit of resistance from both Dr. Wexler and Sarah. I'll need your support. You can leave now," he tells me.

I can't wait to leave. I agree completely with being "pharm-free"—walling off pharmaceutical companies from using incentives to shape Psychiatry's clinical practice around prescribing the latest and most expensive drugs. I'm not sure what they want me to do in support of this change. Clearly, I also have no intention of serving as hatchet woman for this administration. As I exit the office, I see Lynne and Sarah Scott, the chief resident, waiting to enter the office to meet with Dr. K. They look ready to do battle. I can only imagine that the subject is the new pharm-friendly policy.

In the evening, I tell Dave about the meeting. "Dr. K and Libby gave me a list today of people they want me to fire. It's a hit list that they constructed using clinical revenue. Of course, they didn't factor in the contract revenue from staffing the hospital and providing the county services. But they have fourteen people on the list. Seven are tenured senior people."

"Well, you're the department administrator," Dave tells me. "Doesn't Dr. K realize that faculty personnel matters are the responsibility of the dean's office? And everything is covered in the union contract? I'd just point him in the direction of HR and the legal department."

"I did tell him that terminating tenured faculty is above my pay grade. I had a phone conversation with Cameron Ellis about the meeting. He seemed not to be aware that this was in the works."

I hear the dryer buzz and run downstairs to empty the laundry into a basket. We continue talking while folding the clean clothes on the dining table.

"I'm no longer concerned that this working relationship may not be satisfactory. I expect it will become untenable. Libby apparently did the flawed financial analysis of clinical productivity that led to making up the hit list. But she doesn't understand that faculty working on contract to the hospitals and places like county mental health also bring in substantial revenue. She's supposed to be a research coordinator, but she has clearly barged in my territory. And I expect this to be her MO."

I tell Dave about Dr. K abandoning the policy of not permitting pharmaceutical companies to hawk their expensive new drugs onsite, giving doctors free meals, expensive fountain pens, and tickets to Knicks and Yankees games.

Several days later, my counterpart in Surgery phones me.

"Hey, Rachel. I don't know if you can talk about this, but we heard that Dr. K plans to terminate a quarter of the faculty. How would he do that?"

"I'm not even sure I should confirm this," I tell him. "Yes, he has said something about it. I sent him downstairs to HR because firing faculty isn't part of my job description."

"Our guys here are up in arms," he tells me. "They wonder if this is K's plan or the dean's. I believe there's to be a faculty union meeting about it. So, how are you doing with the new regime up there?"

"It's a new regime. I can confirm that. Nothing else," I tell him. "Must go."

CHAPTER TWELVE

NOVEMBER 2004

The move to Scarsdale goes as smoothly as any family relocation can. The boys like their new rooms. We keep Jacob in his crib for several weeks, but he's anxious to be in a big-boy bed. After all, he's going to be two! The boys now have a playroom in the basement that looks like it could be a set for a fifties sitcom, complete with knotty pine paneling and plaid carpeting. When the weather is good, Sandra walks Adam to school and pushes Jacob in the stroller. I know that Adam wants to walk the three blocks to school on his own, but I'm not quite ready for that yet.

I love having our own bath off the master bedroom, not having to share the space with Jacob's potty chair. It's true that the house is quite dated, with its pink bathrooms and drummer-boy kitchen wallpaper, but there's a funky charm to it. Most important, we have more room. I even have a little sunroom off the dining room that I can make into my own study and craft room—if I ever find any time again for sewing and quilting. Above the garage is a dusty studio apartment that we could fix up and use for a live-in au pair or nanny in the future.

Jacob has his second birthday, complete with a tiny tricycle with push bar, a ball pit for the playroom, board books, and puzzles. We are less worried about him and more able to enjoy just watching him discover things and acquire new skills.

But I wonder if buying a new house was the smartest thing to have done now that I'm in what can best be described as an unstable period at work. I didn't contemplate that a new chair would usher in such radical changes or that he would appear not to value having a close working relationship with me and would bring a staffer who undermines me. When we took on the new house, we calculated in my salary as well as Dave's. In our smaller house in White Plains, we could have managed on Dave's salary alone for a year or two, but now I no longer have the option of quitting without having something else lined up.

At work, there are consequences to ending the "pharm-free" policy of Psychiatry. Much of the reaction consists of grumbling by faculty at being hounded by dark-suited drug reps outside their offices and in the outpatient clinics. The residents are quietly delighted by the upgrade to catered breakfast and lunch meetings, although they are acutely aware of the ethical problems with allowing unfettered pharmaceutical marketing in an academic medical center. Three weeks after the chief resident and Dr. K face off over the change in policy, Sarah resigns to take a fellowship at NIMH with Dr. Costa in Washington, DC. She was one of Psychiatry's stars. It will be difficult to replace her midyear.

Libby and I continue to have an uneasy relationship. She doesn't want to acknowledge that I'm the administrative head of the department. Purchasing and human resources keep returning requisitions to me because Libby signs as department head when she isn't. She attends monthly meetings with the supervisory staff but looks bored and leaves early each time.

My relationship with Dr. K is businesslike but remote. He seems to be pleased with the regular reporting I do on finances, clinical operations, and research activity, but he isn't much interested in talking with me. The division chiefs tell me that he is similarly remote with them, preferring regular written reports and minimizing meetings. The Child Psychiatry chief tells me that even after three months, Dr. K still has not visited the children's hospital.

In December, I receive a printout of research activity, but I notice that there are no reports for Dr. K. When I call over to sponsored programs to point out the error, I'm informed that Libby has directed that she receive any funding reports for his projects and that his printouts not be sent to me. I stop at Susan's desk to ask if I can have a minute to speak with Dr. K. She asks for the subject, and I state that it's about his research accounts. She tells me that she will set something up. Instead, after returning to my office several hours later, I find a sealed envelope on my chair. I open it and read:

Rachel:

Effective November, sponsored programs is directing all reports and correspondence regarding Dr. Katsaros' grants and clinical trials directly to me. You are not to request any of this information from sponsored programs. If you do, there will be consequences.

In future, you will prepare your research report and spreadsheet up to the point of including data for Dr. Katsaros' grants. Send the spreadsheet to me and I will complete it for the chair.

Libby Brown

I'm furious. Taking a deep breath, I realize that this is not something to answer in anger. I need input from some of my colleagues. I also need to show this outrageous note to Dave, which I do in the evening after the kids are in bed.

"Work isn't going in a positive direction. Today, I asked for some time with Dr. K because sponsored programs is apparently no longer going to send the printouts for his studies to me but rather to Libby. Instead of a meeting, this is what I found on my chair. In a sealed envelope."

I hand him the letter. Dave reads it, his jaw tightening as he grasps the hostile tone.

"Now, this is obviously sanctioned by my boss. Complaining to him isn't going to get me anywhere, Dave. Bringing her into my office and dressing her down over its tone is likely to invite my boss's ire. I think that my only recourse is to speak with Cameron Ellis. But I think that the handwriting's on the wall, so to speak."

"I don't quite know why your boss would want to sanction this, Rach. It sounds as though he depends on you to keep things running smoothly. Libby's background is limited to research. She doesn't know how to manage clinical or educational activities. This may be more her doing than his. I'd say the best approach is to see Cameron."

Dave reaches over and hugs me. We look at each other. I know that we can weather this, but it's clear that I need to be looking for another position. Getting another job is always easier, I know, if I stay employed. I resolve to handle this situation in a nonconfrontational way. I count the months until May, when I'm vested in the pension plan, and could take those funds with me to a new job. But a new job is also likely to be a commute away; it's unlikely to be the convenient ten-minute drive that I have now.

Hanukkah begins the next week. We'll spend the weekend in Boston so the boys can celebrate the third and fourth nights with Grandma Ellen. Adam is excited because he'll sleep in the top bunk in Dave's old room. Jacob will be in the bottom bunk for the first time. They're also both looking forward to winning money playing dreidel with Uncle Ben.

A new acquisition is my pre-owned minivan. Dave still has the elderly VW wagon. But I need room for Adam, Jacob, groceries, and often Adam's buddies. The minivan certainly gives us more space for our trips to

Boston. Jacob still naps in the afternoon, so our hope is that he'll fall asleep during the drive to Brookline. Adam is now in the van's third row of seats with his Gameboy. Out of respect for Ben and Ellen, we always try to time our departure to arrive in Brookline before sundown so that we aren't driving during the beginning of Shabbat. We explain to Adam that at Grandma's we don't watch TV on Shabbat. We also don't play video games, even though we do this at home.

I've noticed that our visits with Ben and Ellen have become far more relaxed over the last year. Where once Ben was tense, on guard for any violation of halacha, or Jewish law, he's now less vigilant, even easygoing on this issue. Ben initially found some of Ellen's kosher kitchen practices lacking and was unable to let go until she corrected them. He also insisted on strict Shabbat observance, including unscrewing any lightbulbs, such as those in the refrigerator, to avoid turning them on by opening the door. It was as if Ben tried to address the disorder in his life by imposing order on his mother and his childhood home. But he has mellowed. Our visits are more enjoyable, without the underlying tension that we might run afoul of some religious restriction.

Our timing on this trip has been perfect. Jacob naps for about two hours, waking as we enter the outskirts of Boston.

"Nana?" he asks. "Nana?"

"Soon, Jake, we're almost there," I answer. "Would you like some juice?"

Jacob makes some unintelligible sounds, so I prompt him, "You need to say, 'juice please, Mommy.'"

"Pease juze, Mommy," he replies.

"Excellent sentence," I tell him, handing back to him the spill-proof juice container. Jacob's speech has taken off, thanks to the four hours of weekly speech therapy, courtesy of New York State. He doesn't yet spontaneously string two or more words together, but he can do so if prompted.

We enter Brookline, turn onto Naples, and pull into the driveway. Dave and I start the process of unbuckling kids and getting them safely onto the front porch. Ellen comes out the front door, hugs both kids, and brings them inside, while we bring in duffel bags and a cardboard box filled with presents. Dave and I touch the mezuzah and kiss our fingers as we enter. I'm reminded that we now have a mezuzah for our Scarsdale house, not something that Dave would have agreed to previously. Ben isn't the only brother who is more relaxed about things religious.

The menorah is on the dining table. Ellen has also set up Shabbat candles and surrounded the window with string of blue and white dreidel lights. Adam brought his own menorah decorated with various sports balls. He also chose a menorah with little animal candleholders that he's giving to Jacob this evening as a Hanukkah gift.

"Ben will be home shortly," Ellen tells us. "He's busy these days. Seems to have grown the practice. He's targeting some interesting nonprofit areas. He's also considering taking a partner. By the way, Ben wants to take you and Dave to brunch on Sunday. I'll babysit, which I don't get to do often enough."

"Ben seems so much more comfortable with himself. Has something happened?" I ask Ellen. "Anything we should know about? A girlfriend?"

Ellen asks me to follow her into the kitchen to get dinner ready. I brought homemade applesauce with me, as well as Hanukkah cookies that the boys and I decorated at home. I put on my Hanukkah apron and begin peeling potatoes for the latkes.

"That's what Ben wants to talk with you and Dave about. It's very positive in terms of making sense of his life. But I don't want to tell you anything more. He wants to tell you himself. I would be patient and wait until Sunday morning.

"I can hear a lot more speech coming from Jacob," she observes. "I'm also hearing what sounds like two words strung together."

"Yes, it's true," I reply. "He's made up a great deal of his delay. But he isn't quite where he needs to be for turning two next week. His teachers cataloged the deficits for me last week. I have to say that they're not the sort of things that regular lay people would be able to identify. Motor planning weakness, gait abnormalities, poor joint stability."

"Are his services authorized until age three, or do they get reviewed every six months or so?" asks Ellen. "I've heard of children in EI who have their services discontinued because they make too much progress."

"Well, I certainly heard this from the mom of the other little boy with Klinefelter syndrome at Building Blocks," I tell her. "When her son aged out of EI, his school district wouldn't authorize continued services because they claimed he no longer had enough disability. But the mom and Building Blocks made a good appeal, and he was able to continue."

Then we hear Ben. He enters the side door with a shopping bag, greets both of us, and heads out into the living room to see Dave and the boys.

"Uncle Ben!" shouts Adam, running to him and hugging him. "Happy Hanukkah!"

Jacob joins in, "Hankah, hankah!"

"I have a surprise for you boys," says Ben, opening the bag. "This isn't your Hanukkah gift, but I bought each of you a special kippah to wear tonight. I even have one for your dad."

Ben pulls out three suede yarmulkes. The boys' are decorated with sports balls—soccer, basketball, baseball, and football. And for Dave, one decorated with legal scales. They all put them on, ready for Shabbat. No argument from Dave.

About fifteen minutes before sundown, I tell Adam to get out the wrapped menorah for Jacob.

"Jacob, you're getting the first present tonight," I tell him. "It's from your brother. Quick, open it."

Jacob tears off the wrapping paper. Flashing a big smile, he holds up his menorah. Dave names each animal for him, Jacob repeats some. Then I motion them over to put the candles in the menorah, starting with the shamash, the candle that is lit first and then used to light the other candles.

Adam asks Ben which candles are lit first, the Shabbat candles or the Hanukkah candles?

"The rabbis have disagreed about this," replies Ben. "There are texts that cover the reasoning for either. But the argument that many of us have adopted is that it's forbidden to kindle a light after Shabbos begins so the Hanukkah candles should be lit right before the Shabbos candles. I could spend more time on scholarly arguments that conclude the opposite, but I don't think the kids can contain themselves."

Ellen hands Ben a matchbox. He takes out a match and lights his shamash, then Jacob's and Adam's. I help Jacob with lighting his candles while Dave helps Adam. Adam proudly gives the blessing with Ben: "Baruch atah, Adonai Eloheinu, Melech haolam, asher kid'shanu b'mitz-votav v'tsivanu l'hadlik ner shel Hanukkah."

Ellen checks her watch, lights the Shabbat candles, and, with help from Adam, says the blessing, her eyes covered and then using her hand motions to bring in Shabbat. Adam copies her. It occurs to me just then that Dave and I still haven't fried the potato latkes, requiring turning on the burners of the stove. I follow Ellen out into the kitchen.

"We haven't fried the latkes, Ellen!" I'm alarmed that we forgot.

Ellen shakes her head and quickly responds, "No longer an issue. Several months ago, I had a sit down with Ben. This is my house, and while I respect his strict interpretation of religious law, and I've been observant my whole life, I've eased certain things. I don't drive or answer the phone or watch TV on Shabbat, but I've always turned my stove on and off. I told Ben that he has his own apartment. If he wants to observe strictly, he can do it there. But he doesn't have the right to impose his rules on his mother."

"Well, Ellen, I do admire you for finally standing your ground!"

"The laws he adhered to so strictly following the divorce," continues Ellen, "were giving him comfort and meaning that he lacked. I think you'll understand when you and Dave get the chance to speak with him privately at brunch. Now, I know it's a mystery, but I don't want to go into what he'll discuss with you. Know only that I am relieved and happy for him. We need to get dinner on."

We all enjoy the Hanukkah celebrations. Ben and Dave and the boys go to shul on Saturday morning. Having the boys with him gives Dave the opportunity to duck out after forty minutes. We play board games and do other unplugged activities for Shabbat. I think about how I might enjoy making Shabbat a day without electronics, or shopping, or driving. Dave and I both wonder what Ben wants to discuss with us. We even dream up the scenario that Ben has a girlfriend who isn't Jewish! Whatever it is has made Ellen quite happy. It's nearly returned Ben to the fun, witty person that he used to be in Washington.

On Saturday evening after dinner, Ben goes out to visit friends. He expects to be quite late and plans to stay with a friend near BU. He'll meet us for brunch on Sunday and then drive us home. Ben gives us the address of the kosher restaurant and the nearest stop on the T, Boston's trolley.

In the morning, Dave and I ride the trolley to the neighborhood. At the restaurant, Ben is waiting. He introduces us to the owners, who are friends of his, and tells us that we'll be upstairs in a private dining room because Sunday morning is busy and too loud for easy conversation. We walk up the stairs and into a small dining room. We're the only ones eating there, apparently, because the long table is set for only three people. Ben recommends various brunch dishes involving eggs and lox, which I love, and he orders for us. Then he begins.

"I know that everyone in my family was surprised when my marriage to Resa ended in divorce, and I gave up my law job to move back to Brookline. I know that I did not, and could not, at that time, explain it. I wasn't sure of who I was or how I wanted to live. It's taken me nearly three years to become reconciled with who I am.

"The truth is that I'm gay. I've always been gay, although I couldn't admit this to myself, because of my religious beliefs, until now. Mom knows all about it; she's known for about four months. I was waiting for the right time to tell you. Dave, I've known this since Brookline

Day, but the thought so horrified me that I denied it. I put tremendous energy into suppressing it. I knew that I was attracted to other boys, but I couldn't see any possible way to act on my urges."

I can tell that Dave is floored by this revelation. He doesn't react immediately but folds his hands and thinks about what to say.

"No, I never suspected, but please know that I only wish you'd told us earlier. That you didn't have to suffer on your own with this."

Ben is quiet, sipping coffee. I'm stunned. That Ben might be gay had never occurred to me. I think back to our times with Ben and Resa. Such a loving pair. No, this was not something that I had thought about as a possibility. It seemed so much less likely than an affair on her part.

Ben continues, "So, I dated girls. I tried. I loved girls, platonically. I loved Resa, deeply. She was my best friend, my soulmate, but I wasn't attracted to her physically. We had sex, but I only managed it because I imagined having sex with men. The family purity laws were a godsend because I only had to perform half of each month. I was relieved when Resa was niddah."

The waiter arrives with our plates and bustles about, making sure that our coffee cups are refilled. We're quiet until he leaves, closing the door.

"Resa suspected nothing. I prayed daily to put these thoughts out of my mind. If I didn't act on my impulses, I wasn't breaking any laws. Rachel, I don't know how familiar you are with Jewish prohibitions against homosexuality. The best known are in Leviticus: 'Thou shalt not lie with mankind, as with womankind; it is detestable.' And 'If a man lie with mankind, as with womankind, both of them have committed a detestable act: they shall surely be put to death; their blood shall be upon them.' So, there was no room for acting on my sexual orientation in Orthodox Judaism."

Dave looks at Ben, clearly astonished. They look so similar. They have the same expressions and mannerisms. The same receding hairline. And they've always been so close. But not quite close enough to have shared this.

"I feel terrible," says Ben. "Neither of you is eating. But I need to do this. I need to explain so that you both understand. All this turmoil came to a head with a legal assistant on one of my all-consuming cases. He and I worked evenings and weekends together. We developed an intense physical relationship. I knew that I had to end it, that I had to cut if off, and that Resa must never know. I needed to return to my disciplined life.

"My turmoil was affecting my work. I couldn't sleep. I was showing all the signs of anxiety and depression. My doctor recommended a therapist. Over several months, that therapist helped me realize that I was mired in an untenable situation. I confessed to Resa and asked her for a divorce."

I feel like I should be saying something supportive, but I'm speechless from what Ben has revealed. I can't say anything that would make sense.

"Resa and I determined never to tell anyone why we ended the marriage. I've broken that commitment, but with Resa's permission. She knows that I spoke with Mom and that I'm speaking with you. She's happily married and loves being a mother. We still love each other as people. She wants me to be able to move on with my life, whatever is required to do this."

Suddenly, I am reminded of meeting the friends Ben invited to Jacob's bris: They were all observant Jews in their thirties and forties, and they were all single.

"Ben, it never occurred to me that you might be gay," I tell him. "Except that I now remember that at Jacob's bris the friends you invited were unmarried. I did briefly think how unusual it was for Orthodox Jews to be unmarried at thirty or forty. But how did you get from DC to Boston?"

"I made the rash decision to quit my job, move to Boston, and try to live a chaste life away from any temptations."

"So, how did that work out?" Dave asks, smiling.

"It didn't," responds Ben. "I was miserable. And then I heard of a group of LGBT religious Jews. I longed for someone who could understand my guilt and desperation. And they've been my lifesaver. My ticket out of . . . whatever. I also found a good therapist again. A formerly Orthodox Jew who came to terms with being gay. What I want to let you know is that I'm in love. With a man. I spend several nights a week at my partner's condo in

Boston and, within the next month, I'll be moving in with him. You've met him."

Instantly I know it's the mohel, Dr. Eli Rubin.

"Dr. Rubin?" I ask.

"Yes," replies Ben. "But not at the time that you met him. I was still new to the group then. We all need to eat. I've given you quite a bit to digest."

I almost reach for Ben's hand, but remembering that I'm a woman, I reach for Dave's instead. I tell Ben, "I wish that you hadn't kept this to yourself. I'm so glad you feel now that you can tell us. Ellen told us that we would understand now how much more at peace you are with your life. She revealed nothing to us except that you wanted to speak with us alone.

"We'd love to meet Eli again." I pause and smile at Ben. "And now I'm hungry."

Ben tells us that he knows that his sexual orientation will become public and that he will have to stop going to the Brookline shul because many of the members will no longer accept him. His law practice has taken on enough new clients, so he isn't terribly concerned about those he knows will leave. A new area of the practice includes non-profit organizations, including several LBGTQ groups, providing a stable source of income.

I now recall some things that my father-in-law said. Fairly typical joking about homosexuals that one might expect from an older man. I hesitate to speak ill of the dead, but I have to wonder if his attitude toward gays kept Ben from confiding in his parents. My father-in-law was a socially liberal man, but I don't think his acceptance and tolerance quite extended to homosexuality. I don't want to ask, but my guess is that Dave will.

After Ben takes us home and goes up to his apartment, Dave and his mother spend time privately discussing the news while I put Jacob down for a nap and play quietly with Adam. We'll be leaving Brookline later than we planned, but this isn't the time to jump in the van and head back to Scarsdale. That can wait until we all process Ben's revelation.

Back at home, we talk frequently of Ben and our new understanding of his life. On the phone with Dave later, Ben tells him that he was hesitant to acknowledge to his parents that he was gay, not only for religious reasons but also because he feared that coming out to them would be too stressful for his father. My father-in-law had experienced baffling neurological symptoms before his sudden death, and Ben feared that revealing he was gay would be unwise.

One morning the next week, my staff greet me with what they tell me will be juicy gossip. When I ask what it is, Karen tells me that not only has Rebecca's plastic surgeon husband left her, but it's also known that he left her for a man. When they ask me if this isn't the most scandalous thing I've ever heard, I tell them that something similar happened in my family. So no, I tell them, I don't think this is a scandal. And then I go into my office and close the door.

CHAPTER THIRTEEN

JANUARY 2005

After New Year's, I'm scheduled to spend the day on the annual inventory of space devoted to research. I accompany a facilities manager to our labs and offices and all the offsite locations, including Dr. K's clinical trials space in downtown White Plains. I've emailed notice to all supervisors, including Libby. When we meet at the clinical trials unit, the research nurse tells us that Libby is in Florida. As she shows us through the facility, the facilities manager enters information in his laptop.

There is a problem, however. Libby's office leads to a file room. Her office has a combination push button lock installed on the door. Only Libby knows the combination. Combination locks require approval from the dean's office, but Libby installed it without asking. In addition, fire regulations mandate that the inside file room have two exits. When we try to enter through the back door of the file room, we find that the second door is blocked by filing cabinets on both sides. The facilities manager calls two workers to move the file cabinets. He then unlocks the door, and we enter. The file room has twelve five-drawer lateral file cabinets, six on each side, and three rows of shelving above the cabinets. They're filled with ring binders identifying various clinical trials. As we walk through the space, I wonder how the eight clinical trials conducted at Hudson Valley can fill so much space. This looks to me like the filing capacity for many more projects than just the eight operating through sponsored programs.

The workers then enter Libby's office and remove the combination lock. Facilities will cite Libby for a safety violation. I decide to write up the facts of the visit and send the memo to Libby, with copies to Dr. K and Cameron. I have a sinking feeling about this.

Cameron phones me after receiving the memo.

"Rachel, I agree that Libby's difficult. I was taken aback when I saw your memo that you are forbidden from requesting to see the chair's sponsored programs accounts. But I can't really do anything about that or about the problem with the unauthorized locks in the clinical trials office, except to insist that Libby follow medical center regulations. Dr. Katsaros has brought in substantial unrestricted revenue from the pharmaceutical companies that he works with—over two million dollars within his first four months. The dean isn't at all likely to approve my intervening here. If Libby's not actually interfering with your getting work done, I think you'll just have to put up with her unpleasant personality."

"Cameron, I really didn't expect you to say anything different. But the atmosphere that Libby is allowed to generate here isn't helpful or healthy for the department.

I wanted you to see the tone of her letters to me, and I wanted to make a record of it, just in case."

Cameron doesn't reply. I end the awkward silence by telling him to have a good day and hang up.

I find myself feeling increasingly paranoid. Realistically, I think. Between Christmas and New Year's, when the office is barely occupied, I copy the disclosure forms from Dr. K's and Libby's personnel files. Libby reports no additional sources of compensation; Dr. K reports only four consulting arrangements, all less than $5,000. I also copy the correspondence listing more than thirty-two clinical trials that Dr. K originally committed to transferring to Hudson Valley. And I copy my entire personnel file. I take the copies home in case I ever need them.

I've started looking for other jobs. I have no desire to stay where I am increasingly uncomfortable and feel I am being marginalized. I fear what I am sure will be Libby's anger at finding the safety violation notification and the removal of the keypad lock. Libby doesn't return until after New Year's, although she reports using no vacation time. It appears that Hudson Valley is financially supporting Dr. K's clinical trials that are still being conducted in Florida. But I don't see myself being a whistle blower.

One morning, I unlock my office door to find another sealed envelope on my chair. Opening it, I see that it's another letter from Libby. The only two staff members who have master keys are Dr. K and Karen. Karen doesn't put letters on my chair, so it had to be Libby or Dr. K. I take the letter out of the envelope and read:

Rachel:

I am disappointed that you chose to enter the Clinical Trials Unit without my permission and without my being present. You also did not brief me in advance of the nature of your visit. As a consequence of your unauthorized visit, the security of our clinical trials records has been compromised. Apparently, you have also directed Facilities to deny my written request for combination pads to secure both my office and the file room.

I am hereby directing that you take whatever action is necessary to secure approval of the locks. I also request that you acknowledge in writing that you will never enter the facility again without my permission and without establishing first that I will be present.

Libby Brown
Director, Research

At home, I show the memo to Dave, who tells me that Libby is "f-ing crazy." We both agree that it's time to respond to her in writing, regardless of her reaction. Her attitude toward me is intolerable. No doubt Dr. K sanctions her memos to me, even though he remains cordial with me day to day. But it's significant that he only chooses to meet with me once or twice a month, while Libby is in his office daily.

These days, I am careful about what I put on my work computer or send by email. Our computers are now networked, and file sharing is permitted, so I suspect that it would be possible for Libby to read through my files. I decide to compose and print my memo of reply on our home computer.

Dear Libby:

I received your memo regarding the facilities inventory visit. First, let me say that the tone of this memo as well as the previous one regarding sponsored programs printouts is unnecessary and inappropriate. I am your supervisor, and your hostility toward me is not helpful. We need to maintain a good relationship in order to provide effective management for the Department of Psychiatry.

Regarding the inventory, on December 20, I notified all supervisors that I would accompany facilities to inventory all space and its use. This is done once per year to calculate our research indirect cost rates. You had ten days' notice that this would happen. You also did not tell me that you would be out-of-state on that day.

You are aware that the file room requires two exits. We sat in the same meeting with the architect when he explained this. In addition, the regulations manual regarding rented offsite facilities states that facilities will maintain locks and keys. Keypads need the written permission of the dean's office, but you never applied for such permission.

Finally, I cannot commit to never entering the clinical trials facility without your prior permission. I will always notify you, as a courtesy, but my responsibilities include all research and all clinical sites. If you are not available, and I need to enter, I will do so.

I trust that this clarifies the situation.

Yours sincerely,
Rachel Gold
Director, Finance and Administration
Department of Psychiatry

Cc: Michael Katsaros, MD PhD
    Cameron Ellis

Dave and I agree that this may compromise things with the chair, but I'm not willing to have Libby steamroll me. I make an appointment to see Cameron prior to sending the memo. Sitting in his office, we have a brief discussion of my relationship with Libby over the last four months.

I hand him my reply and say, "I don't think that I have any option but to set her straight. If I don't, I have no hope of being able to serve as her supervisor in the future. I will have, essentially, given up my research oversight role. I realize that this may make both Libby and Dr. K very unhappy. But, quite frankly, if I need to lie down and permit a direct report to treat me like this, and my boss approves, then I don't value this job much."

Cameron reads through the memo, frowning. Then he responds, "Well, as long as you understand that Dr. Katsaros has brought in two large federal grants and attracted millions in donations and other philanthropy. The dean is his strong supporter. If Dr. Katsaros needs to choose between you or Libby, it's apparent that he is most comfortable with Libby, and you're expendable. You need to realize this. Please understand that it would make my job very difficult if you left. Not only is Libby's expertise limited to research, but it would also be difficult to recruit another administrator who would agree to take a hands-off attitude with her. But Dr. Katsaros is quite a favored chair right now. I can't protect you. He may choose to give you a notice of nonrenewal in May."

I tell him that I understand. I have lots of options. I don't doubt my ability to obtain another job equivalent to this one. Briefly, I consider bringing up the issue that less than one-third of Dr. K's clinical trials have transferred to Hudson Valley. Libby continues to work on them in Florida on Hudson Valley's dime. But I don't have clear evidence of wrongdoing, so I drop the idea.

After returning to my office, I ask one of our office assistants to take a memo to Libby's office on her way home. I also give Susan a copy of the letter in an envelope and ask her to put it on Dr. K's desk. I tell her that I would like to speak with him as soon as possible. The next day, Susan tells me that Dr. Katsaros would like to see me. When I walk in, he's sitting at his desk and tells me to sit in the chair opposite. He eyes me, unsmiling.

"If you and Libby are going to engage in a cat fight, please leave me out of it," he says. "I don't have time for this nonsense. I expected more from someone of your qualifications."

"Dr. Katsaros, I'm telling Libby that her memo and her accusations are unacceptable. This isn't a cat fight. She needs to adhere to medical center regulations; she isn't exempt. I thought you needed to know, given that the clinical trials space is your project. That's why I copied you on the memo."

He is now looking at other papers, ignoring me. I stand and walk out of his office.

At home, I tell Dave about my meeting and my conclusion that I've got to find another job. I regret having bought the larger and more expensive house in Scarsdale. If we were still living in our little Cape Cod in White Plains, we could manage on Dave's salary. For more than a month, I have been sending out applications. I'm also active in several professional organizations, so I let my network know that I am now looking.

I really don't need all this career stress as well as worries over Jacob's development. Dave plays basketball twice a week and recommends that I also get in some exercise that I can do when the weather is cold, so I build into my calendar regular hours at a nearby gym that also has an indoor track. Maybe regular workouts will relieve some of my anxiety.

Although I haven't worked from home since the fall, I usually spend an hour on Friday mornings with Jacob's therapy team getting coaching on Jacob's "homework" and trading progress notes with them. Karen knows to tell anyone who makes an inquiry about where I am to say that I am in a meeting at one of the off-site locations. This morning, Dave and I are both meeting with his therapists at our kitchen table when my beeper vibrates. It's Karen's number. I wait to call her back. Then it vibrates again and reads, "911." I excuse myself and call her back from the kitchen phone.

"Rachel, Libby is stomping around here demanding to know where you are. I told her you're at a meeting off-site.

She wanted your beeper number. My suggestion is that when she pages you, call back from your cell phone, rather than the home phone. These new phones show caller ID, and she'd be able to tell that you're at home. I don't know what's wrong with her. She's all huffy lately and trying to check on your whereabouts if you aren't in your office when she happens to be up here."

I thank Karen and go back into the meeting. Five minutes later, my beeper vibrates. Libby's number. I'm so irritated that I'm not engaged except to note that Jacob is making progress. Building Blocks has requested another six months of therapy services for him, dropping physical therapy but keeping speech and OT. The meeting ends, and I phone Libby from the cell phone. She answers and I ask what she needs. She wants to know who I've been meeting with, but I don't answer right away. I consider what to say.

"Libby, I have all sorts of reasons to meet with faculty and staff off-site. None of what I'm doing here this morning concerns you. What do you need?"

"Well," she says, "I want you to apply for locking keypads for my office and for the file room. And Dr. Katsaros would like you to apply for one for his office."

I respond, "I can certainly apply for the chair's office. But clinical trials is yours, and you know best how to justify it. The forms do need to come to me so that I can sign off."

I explain to Dave that I needed to use the cell because Libby apparently checks up on me now. He gives me a sympathetic kiss and tells me, "Rach, I know you're wound pretty tight."

He looks at me with concern. Yes, I'm often feeling miserable. We know our nanny's daughter is having a baby in July and that we need to find replacement child-care. I decide that if I haven't found another job by then, I will seriously consider resigning and spending the summer being a stay-at-home mom. But I need to continue working at least through May. And if I can hold on, I do need to bring in more income. We have some expensive and non-optional repairs that we discovered once we moved into this house. It was built in the twenties, and its age shows: a leaking water heater, substandard wiring in the basement, a refrigerator freezer that doesn't keep things frozen, and an old oven that likes to turn itself off in the middle of baking.

There are no additional overt incidents with Libby and Dr. K through the winter. I just have a general feeling that Dr. K would prefer not deal with me. Libby continues to spend time away on "research business," according to her clinical trials staff. She doesn't seem very popular with them, either. I'm being left alone, however, to do my work and to look for a new job. I have several interviews, but I'm not particularly interested in the positions. I get an offer from a non-profit public health organization, but the pay is not worth a daily commute to and from Brooklyn. I keep looking.

CHAPTER FOURTEEN

FEBRUARY 2005

In February, Ellen goes to Florida to spend the coldest weeks of the winter in Miami. She and my late father-in-law always rented the same apartment in a high-rise building with a view of the ocean. Ellen wants to continue that tradition but now include her sons and their families. The apartment cannot accommodate our family as well as Ben and Eli all at the same time, but we arrive for Friday through Thursday. We overlap for two days with Ben and Eli, who stay in a hotel in South Beach until our family vacates the guest room. The boys are on school vacation, and Dave rearranges his legal clinics around our vacation days.

I'm not a great fan of sitting on the beach; my Irish heritage and light complexion make it too easy for me to get a sunburn, but I do appreciate the break from New York's winter, with its cold winds and dirty piles of snow. Here, there's a sea breeze on my face, kids are flying kites on the beach, and there are colorful windsurfers in the water. But away from the ocean, it's hard to appreciate the attraction of Florida. I tend to see everything through the lens of a parent, especially one with a child with special needs. The Klinefelter listserv is full of parent complaints that special education services are greatly underfunded in Florida, so that colors my view of this semi-tropical state.

I wish that Ben had opened up earlier with us about his sexuality and about Eli. But I can understand how he struggled with his gayness and his observance of Judaism, at least the more conservative and fundamentalist version. I know it took years for him to be ready to reveal it to his family, however tolerant and understanding we are. He and Eli are perfect for each other. Ben is relaxed, funny, and entertaining once again. Eli is a great hit with the boys. He's totally comfortable with them, as one would expect a pediatric specialist to be. He does magic tricks, builds sandcastles, and teaches them to toss a Frisbee. Standing on the terrace, I can just barely see Ben and Eli with the boys on the beach. Each one has a boy by the hand and wades into the water then lifts them up each time a wave comes crashing in.

Although South Beach is a gay mecca, Ben and Eli are conservative, observant Jewish professionals, so the bar scene is not of great interest. But they do enjoy being able to walk hand in hand without anyone staring. And Miami has many kosher restaurants where they can indulge in great food. One evening, Dave and I go to dinner with Ben and Eli while Ellen babysits. We're in a kosher Cuban-Japanese fusion restaurant, certainly not something we'd get in White Plains.

I learn that Eli has not had the acceptance from his family that Ben has; in fact, Eli is currently estranged. The estrangement began well before Eli revealed to them that he was gay. Eli grew up in a large family, members of the Belzer Hasidic sect in Brooklyn. He attended yeshiva and spoke mostly Yiddish as a child, although he made himself become fluent in English. But past ninth grade, there was no science education. He could not have passed New York State exams required for a college-prep high school diploma.

As an obedient, young Hasidic man, Eli went to Israel in the year after high school graduation to devote himself to religious learning. But he also decided that once he returned, he would not pursue the scholarly career of Jewish learning expected of Hasidic men. Instead, he determined that he would attend community college to gain enough science and math knowledge for four-year college admission. His parents could not support college education in a secular environment, taking classes with women. But finally, they allowed him to live at home while taking his classes as long as he agreed to pray three times a day, attend shul, and live according to halachic law.

Eli tells us, "I'd never heard of SAT prep courses, so I bought two different books and took all the sample tests in both. The only college that I could reasonably consider was Yeshiva University in Manhattan. Attending a modern Orthodox university was not considered quite as dangerous as 'going secular,' or off the derech, but it was still considered suspect. I'd be exposed to computers, television, the internet. I also insisted on living in the dorms, telling my parents that it would reduce time spent commuting. By this time, I knew that I was gay."

"I'll bet your parents were actually more concerned that you'd be exposed unchaperoned to women," says Dave, dipping a chip into a chili-soy salsa.

"My parents, of course, wanted to arrange a marriage for me. In our community, both men and women marry early, the women in their late teens and the men usually before the age of twenty-three or twenty-four. This would be difficult because I was pursuing higher education, which isn't typical of Hasidic men. It's not unknown, but it's unfamiliar to the community. Academics is simply not a goal for the ultra-Orthodox. My ready-made excuse for why I couldn't contemplate a marriage was that my studies were all consuming. I couldn't provide the funds to care for a wife and the children that would soon follow.

"Yeshiva provided me with distance from Borough Park. Initially, I traveled home each Friday afternoon for Shabbos with my family; Attended shul with my father and brothers; Returned on Saturday evening to Manhattan. At Yeshiva, I was determined to remain celibate, completely focused on my pre-med studies and my job in a biology lab. Most of my fellow students were modern Orthodox. They understood where I was coming from, with my white dress shirts, black pants, and peyot. Rachel, those are the side curls."

"Yes, I know," I tell him. "Even in Wisconsin, we knew a bit about Hasidim. So, did you change over to identifying as modern Orthodox while you were an undergrad? How did you transition away from the Belzer community?"

The waiter arrives to present us with a variety of appetizers, melding fish, tofu, and tropical fruits. Dave scoops some onto a plate and hands it to me, grinning. I take a bite. Delicious!

"I continued to go home for Shabbos, but I was considered an oddity. My parents simply could not imagine my life at Yeshiva or understand why I wanted to spend so much time studying science."

Dave interjects, "I know. Effort that's not concentrated on religious study is merely a distraction from a pious life. A superior brain should be devoted to God, not to science. I'm surprised that the rebbe didn't get hold of you."

Eli laughs, "They tried. More than once. In our community, you know, the rebbe holds sway over every life decision. They found a yenta, a matchmaker, to propose Hasidic girls, or I should say, young women, who had some college, for me to consider for marriage. I was completely uninterested, angering my parents. I did have to sit through several heart-to-heart counseling sessions with the rebbe, but he started circling in on sexual orientation issues. When I stopped coming home because of the increasing pressure, the rift began. I hadn't yet begun dressing more casually—in T-shirts, for instance.

The only thing I'd done was to shave my beard and peyot because of the danger of setting them on fire in the lab."

"Are all your siblings still in the community, still Hasidic?" I ask.

"Yes, I'm one of seven. Two boys and five girls. Only one of my sisters went to college. She has an MSW. Her husband's a pharmacist. They're Touro graduates. So, they have far more contact with the outside world than the rest of the family. But they remain firmly part of the Belzer community.

Another waiter rolls up a platter of chicken skewers, douses it in a liquid, and lights it aflame. Then he serves us a mixture of rice, beans, and delectable peanut-sauced chicken.

"How did you hear about this place?" I ask, tucking into my fusion entrée.

"Oh, it's on a national kosher restaurant website," says Ben. "Miami has perhaps the largest listing of kosher restaurants serving truly good and innovative dishes."

"But go on, Eli," I tell him. "Your story's fascinating."

"My solution—putting even more distance between me and the Belzers—was to take my junior year in Israel at Technion in Haifa. Haifa's a beautiful, liberal city, and I didn't need to fear being seen by anyone from Brooklyn. I shed my Hasidic dress and began exploring my sexuality. I made the decision not to return to Yeshiva. Instead, I stayed at Technion for both undergrad and medical degrees. I only returned to New York twice for my sisters' weddings. When I visited, I dressed traditionally and revealed nothing of my new life. Fortunately, my family didn't visit Israel. My father was a clerk in a hardware store. They never had the funds to fly over to visit me."

Ben adds, "In Israel, Eli maintained his observant life. He wasn't open because the Orthodox there are no more tolerant of homosexuality there than they are in the US, but it's easier to hide in Israel."

Eli continues, "It was acceptable for my parents to tell people that I was studying medicine in Israel. There were questions about why I hadn't married, but it wasn't so immediate as it would have been if I were still living in Manhattan. Then I had to decide on my residency. I knew that I wanted to do urology—probably pediatrics—and I chose a Boston program—Mass General. But that also meant going home. And disclosing to my family that I was no longer part of the Belzer community nor Hasidic, that I now identified as modern Orthodox."

"Certainly, I've read about people who escaped their Hasidic upbringing, but it was always for a secular lifestyle. Not just sort of dropping down a tad in observance to modern Orthodox," I say. "Was this also suspect?"

"It was difficult. They tried to be accepting of me, but they had absolutely no idea how integrated in modern life and modern norms I'd become. Much of the ultra-Orthodox approach to life is to be totally separate from the sinful ways of contemporary America. No internet, no TV, no close relationships with those not part of the community," Eli says.

"In Boston, I completed my urology residency and then my pediatric fellowship at Boston Children's. Now I had a group of gay Jewish friends, some of whom remained observant, as I was. There's a whole network of us. We still don't have an Orthodox rabbi willing to lead us as a group, but we're able to manage as a chavurah, a home-based group for prayer and worship, aided by Reform and Conservative rabbis. We label ourselves 'Conservadox.'"

"And the two of you met through this group?" Dave asks.

The waiter approaches to ask if we want our glasses of sangria refilled and then to ask if he can bring us a second pitcher.

"No, thank you," answers Ben. "But let's try the iced coffee. It's Cuban coffee and coconut milk. Sort of Cuban-Thai fusion.

He responds to Dave, "I was in bad shape when I arrived in Boston, having resigned from Sieberg, Black and left my marriage. While I immersed myself in prayer and study, I also began to explore Judaism and LGBT issues. It led me to this group at Boston University. They helped me enormously, befriending me, praying with me, and referring me to a therapist. The therapist had also left Orthodox Judaism. I told the therapist that I wanted to accomplish the impossible: continuing to live my life as an Orthodox Jew while acknowledging my sexual being. It took me two years to reconcile the two. During this time, Eli was one of my greatest supports, and we grew to love each other."

Eli interjects, "But enough of us. I love your kids. Jacob's speech appears to be coming along well. By the way, I've been asked to speak at the KSA family conference in Boston this summer. As a urologist, I probably follow forty patients with Klinefelter syndrome. I'm interested not only in hormones and sexual development but also in psychosocial issues. Ellen tells me that you'll be attending. I hope you'll bring the boys' nanny, because Ellen also wants to attend. Has she talked with you about this?"

"Yes, she has," I answer. "But Dave and I also want to talk with you, as a physician, about what seems to be a stigma attached to Klinefelter syndrome. We first learned of it from the medical geneticist, the one who advised us to abort. Do you see it as the product of the supposed relationship to criminality? Or to infertility? Or to what seems to be a number of gay and transgender XXYs?"

Eli answers, "All of the above. As I said, I follow approximately forty boys and young men with Klinefelter syndrome. Of those forty, and this isn't scientific, eight tell me that they are gay, and two are transitioning to female. Of course, having one-quarter of these patients identify as LGBTQ may also be a product of knowing that I'll be an empathetic physician. I don't hide the fact that I'm gay. That might also keep some families from bringing their kids to me."

"Maybe we can strategize on effective advocacy for the Klinefelter population," Dave suggests. "We've told the genetic counselor that we don't tolerate stigmatizing HIV anymore. Why should Klinefelter syndrome be something to hide, to avoid discussing? Of course, the issue of sexuality is pretty remote for us at this point, since Jacob is a preschooler."

After our coffee arrives, we continue to talk about Klinefelter syndrome, kids, Ellen's eventual plans to sell the house in Brookline. I'm so glad that Ben and Eli found each other. And I suspect that Eli will be an invaluable resource for us in the future—an in-house XXY expert!

CHAPTER FIFTEEN

MARCH 2005

Once back in New York, the cold, gray weather is a downer. I think the boys feel cooped up inside. Jacob has become more difficult lately, with lots of crying and tantrums. I tell myself that he's in the midst of the terrible twos. Lately, however, he seems to cry as soon as his therapists arrive, and he spends a substantial part of each session resisting working with them and clinging to Sandra. It's a source of worry because he hasn't made as much progress recently. He's happy and engaged when we aren't trying to get him to work on skills, but any attempt to do his "homework" puts him in tears. I had hoped that the vacation to Florida and ten days away from therapy during the school break would reset things, but it hasn't.

I attend my first support group meeting held at a church in Brooklyn, driving with Star, Donny's mother. Between drive time, the meeting, and a dinner afterward with other parents at a Chinese restaurant, I spend more than eight hours talking and thinking about XXY, as well as the related conditions, 47,XYY, and 47,XXX.

Star's son was diagnosed last month with a form of mild autism. Star explains that while Donny has many characteristics of autism, he doesn't show the full range of disability. He has functional language but odd social skills and numerous sensory issues. He won't wear socks. He eats only three different foods. And he engages in lots of repetitive activities, preferring toys that spin like pinwheels over anything else. I've never read anything about an association between autism and Klinefelter syndrome, but of the twenty families of school-age children who attended the support group, three boys have an autism spectrum diagnosis, as well.

Driving home to Westchester County, Star is upset about the presence of three XXY men who attended. Each man told the support group that he had come to realize that he is gay. She tells me that there were also openly gay men at the previous meetings she attended. Star says that if gay men continue to attend the meetings and openly discuss their sexuality, she won't be able to bring her son when he is older because she doesn't want him hearing about homosexuality.

Considering my words carefully, I tell her that my brother-in-law is gay.

"I love him dearly," I tell Star. "He's a great guy. He didn't choose to be gay. In fact, he was even married and tried very hard to live as a straight person. Believe me, he'd be the last person to want to try to influence anyone to become homosexual. I don't even think that's possible.

I think you're born gay. Genetics must be a strong influence, particularly with XXY."

Star is quiet. Then she says, "I believe it's deviant. I'm sorry. I hope my son doesn't turn out to be gay. My husband would disown him. And Donny couldn't take communion."

Changing the subject, I ask her, "Will you be attending the family conference in Boston in July?"

"I'd like to, but if we do that, there won't be money left over for a vacation," Star answers.

"Make Boston your vacation," I tell her. "There's a great children's museum. You can walk the Freedom Trail, see Paul Revere's house, visit the Old North Church."

"No," she says. "If it doesn't involve fishing for my husband, it's not a vacation. And I'd rather that my husband not meet some of the men who come to these conferences. He will lose hope for our son's future."

Apparently, I haven't been successful at changing the subject after all. Star is fixated on the sexual orientation of some XXY men. It certainly won't help much for me to tell her that my brother-in-law's partner will be one of the doctors presenting at the conference! We don't talk much for the rest of the drive.

At work the next week, I have a faculty practice meeting. These meetings are always somewhat humorous. Rebecca Kahn puts on a well-choreographed show of being the sophisticated female executive. She usually begins each meeting with a PowerPoint presentation of the metrics of FPA. Word has it that Rebecca is afraid of computers and software. For this meeting, she has a young tech who not only creates the slides for her but also sits at her side during the meeting so that she doesn't have to change the slides while speaking.

We all cringe during these meetings when Rebecca makes insulting, condescending remarks to several administrators whom she has targeted. They are sweet, older women who are practice managers because they were loyal medical secretaries, not because they have graduate degrees. Rebecca bullies them, asking them questions about return on investment and other technical matters to demonstrate how much more she knows than they do. This meeting is no exception. She focuses on Eleanor, who is nearing retirement, asking her to discuss Neurology's practice mix and then waiting for Eleanor to ask what a practice mix is.

Before the meeting is adjourned, her tech brings me a note. It reads, 'If you have a minute, I would like to have a word with you in my office. Rebecca.' When the meeting ends, I walk over to her and follow her into her office. She closes the door and tells me to sit down in her conversation area, where she joins me.

"So, how are you, Rachel?" she asks.

Rebecca has a tendency, on occasion, to be too familiar with the administrators. None of us are friendly with her, and she is usually haughty and superior. But sometimes she will invite one of us into her office and then share something very personal, such as the time several years ago when she shared about going through IVF, knowing

I was doing so. I fear that this is one of those occasions, and I'm correct.

"Rachel, you undoubtedly know about my recent trauma?"

"Yes, Rebecca, I do. I'm so sorry. I know it's a difficult thing to go through. And it's hard to have people know about your husband's orientation. But these circumstances are increasingly common. Our family's had personal experience with this issue."

"Well, yes, I knew that you were facing the same thing," says Rebecca, although I wonder how she could possibly know about Ben. I never mentioned him at work.

She continues, "It's particularly heartbreaking when it involves a child."

"A child?" I ask. "What do you mean?"

Rebecca looks uncomfortable but she continues, "Forgive me if I have this confused, but I was told that your little boy has a genetic condition that makes his sex ambiguous. That he's both male and female. But that you and your husband are accepting and supportive."

I'm speechless. I need to set her straight as well as anyone else who may believe this. I can't believe that people are spreading this rumor when they have no idea what they are talking about.

"Jacob has an extra X chromosome," I tell her. "It's a condition called Klinefelter syndrome. But he is absolutely a boy. He has a Y chromosome, so that controls his physical development as a male. I need to know who told you this. It's very damaging for people to spread untruths regarding a child's gender. I don't care if this person or persons claimed confidential information."

Rebecca looks stricken. "I don't know who spread that word from your office. My assistant told me. She was probably the one who told people from Psychiatry that my husband left me for a man. Medical center gossip can be pretty cruel. I'm glad that what they said regarding your little boy turns out not to be true. I only wish that were the case with the man who will be my ex-husband. I'll certainly correct things with Barbara. And you may need to have a meeting with your staff."

I tell Rebecca that I'll do that this afternoon.

She then adds, quickly changing the subject, "Actually, what I called you in to talk about is a visit that I had from Libby Brown and Alyce Bryson. Libby scheduled it. I understood that the subject was the advisability of seeing fee-paying patients in the clinical trials office in downtown White Plains. I explained that this practice isn't appropriate. The clinical trials office doesn't meet Department of Health standards for a hospital satellite clinic. But then Libby also wanted me to explain the financials of faculty practice. Does Libby have any background in health care?"

"Not in clinical health care," I answer. "She holds an MPH, as I do, but her entire career has been spent as a research administrator, most of that time for Dr. Katsaros."

Rebecca continues, "For instance, Libby wondered why we aren't billing Medicaid patients for the balance of what they owe after Medicaid pays. I told her that the regulations regarding Medicaid prohibit balance billing. She seems completely unfamiliar with anything to do with medical practice. And she also wanted me to give her copies of the Psychiatry contracts with Westchester County. I referred her back to you. It wasn't clear to me why she had the residency coordinator with her. Is there some reorganization going on up there? I've left messages for Dr. Katsaros to call me, but I'm told he's traveling."

I tell Rebecca that I'm not aware of any reorganization, but that if Dr. K has decided on one, I would probably be the last to know. I also tell her that Dr. K doesn't consult with anyone else in the department when he makes major changes, which has resulted in great unhappiness with him on the part of Psychiatry faculty. Rebecca has already heard all of this from the physicians, she tells me. But at this point, what I'm disgusted by is the rumor mill that has labeled my son as intersex. The implications of having Libby intrude on my job responsibilities are awful but not nearly as bad as this rumor about my child.

We are quiet. I think she realizes that she has opened two terribly awkward and painful realities for me. She doesn't quite know how to end this conversation. Then Rebecca once more adopts her female executive persona, no longer concerned with my family or career. She walks over to her phone, summoning an assistant to bring in her fur coat. Even her voice has changed back from Queens accent to carefully coached pronunciations, yet still not covering her origins completely. A moment later, the young tech enters holding a full-length mink coat.

"Oh, thank you so much, Ming," she says as Ming helps her into the coat.

"Will there be anything else, Ms. Kahn?"

"No, that will be all, Ming."

As soon as he leaves, Rebecca asks, "Isn't he adorable, Rachel? I am so sorry, but I have a meeting in the city, and I have to run. Please let me know if I can be of any assistance."

And she sweeps out of her office. I'm stunned at her behavior, at the rumor about Jacob, at the audacity of Libby and Alyce visiting Rebecca to get the scoop on what is my area of responsibility. I sit for a minute collecting myself. I'd like to go home, but first I need to address the rumor mill. I take the elevator up to my floor, enter the office, and tell Karen that I would like everyone in the conference room immediately for a short meeting. I take my place at the conference table as staff drift in, mentally taking attendance. Everyone is here except Alyce.

"Karen," I say. "Tell Alyce to get in here. This is a mandatory meeting."

Karen leaves and returns with Alyce following her. I look around the table.

"Today, I learned from Rebecca Kahn that there's a very disturbing rumor circulating regarding Jacob, my two-and-a-half-year-old son. Most of you are aware that he has an extra X chromosome, which is a genetic condition called Klinefelter syndrome. In Jacob, it has resulted in a speech delay, but he's made up most of that delay with speech therapy.

"What I learned is that people have been told that we, his parents, are not sure whether he's a boy or a girl. That he has ambiguous genitalia. That he's intersex or has both male and female sex organs." I stop and look around the room at the staff. Some are staring down at the table. No one is making direct eye contact with me; it must be a widely held belief. How did this get started?

I continue, "All fetuses have the default sex of female. If the fetus has a Y chromosome, however, the fetus will develop as a male. There's no question about Jacob's sex. Children with Klinefelter syndrome are occasionally intersex, but that is only the case for a tiny percentage. Before gossiping about this, people should know what they are talking about, scientifically.

"Now, Rebecca Kahn tells me that the sources of this information are staff members from Psychiatry. If any of you have spoken with anyone anywhere in the medical center or in the community, and you've spread this misinformation, you have a moral obligation to correct what you said. It's unfair to a toddler. It's unfair to our family. I want any of you who spread misinformation to do the right thing. Does anyone have any questions?"

They are all silent.

"Then this meeting is over."

I stand up and leave. Next, I will speak with Alyce, but first I need to see Lynne, since she works most closely with Alyce. When I get to Lynne's office, I can hear others inside with her. I pop my head in and tell her that I'll return but she motions me in.

"Dr. K didn't even have the courtesy of telling me himself," she says, waving a paper at me.

I take it and read. The letter gives her notice that her contract will not be renewed. And further, effective immediately, he has appointed a new associate chair for education. Lynne must vacate her office next week and assume a rotating inpatient attending schedule every other weekend in the Psychiatry ER.

"What an asshole he is," she tells me. "But I've accepted a great offer from Columbia. Next week, my husband and I are flying to St. Maarten for a week's vacation. Then I'm taking off a week to do things with my kids and to do some work around the house. And then I'm taking on my new responsibilities with Columbia. So, I don't care. And he isn't back until Tuesday, so I'll never have to see his arrogant face again."

Lynne's angry. There's no reason for me to tell her about Alyce. Instead, I tell her that she deserves better and that I'm glad that she has a great job lined up. I walk two doors down to Alyce's office. I don't bother to ask her if I can come in. I walk in and close the door.

"Do you want to tell me what you and Libby were trying to accomplish meeting with Rebecca Kahn?" I ask.

Alyce just looks at me.

"You do report to me, so you need to answer my question," I say.

She replies, "I'm not at liberty to tell you."

"Alyce, that's bullshit unless you've taken another job. But if you have, you need to tell me that. By the way,

Rebecca said that neither you nor Libby has any idea what you were asking or talking about. And further, she referred both of you back to me. What is it that you want to know?"

She doesn't say anything.

"Well, Alyce, Dr. Wexler is leaving the department as of next Monday for a terrific new position at Columbia. I hope that you're ready to function independently starting next week. And you will have a new boss next week. I hope you're up to it."

Alyce looks surprised. Apparently, Libby hadn't told Alyce that Lynne was not being renewed. I leave, feeling nauseated. I let Karen know that given what's occurred today, I'm taking the rest of the day off. I grab my brief-case and leave.

Once home, I tell Sandra that I've decided to take the afternoon off. I briefly consider discussing the rumors with Sandra but decide that there's no point in angering her. She dearly loves Jacob and has given him so much attention, taken the therapies so seriously. Sandra would be heartbroken to hear that this sort of gossip was circulated.

I call Dave and find him in his office. When I tell him about the rumor, he's furious. He starts considering what sort of damages he could extract from the guilty parties if we can determine who they are.

"Dave, I'm not interested in suing anyone. It would publicize the situation rather than correcting it. I called a ten-minute staff meeting where I outlined what I heard. I asked any of them who spread the rumor to go back and acknowledge that what they said was incorrect. I know my staff, and I predict that they'll do that."

"Okay, Rachel, I'll stop threatening litigation. You need to do something to relax right now. Maybe get a pedicure. Go shopping for new kitchen appliances. I'll try to be home early. How about if we ask Sandra if she can stay a bit later tonight? We can go out for a glass of wine together, maybe early dinner."

I like the idea of the pedicure and the wine. We sign off. I hang up the phone and go into the living room where Sandra is sitting, knitting a baby sweater for her grandchild-to-be. Jacob is napping upstairs.

"Dave and I need to have some serious discussions about these house renovations. We don't seem to get around to it when we have dinner, baths, and bedtime to get to. We're wondering if it might be possible for you to stay tonight until about seven thirty while we go out for an early dinner. Just get the kids ready for bed. Dave will drive you to the station. We'll make sure that you get on the 7:48 back home."

"Oh, yes, that's no problem at all," she says in her lovely Dominican lilt. "Love bedtime with these little men. You know, I will miss them so much after I leave to be a full-time grandmother. Also, I've put the weekend in July on my calendar. I'll be able to go with you to Boston."

Sandra is such a gem. I wonder if we'll be replacing her in August. Will I even have a job then?

Dave arrives home about four thirty. We spend some time playing with both Jacob and Adam before telling them that for a special treat, Sandra will be doing supper and bedtime with them.

There's nothing that Dave can say that makes the situation better. The thought of leaving without another source of income panics me. Between my hurt at the hermaphrodite rumors and whatever Libby and Dr. K are plotting, I know that I want to leave my job. But we also discuss the practical consideration that makes remaining through May desirable. When I get to my five-year anniversary at Hudson Valley, I'll be vested in the retirement plan. That means having those funds once I reach retirement age or being able to borrow from them for another graduate degree. If I leave now, the funds will be gone. Toughing it out for a few more months is worth it. Even if I am fired by Dr. K, and it strikes me that this is becoming a possibility, I've been in my position long enough that Hudson Valley owes me six months of severance pay.

"Rachel," Dave advises me, "I think you've got to adopt an attitude that you're not invested in this job anymore. You have time to find another position or even to do less than full-time consulting. The problem with the sort of position you're in now is that it's entirely dependent on the personality of the chair. Medical school departments are unlike any other academic units. Their chairs are essentially noblemen provided with a duchy. They have latitude unequaled in other schools, not to speak of access to dollars from clinical work, something that occurs nowhere else in academia. Whatever you choose to do in the future, it can't be that sort of job, because it all can change radically in a few months with a new person at the helm."

I agree. I tell him that I'm wondering if I want to take a completely different direction. I've given some thought to genetic counseling, which would require a second master's degree. Reading up on genetics has fascinated me. And since I explored biochemistry as a possible career before turning to public health, I've already determined that I lack only one college prerequisite for the graduate program, a basic course in genetics. As always, Dave encourages me to go for it if that's what I want to do. We can live with our retro kitchen and bathrooms for a few years while I attend school. Now that Dave is beginning to get royalty payments from his textbook, if we're careful, we can manage on his salary using some of my retirement funds. The wine and the pep talk from Dave reduce my panic considerably.

For the next two days, I am surprisingly relaxed and unperturbed by the organizational uncertainty of psychiatry. Several staff members visit my office and tell me that they had spoken with others about Jacob's genetic condition, passing on incorrect information that his gender was uncertain. They've now corrected what they said about Klinefelter syndrome. The staff are all so apologetic that I forgive them, genuinely. I help plan a farewell dinner for Lynne. I'm no longer on the warpath over Libby's undermining of me. It probably is that I don't care anymore. If she thinks that running a department of this complexity will be easy, she'll find out that she's in over her head if she needs to do this by herself.

Later that morning, Karen comes into my office and closes the door. She tells me that when she arrived this morning and walked toward her cubicle, she could see that Libby was sitting in her chair. Libby didn't hear Karen until Karen was no more than ten feet away. Libby had been looking at the calendar that Karen keeps for me!

"She looked totally flustered that I caught her," says Karen. "I nonchalantly asked if I could help her with anything. She said that she was only trying to see your general availability for a meeting with Dr. K. That is bullshit, of course. You also need to know that Libby and Alyce have become extremely buddy-buddy. They sit in Alyce's office with the door closed; they go out to lunch together, which is probably good for them since neither is very popular in the office."

I have the distinct feeling of waiting for the other shoe to drop. I'm being undermined, and Alyce and Libby are plotting to take over my responsibilities in Psychiatry. The atmosphere seems abusive to me with the nasty letters left on my chair, and Libby checking up on my whereabouts. Briefly, I consider going to Hudson Valley's union representative. I need to make sure my administrative ducks are in a row in case I am fired. The strange thing is that I would almost welcome being able to leave this hostile, poisonous atmosphere.

CHAPTER SIXTEEN

On Friday, I'm at my desk working on a computer tutorial on the new web-based HR system. Suddenly, I notice Cameron in my doorway.

"May I come in?" he asks. "I've brought Dorothy O'Connor with me. May we sit down?"

He closes the door. I know instantly that this isn't a good situation. This is what happens when a senior-level person (that would be me) is fired. I turn my desk chair to face them. "Am I being fired?"

Cameron looks uncomfortable, as he should. I know this isn't his decision.

"No, Rachel, you have a term appointment, and you can't be fired without at least six months' notice. But we're reassigning you. Effective today. Dr. Katsaros prefers to choose his own administrator. We're moving you so that he's free to do that."

"Where am I being moved?" I ask.

"Eleanor White is retiring in six weeks," Dorothy explains. "Neurology needs someone to serve as acting administrator while they recruit for a replacement. When we proposed placing you in the position, at least tempo-rarily, Dr. Weiss welcomed it. You have a good reputation, and Neurology certainly needs someone with up-to-date computer and organizational skills, which Eleanor has never had. Now, there's no guarantee that Dr. Weiss will appoint you if you choose to apply, but I think you'd be a strong candidate. And there will be no reduction in sala-ry, no reduction in title. They don't have a desk available yet for you, so it may be a few days before you can move in up there."

"Rachel," says Cameron. "We're sorry about the way that we must do this, but Dr. Katsaros was assured that he could select his own administrator, and we need to honor that commitment. If Dr. Weiss doesn't hire you, or you choose not to take the position, you'll be given six-months' notice of nonrenewal of your appointment. But we do value you and want you to have a satisfactory position to move into."

There's an awkward silence. I look at them both. This sort of thing has never happened to me before. I have no idea how to react. I'm not even sure what emotions I am feeling. My chest and forehead tighten. I feel slightly nau-seous. I'm aware of gripping the arms of my chair.

"I'm not surprised," I say. "I was given a hint last week by Rebecca Kahn, who told me that Libby visited her with Alyce, our residency coordinator, asking all sorts of questions about the clinical practice and about contracts with Westchester County. Rebecca asked me if there was a reorganization in the works. When I confronted Alyce about it, she told me that she wasn't at liberty to tell me. I knew something was up."

Dorothy looks at Cameron and raises her eyebrows. I can tell she's not pleased.

"Rachel," she says. "That's unfortunate and unprofessional on the part of both Libby and Alyce. You can be assured that I will express my unhappiness to Dr. Katsaros."

"Also," I continue. "I need to let you know that at the same meeting, Rebecca told me about a disgusting, mean rumor circulating about my two-year-old son, Jacob. He has a genetic disorder called Klinefelter syndrome, an extra X chromosome. But someone spread the rumor, which is untrue, that my husband and I don't know what his sex is. That he has an intersex condition. That he's a hermaphrodite. I know that this is a titillating piece of gossip, but it's cruel and very damaging. I've already spoken with my staff. I don't know who's responsible, or if it's just more of the harassment that I've had to endure now from Libby for a number of months."

I stop talking and look at both directly. Dorothy takes a deep breath again. Cameron seems unsure of what to say. I'm disappointed in him, although I realize that he has no choice except to follow the dean's direction.

"I can also say that Libby, at least, is totally unprofessional. Her means of sending me messages regarding management is to place nasty letters on my chair. And I don't know why she thought she could involve Alyce and Rebecca in a premature discussion of a change in the organization without my hearing about it. That's irresponsible and shows her inexperience." I stop. My reaction right now is anger. I think about what to say next. "Quite frankly, if you recruit another administrator, I suspect that Libby will sabotage the new hire. I'm very angry about the way that I've been treated by Libby and Dr. K. The medical center owes its employees better treatment than I've received since they arrived in October."

I stop and look at both again. My heart pounds. My fists clench. Will I be escorted out of the office? What happens next?

Another awkward pause. Then Cameron speaks, "I'm truly sorry that you've been put through this. Libby, I know, is a difficult person, and I recognize that you used great diplomacy in handling her." Cameron nods at Dorothy. "I think that we should move downstairs as quickly as we can."

Dorothy gets up, opens the door, and brings in a flat cardboard box that she must have stowed in the hall. With the door open, I can hear what sounds like staff walking toward the conference room. Dorothy closes the door and starts assembling the box.

"You don't mean that you're going to ask me to walk out of this office holding all of my possessions in a cardboard box!" I exclaim. "Having to walk past my staff is humiliating. I can't believe that you think this is humane."

Cameron looks at Dorothy. Dorothy is quick on her feet.

"No, you don't have to do that. Just pack what you want to take," she says, finishing the assembly. "I'll send someone upstairs to pick it up. Is the poster yours? They can take that down to HR, as well."

I silently take Dave's and the kids' photos, the few personal things that I have in the office, and put them in the box. I pick up my Rolodex, tell them that it's mine, that I brought it from Michigan. A pack of my business cards. What they don't know is that my increasing paranoia caused me to bring home copies of my personnel folder, as well as Libby's memos, the disclosure forms for Libby and Dr. K, and an accounting of the "missing" clinical trials. I put the cover on the cardboard bank box and place it on my chair. I take down the framed poster so that it isn't missed and then Cameron, Dorothy, and I leave what has been my office for nearly five years, walk past the empty secretarial desks, and out of Psychiatry.

When we arrive at HR, Dorothy points out an open, highly visible cubicle where I can sit for two days while the Neurology staff readies an office. I tell her that I'd rather take two days of vacation until I can go directly to Neurology. I can't imagine sitting in an open cubicle with colleagues passing by. Either they will stop to offer their sympathy at my sudden removal from Psychiatry, or I'll have to watch people try to avoid me. Dorothy agrees. She tells me that she will have my possessions locked in her storeroom until then.

This time, when I arrive home unexpectedly at noon, I tell Sandra exactly what has happened. Sandra is motherly. Right now, that's what I need. She points out that there may be a silver lining in all of this. At least I still have a job to go to. But a few days of unscheduled vacation also presents an opportunity to have lunch with Jacob, pick up Adam at school, and get various errands done that I never seem to have time for.

I try to phone Dave, but his assistant picks up and tells me that he's at a hearing at the county center. She expects him to go home directly from the hearing. We have so far resisted getting a second cell phone. We still share one, trying to economize wherever possible, but that doesn't work at times like this. Dave will have to hear about my day when he gets home.

Adam has a homework assignment that we work on after school. Then we make muffins to have with dinner. The boys help me prepare butternut squash soup, taking turns pulsing the cooked squash in the food processor. I may be in shock, but I feel relieved and grateful to be enjoying time with my kids. Grateful to have a loving family.

Sandra leaves as I hear Dave's car in the drive. He enters the house, first hugs Adam, and then picks up his "big little man," as he calls Jacob. Walking into the kitchen with Jacob, Dave kisses me and asks me about my day.

"Probably not what you think I did today, Dave. About ten thirty, the associate dean—Cameron Ellis, whom I've talked about with you—showed up unannounced at my office. He had Dorothy O'Connor, the HR director, with him."

Dave looks alarmed. I tell him that they informed me I am being reassigned immediately, that I was given a box in which to pack my personal items and walked downstairs to HR. I repeat the angry things that I said to them and tell him I am home for two days until an office is ready for me in Neurology. Then I cry, my first tears.

Dave walks over to me, envelops me in his arms, and just holds me.

"It's going to be okay, baby. I think this is a soft landing, and you—we—can figure things out from here." Dave walks over to the sofa with me, and we sit silently for a few minutes until my tears stop.

"Yes, it's a job I can do while I figure out what I want to do next," I tell him. "But it isn't safe. Many academic centers combine the Neurology and Neurosurgery departments. Neurosurgery at Hudson Valley is a powerhouse; Neurology is sort of schleppy. The chair is older, and the faculty is adequate, but there are no stars. When Dr. Weiss steps down, and he's at the age where this will happen soon, I see Neurosurgery making a move to absorb Neurology. So, no, I don't think this offers a spot for me. Frankly, Dave, after everything, I have no desire to keep working there."

We get dinner on the table then go through our evening routine of baths, pajamas, bedtime stories, and tucking in. I've finished with getting Adam settled down, and checked on Jacob, tucked into his toddler bed, when I hear the phone ring. I go downstairs as quickly as possible so that I can pick up in the kitchen. It's Karen.

"Gosh, Rachel! How are you? That was a terrible thing that they did to you!"

"Karen, it's probably for the best. I know that you were all called into a meeting so that you didn't have to see me walked out of my office by Cameron and Dorothy, carrying my cardboard box. What did they tell you? Who ran the meeting?"

"It was called by Libby," answers Karen. "She introduced herself as the new acting administrator for finance and administration. We both know she doesn't know anything about finance or administration, but that's what she's doing for now. She told us you'd been reassigned, but she wouldn't tell us where. Then she said that she and Dr. K are directing that none of us have any contact with you at all, or there will be consequences. No phone calls, no visits, no having lunch. She implied that you're a bad influence on all of us. I'm defying orders by calling you. Even worse, Libby is moving into your office. I'll be her assistant. So, I think I'll be looking for another job because I can't stand her."

"They are such schmucks!" I almost yell. "I don't know why they couldn't have done this more directly, more professionally, rather than harassing me for weeks before handling things as they did. I'll keep any contact strictly confidential. I'm going to be in Neurology to take over once Eleanor retires. She leaves at the end of June. I'm really okay. I'll miss all of you. I'm not sure that Libby is at all competent, but that's for Dr. K to find out."

We talk a bit more and hang up.

The next day, Beth phones me. She tells me that Dr. K and Libby called her in and told her that the Faculty

Practice Association will be taking over all Psychiatry billing. Beth was moved downstairs to manage the department's billing activity, working directly for Rebecca. Beth refers to Rebecca as the "she-devil." I know that Beth is beside herself, but I tell her that she has lots of options, both inside and outside the medical center. She will do fine, I reassure her. We agree to have lunch next week to compare "notes of the reassigned."

CHAPTER SEVENTEEN

MAY 2005

After my unexpected and involuntary departure from Psychiatry, everyone in Neurology tries to soften things for me. I discover that Neurology is run by Eleanor and Dr. Weiss in a mid-twentieth–century manner, dependent on paper ledgers, vintage word processors, and one lonely computer. Patient billing is haphazard, at best. Schedules are kept on a blackboard in the conference room. There seems to be no systematic way of keeping personnel, teaching, or research records. The Neurology faculty is pleased to have me to start upgrading systems. I'm able to throw myself into modernizing the department. I also let Dr. Weiss know that he should do an open recruitment for an administrator to replace Eleanor because I'm not sure of my long-term plans.

Eleanor assumes that I will stay in the job permanently. I don't believe that she or anyone else appreciates how I never want to feel so vulnerable again, so dependent on the whim of a department chair. And more than that, I'm not sure that this field continues to interest me. It's a management support role, not one in which I have ownership of the substance of the organization. I continue to look at options for changing careers, the prime candidate being genetic counseling.

I decide to speak with Heather, the genetic counselor who guided us through our prenatal finding of Klinefelter syndrome. We schedule a meeting at her office.

When I arrive, she greets me, wearing her signature Birkenstocks and a jean jumper. She asks me to sit at her small conference table, where I notice a photo of her daughter and a man who must be her husband. He has shoulder-length hair and a full beard, and he is holding a blue ribbon with one hand on the head of a goat standing between the two. I ask if they farm.

"We're just hobby farmers," answers Heather, smiling. "Eric's a microbiologist, but he's really into having chickens for eggs and goats for milk. So, our alarm clock is a rooster that gets us up these days around 4:30 a.m."

After filling Heather in on Jacob's progress and showing her photos of the boys, I tell her of my disillusionment with academic health center administration and my growing interest in genetic counseling. She's my inspiration for thinking of this career path, I tell her.

"It's not unusual, Rachel, for an entering class to have students who hold master's degrees in disciplines like social work and nursing, or in the basic sciences. You need to understand that it's a very competitive graduate program. But you hold an MPH from the University of Michigan, and that's certainly prestigious. And you've already completed all the science prerequisites except introductory genetics. If you have a strong GPA, you should be in the running. I think you'll also want to use your family's experience in developing a persuasive argument for why you'd make a good candidate."

"I always felt that the personal interactions I had with patients, with the public, while I was in graduate school were the most satisfying," I tell her. "I could use my knowledge of public health or epidemiology to educate or counsel families. I never doubted that I was a good administrator, but I missed the interpersonal relations. Genetic counseling would give me the opportunity to return to that."

"I think that's as convincing an argument as you'll need for justifying a career change," Heather responds. "You probably know that, unfortunately, there are only two genetic counseling graduate programs within commuting range for you: Sarah Lawrence in Bronxville and Beth Israel in the city."

"Yes, I'm aware," I say. "We're not able to relocate, but I think I'll apply to both and see what happens."

We continue talking about various roles and specializations for genetic counselors and the very strong job market for counselors. She gives me information on the time demands of the programs, including clinical internships and research requirements. Then, noting the time, I thank her for being so generous in meeting with me. I promise to let her know if I'm accepted into one of the programs.

"And I love nothing more, Rachel, than being able to hear about my prenatal patients. Jacob sounds like he is doing so well. A prenatal diagnosis can be enormously valuable, especially with getting early intervention services."

We hug again before I leave her office.

It's late spring. As I drive back home, I'm impressed with the riot of spring color from azaleas, rhododendrons, hydrangeas. Before moving to New York, I had always lived in places where winters are too cold for most of the flowering shrubs that surround the older homes in wooded suburbs like Scarsdale. Just like the colorful spring is a new beginning, I feel as though some things in my life may be settling into a new pattern that makes sense. For a while this winter, the stress at the job, on top of worries about Jacob's development and behavior, was simply overwhelming to me. I felt constantly distracted at work, around my kids, around Dave. The new position is a demotion, even though it didn't come with a reduction in salary. The change could have been so humiliating, but it wasn't. It has given me a chance to breathe and reflect on what I really want. I understand that this choice will be costly and put the family under several years of very tight budgets.

I'm also looking forward to next week when our family will fly to California for five days of relaxation. Dave has a conference at the University of California, Davis. The boys and I hadn't planned to go with him because of the expense of a cross-country family trip. After my reassignment, however, we decided that a family vacation is what we need. I've never been to the Lake Tahoe area, in the Sierra Nevada mountains, which is an easy drive from

Davis. When I called Sarah to let her know that we were planning a trip to California, she told me she would book a rental house on the lake large enough for two families, plus Grandma and Grandpa.

On the date of our flight, we drive to JFK and park off-site in a quasi-affordable lot that has a school bus shuttle to and from the airport. The boys are equipped with backpacks holding portable battery-powered games, books, crayons, and paper. While we wait in the gate area, they are mesmerized watching planes take off and land. During the five hours on the plane, both are delightful. I marvel at how lucky I am. I've never had to deal (yet) with a crying child on an airplane. No one even spills anything when eating lunch.

"Mommy," calls Adam from his window seat next to Dave. "Have Jakey look out the window at the mountains. Those are the Rocky Mountains. Daddy, are they as tall as Mount Everest?"

"No," answers Dave. "Maybe half the height of Everest. We'll also be in mountains in California. The Sierra Nevada mountains."

I help Jacob unbuckle his seatbelt so that he can peer out of his plane window.

"Mountain," says Jacob. Pointing down, he repeats, "Mountain! Evwest! Cafornia!"

Hugging him, I tell him, "Good job, Jake! Yes, we're going to see mountains in California."

We land in Sacramento and collect our luggage. Sarah and Oren are waiting at the curb outside in their twelve-passenger van to drive the boys and me to Lake Tahoe. Dave will pick up a rental car to drive to his convention in Davis, meeting us two days later at the lake. Sarah jumps out of the van, hugs all of us, and helps get Jacob into his car seat while Dave and I load the luggage. I sit between the two toddlers. Adam has a seat next to Porter, who also has a Gameboy, as do his brothers, Wallace, and Oliver. And we're off!

After updates on the kids and school, Oren asks me, "So, how are you doing, Rachel, now that you've made it out of the snake pit?"

"I'm doing all right. Neurology is full of very decent people who have no idea how technology can help them. They have some old IBM word-processors with floppy disks that are the backbone of their clerical system. I have no idea how they keep them running. Also, of course, IBM Selectrics. And there is one IBM PC-XT to access various systems. You'd better believe we're doing some computer purchases and networking, because soon everything—the HR systems, the budget, research—will be accessible only by computer. Oren, you must think this is very quaint.

"I no longer have to fear being harassed by the research administrator that the new chair brought with him," I continue. "She was awful. Couldn't speak with me directly about anything. Instead, she'd write nasty letters, seal them in envelopes, and leave them on my chair. Ostensibly, she's the new interim administrator. But I can't believe that she's going to allow someone else to come in who has any supervisory authority over her." I explain to Sarah and Oren my suspicions about missing clinical trials. I tell them that when Dr. K was recruited, he provided a list of his research activity, but a small fraction of the projects actually transferred to Hudson Valley. Some are being completed in Florida, but it's been nine months now, and Libby and Dr. K are still traveling regularly to complete them. Although it all seems very fishy to me, I don't have any clear evidence that something dishonest has occurred, and it's no longer my concern.

I've never been to Lake Tahoe, which is very blue and very clear, and still very cold due to its depth and elevation. There are even spots of snow still on the ground. We're sharing a cedar-sided house with floor-to-ceiling windows looking out over the lake. The house has two canoes that we can use. The kids can fish off the dock. Fortunately, Oren is an experienced fisherman, which Dave is not. But the main challenge with fishing is to keep kids from casting their lines and hooking each other or getting their lines tangled.

We take turns cooking. Oren and Sarah make a Chinese food buffet, Dave and I make pizzas, and Mum and Dad barbecue on the deck. We all play mini-golf, swim at a small (and warmer) nearby lake, and take short, little-kid hikes. One evening, Mum and Dad babysit the six kids, with assistance from a movie on video, while Sarah, Oren, Dave, and I take a sunset sail.

The four older boys occupy a bunk room. They need constant monitoring because pillow fights, tickle attacks, and all sorts of elementary school nonsense break out, requiring stern warnings and threats to separate and move them. This is the best low-key vacation ever. My favorite moments, however, are afternoons when Sarah and I stay behind while Noam and Jacob nap. We get generous glasses of chardonnay and lower ourselves, sans bathing suits, into the hot tub on the deck. During one of our afternoons, I ask Sarah about the affair and its aftermath.

"Don't feel that you need to tell me about it. I know it shook up your world. But you both seem very together. Are you okay?" I ask.

Sarah takes a sip of wine. "Yes. We are now. We're still seeing a marriage counselor. It was rough for a while. In counseling, Oren admitted that there had been others. The same addiction problem that he had with alcohol, he appears to have with hot, young women. I gave divorcing him long, careful thought because I didn't know if I ever would be able to trust him again."

She stops, looks out over the lake, where we can just see the guys in their canoes, and continues, "But the logistics of divorce are awful. The shared custody and its impact on the kids. What would it do to my relationship with the boys? When I talk with friends who've divorced, it seems that mom gets the kids during the week, so it's all the hard work of school and homework and enforcing bedtime. Dad gets them on the weekend and treats them to fun and games. He's the fun parent, and mom is the drudge. Do I want this?"

Sarah looks up at me as though she wants my understanding and approval.

"I get it, Sarah. I've noticed the same dynamic with the few divorces I've observed. Once kids are involved, that decision can't be easy."

"Also, I still love Oren. He claims to love me and says he never wanted to hurt me or the family. So, why can't he exercise a little discipline when he happens to see someone who has a flat tummy and perky breasts? In fact, Oren knows he needs help saying no. He's working on leaving any thoughts to fantasy when he's around these young things, and especially not acting on those fantasies. He even mentioned dabbling in spirituality as a family. Not Mormonism—he would never ask me to commit to something so all encompassing. But possibly Judaism. There are several synagogues that welcome intermarried families in our area. I'm thinking that if it can help strengthen his resolve, then we should do this as a family. Although, I think his parents would go into mourning."

"We're all over the map, aren't we?" I comment. "Dad grew up Orthodox. Mum is a converted former Presbyterian. Oren is a lapsed Mormon. Our family is Reform, but Dave grew up modern Orthodox. My brother-in-law has a same-sex partner who's a former Hasid, and they belong to a Conservadox gay chavurah! We can have quite the Seder, can't we?"

We laugh. I pull the wine out of the ice bucket next to the hot tub and top up our glasses. Sarah and I clink and toast to the Zimmerman family Seder.

"But one thing that's come out of all of this angst," says Sarah, "is that I need to go back to school to get my teaching degree. I need a career. I can't be dependent exclusively on Oren's money. It's not my money, although we hold our assets jointly and California's a community property state. I can never quite trust that I will always be one partner in a marriage. That's gone."

I look at Sarah. She's really suffered. Oren's a schmuck, I think to myself. Sarah's been such a wonderful wife and mother, doing all the heavy family lifting while he built a multimillion-dollar company.

"I've applied to return for my teaching certificate at San Jose State. It'll take me two years because I want a bilingual certificate. It makes me more marketable. Now we need to find a nanny so that I can go off to classes for about thirty hours a week. I won't feel secure until I have this credential and get a real job. Not that I think being the mother of four boys isn't a real job."

I tell Sarah about my plans to change careers from public health and medical administration to genetic counseling, having been sufficiently traumatized by my treatment in Psychiatry that I have no desire to stay on my present career path.

"On the issue of genetics, I want to ask if you've seen anything about Jacob that you think is unusual. Be honest, please. Sometimes I think I over assess behavioral or physical things that might be associated with Klinefelter syndrome."

Sarah thinks for a minute, then says, "Of course, I compare him with Noam. Noam seems to have more physical competence. Jacob is more hesitant. Getting into the canoe, for instance. Noam jumped in, but Jacob looked scared. Dave lifted him in. Jacob, of course, is quieter, but that's probably just his personality."

The truth is that I know a major difference between the two boys, verbally, is that Noam can easily string together three- or four-word sentences, whereas Jacob still manages only two words.

Sarah adds, "One thing that I have noticed, and I don't know if you have, is that when Jacob gets at all excited, he flaps his arms and hands. Mum also mentioned it to me. Do you think that has anything to do with Klinefelter syndrome? Also, Mum's noticed that Jacob rarely looks you in the eye. Even when he's talking to you."

Yes, I've noticed all these things: the hand flapping, the lack of eye contact. I know that they may be indicative of the autism spectrum. I keep hoping it's only a phase, but I've heard enough parents of kids with extra X and Y chromosomes discussing this at the recent support group that I'm concerned. We'll speak with his therapists about it again at his next review. I can't bring myself to tell Sarah our fears that he's also on the autism spectrum, as if not acknowledging it verbally will somehow make it less real.

"Jacob has a review every six months. The next one's in July. I'm going to see what comes up as concerns to be addressed. It's amazing, this early intervention program. He gets eight hours per week of therapy, and the county doesn't even charge our insurance. He'll also have a six-week summer program. For the fall, we have the option of having him go to the center every morning from nine to eleven thirty. I think that we'll take advantage of the preschool program. He loves being around other kids, and it will give me a few hours.

"At this point, unless something truly attractive comes up, I'm thinking of quitting in August, when we'll be losing Nanny Sandra, anyway. Her daughter's having a baby, and Sandra wants to take care of her grandchild. If I'm admitted to a genetic counseling program for the fall semester next year, I'll have to take a college-level genetics course, so I'll need time for class and studying."

I don't discuss with Sarah our need to economize if I give up my income: no cleaning woman, a much tighter grocery budget, no more vacations or meals out. And forget replacing our aging cars or furniture. We continue to sip our wine and talk about our mid-life returns to college, and how to manage a household and school events while also attending class, studying, and writing papers. I tell Sarah about the KSA family conference that I'll attend with Ellen next month. And the fact that Ben's partner, the pediatric urologist who was the mohel at Jacob's bris, will be one of the presenters. Then I hear Jacob on the baby monitor and go into the house to get him up before he wakes Noam.

When I enter the room, he's sitting up in bed, with a big smile on his face.

"Noam seeping. Still seeping. I get up."

God, he is just so adorable. And that last phrase was a three-word sentence!

CHAPTER EIGHTEEN

JULY 2005

Neurology can best be described as the sleepy department of the medical center. The chair and most of the other faculty all seem to be older. Even those who are more recent graduates appear lacking in initiative. There's almost no research taking place and little clinical innovation. It isn't an exciting place—no clinical outreach, innovative teaching, or patient care models. But it certainly is predictably pleasant. Right now, that's what I need.

I start the process of recruiting a new administrator. Since my reassignment and Beth's transfer to the Faculty Practice Plan, we've met weekly for coffee or lunch. She's very unhappy reporting to Rebecca. Rebecca is condescending, giving her no positive feedback, only criticism. Rebecca also implies to Beth that there are no advancement opportunities for her, that she wouldn't be competitive in the health care employment marketplace, despite a master's degree.

Beth married young, had two children, and went back to college after her husband left her. She earned both bachelor's and master's degrees while working to support her children. But Beth's lack of sophistication, characterized by her casual dress, is viewed by Rebecca as limiting her to no higher-ranking position than billing supervisor. I know Beth's abilities, however. She's a fast learner and a good supervisor. She'd be perfect for a small clinical service like Neurology. I tell her that I want her to apply. In confidence, I let her know that I won't be staying on in Neurology, even if offered the position, because I intend to change careers.

The KSA conference takes place on a weekend in Boston. Sandra, the boys, and I leave on Friday morning for Brookline. Sandra will babysit while Ellen and I go to the hotel in Boston for conference activities. There's an opening reception on Friday evening. Ellen doesn't ordinarily ride in a car on Shabbat, but she's always made exceptions—and she decides that learning about her grandson's genetic condition will be one. Ben and Eli, on the other hand, won't attend until the Sunday morning sessions.

Ellen and I park and walk into the hotel off Storrow Drive overlooking the Charles River. A sign directs us to the conference center where we see a registration table.

"Welcome! May I have your names?" asks one woman at the table.

I tell her my name and introduce my mother-in-law. We're handed our name tags and a binder. The woman registering us opens another binder and points out the schedule for the conference.

"Our opening reception will be in the ballroom behind us," she says. "This is an appetizer and refreshment 'meet and greet.' We have coffee and soft drinks. If you want alcohol, you may pick up a drink at the bar through those doors. The tables are marked with approximate ages of the children or adults. I see that you have a young child, so you'll want to sit at one of the tables with a sign that says 'preschool.'"

Ellen and I enter the ballroom where we find a pre-school table. We put down our binders and seat our-selves. There are three couples already at the table; one of the women is pregnant, and another couple has an infant in a stroller. We introduce ourselves. I tell the others that I have a two-and-a-half-year-old son, diagnosed prena-tally, and that Ellen is his grandmother.

"We found out two months ago that our baby boy has XXY," the pregnant woman tells us. "We were terrified. Our obstetrician told us that he'd likely be a criminal and that we should terminate. But then the genetic counselor told us there's no evidence that XXY men have criminal tendencies. That XXY boys may have learning disabili-ties, but it's nothing like Down syndrome. She put me in touch with Lisa. That's the woman who organized this as-sociation. After I talked to her by phone for an hour, we decided not to end the pregnancy. But I'm still scared. How's your little boy doing?"

I ask, "Are you still going to that OB?"

"No," she says. "He told us that he doesn't take care of high-risk pregnancies and referred us to the University of North Carolina. UNC said this isn't really a high-risk pregnancy. They're taking good care of me, and I didn't want to continue with him, anyway, after he described our baby as some sort of monster. The Chapel Hill doctors are great. They told me that XXY babies are usually pretty normal. I wanted to come here to meet other parents. Confirm that's really true."

"Our little boy, Jacob," I tell them, "developed completely normally until about sixteen months. He was a little slow to walk. Still within normal limits. Where we noticed the delay was in speech. At about twenty months, he still had no words at all. But in early intervention, he largely caught up. There are still some lingering problems, and he still gets speech and OT."

I decide not to go into our fears that Jacob may also have autism spectrum disorder, or ASD. This woman is pregnant, and I don't want to worry her unduly. It also seems that less than a quarter of the XXY boys have ASD, so it's not typical.

"And what are your names?" asks Ellen of the couple. The name tags are on long strings so they all hang below the tabletop, and we can't read them.

The woman holds up her tag. "I'm Jessica McCloud, and this is my husband, Craig. We're from the Research Triangle area, in North Carolina."

The mother of the little boy in the stroller, Maryellen, tells us that her baby is a year old, one of twins born very prematurely. The other twin died shortly after birth. Because of her son's low muscle tone, he was tested and found to have XXY. He appears to be small for his age but has been in early intervention since he was three months old and is catching up with his milestones.

A third couple flew from Ireland to be here. Their toddler is at home with his "gran." They show us a photo of their red-haired two-year-old, also prenatally diagnosed. Other parents join our table and we compare stories of diagnosis, early intervention services, and whether we've disclosed XXY to anyone.

Then a woman at the front of the room picks up a microphone and introduces herself as Lisa, the mother who started this organization. She tells her story of a child with severe learning disabilities and tantrums, who was labelled with a myriad of misdiagnoses: ADHD, depression, anxiety, schizoaffective disorder, bipolar disorder. Finally, a developmental pediatrician suggested genetic testing, which showed 47,XXY. She cries and needs a minute to compose herself.

"I'm sorry. People who get to know me know that I'm a crier. Sometimes when I get up in front of a room to talk about our diagnostic odyssey, I can't help but sob and sniffle like this. Forgive me. We have over sixty families here and about twenty-five adult men with XXY. People are finally hearing about KSA and identifying themselves so that they can learn about how to cope with the challenges.

"We have some excellent speakers this weekend. Some of the early research on children and adults with XXY has been done in the Boston area. Some of the clinicians who'll be speaking have practices with significant numbers of these patients. But what I want to do this evening is listen to your journeys. I ask you to limit yourself to one minute. Please tell your name, where you're from, and what you're hoping to get from this conference."

Several hands go up, all from a table of adults. Lisa calls on one to start, and tells the others that they can follow, reminding them of the one-minute rule. She walks over to their table and hands off the microphone.

"My name's Steve. I'm forty-two, a computer engineer. Always had learning disabilities and trouble in school. In fact, I dropped out of high school. I always thought I was stupid and that I might as well go to work. After drifting from one job to another, I earned my GED and then I decided to try for a computer certificate in junior college. I needed a physical for admission, and my doctor noticed—I guess we are all used to talking about private things—very small testicles. He asked me some other questions and told me he thought he might have an explanation for my learning disabilities, my lack of a beard, my inability to build muscle no matter how hard I worked out. Oh, and I'm from New Jersey.

"After I learned that I have Klinefelter syndrome, everything fell into place. I started taking testosterone shots and slowly I grew up. I was maturing to the point that I could study. I finally finished my degree when I was thirty. I want to meet other men like me."

Steve sits down, and another young man takes the mic and stands up.

"My name's Mark. I'm from Chicago. I work in customer service. I'm thirty. My wife and I were trying to start a family, but nothing was happening. We went for an infertility workup. That's when we discovered that I have XXY. I've come to terms with being infertile. My wife isn't here because she's eight months pregnant and can't fly. We used donor sperm. I want to hear what the doctors have to say."

Hands go up at other tables. Lisa moves the mic from one attendee to another as they tell their stories. Many of the parents of elementary and older children speak of struggling for years to find the reason for speech delay, learning disabilities, behavior problems. They describe their difficulties obtaining special education services and therapies, tell stories of doctors and teachers blaming them for their children's constellation of developmental and emotional problems, and talk about their relief at finally getting genetic testing for their children that revealed extra X and Y chromosomes and the diagnosis of Klinefelter syndrome or one of the less common conditions such as Trisomy X or XYY.

"Ellen," I whisper. "We were lucky to have had a prenatal diagnosis so we avoided all this."

After the opening reception, we drive back to Brookline, returning to the hotel the next morning for the first speaker. Ellen was told to look for a young man who's a member of Ben and Eli's chavurah of gay Jews. Ben tells us that the man will be coming to the conference sometime during Saturday. Ellen looks at the registration desk, but his name tag is still there, so she knows he hasn't arrived yet.

Entering the hall where chairs are set up in rows facing a screen and a podium, I see Star. She'd told me previously that she couldn't attend, but after I introduce her to Ellen and we sit down, she tells me that her husband told her she should go. She's staying with a cousin in a Boston suburb.

Lisa welcomes us all back for the Saturday program. She talks about the five families who've come from overseas. She also tells us that some families in attendance represent Trisomy X, a condition in which a female has three X chromosomes, rather than the typical two. Also, several boys with 47,XYY, which has many similarities to XXY, but without infertility. There are two families of boys with 48,XXYY. I've read about high-grade aneuploidy, variations with forty-eight and forty-nine chromosomes. These boys, I know, often have more severe disabilities. I make notes in my folder because much of this is new information for me.

The first speaker is a developmental pediatrician discussing research into cognition and communication. I'm glad our binders include copies of the speakers' slides so that we don't have to try to write down so much. There are scientists from NIH recruiting subjects with extra X and Y chromosomes for neuropsychological testing and MRI studies of the brain. Jacob won't be eligible for such testing until he's six and can hold still in a scanner.

I look at one group of young adults who seem to gather off to one side, sitting at a distance from people who are clearly parents. I notice that many of them are tall and wonder if two women in the group may be transgender. They have women's hairstyles, are wearing makeup and long maxi-dresses, and carry purses, but their faces and shoulders still have a masculine look. I catch myself and look away at the stage. I've read on the listserv that some adults with XXY identify as female. I just haven't observed it before as an occasional occurrence.

After the large group presentations, there are smaller breakout sections. Ellen and I split up to cover more topics. She attends a talk on the basics of sex chromosome aneuploidy genetics, while I attend one on the IDEA, the Individuals with Disabilities Education Act.

For lunch, we're seated at a table with other families of younger children. Star and others discuss their experiences with special ed. Donny will be in kindergarten in the fall. Star says that IDEA sounds great but that their school district is trying to have him attend an out-of-district placement instead of going to his home school. She is having great difficulty getting an individualized education plan for him because they don't seem to know what pigeonhole he fits into. An IEP is supposed to be individualized, but the district doesn't seem to understand that.

Just then, Lisa stands up and makes a ringing sound with a spoon on a glass, meant to quiet the room.

"I'm so happy that we now have thirty-two adults with Klinefelter syndrome attending. More checked in today. I think that this is the largest number of XXY adults ever assembled in one place," Lisa says. And suddenly, she's crying again. "I can't believe that we have been so successful in bringing all these people together. It's too much. It gets to me."

The audience laughs while she dabs at her eyes and takes a sip of water. Then she adds, "Now, this may be a little controversial, but after the conference last year in California, some of the men—or I should say, adults—requested a room for themselves for private discussion. There are those who specifically have asked that we set up a lifestyle room for XXY individuals, regardless of orientation or identity. So, we've set aside the Back Bay conference room off the lobby as the lifestyle room."

There are a few claps from some of the tables of adults. I'm a bit confused.

"What does 'lifestyle room' mean?" I ask the table.

I quickly get my answer from Star. Looking very sour, she explains, "KSA is setting up a room where a group can talk to our boys about being gay or transgender. If it gets out that Klinefelter men have a good chance of being gay or of thinking that they're women, then anyone who's pregnant will have an abortion."

One of the other parents at the table comments, "I've never heard that XXY causes a man to be gay."

"This is deviant, sinful. The Catholic church forbids it." says Star, looking sternly around the table. "Life is hard enough for these men because of their learning disabilities. And I'm afraid that young, impressionable kids who may have questions about sexuality anyway will go there and be convinced that they are gay or female or whatever."

Ellen's jaw tightens. I know that she won't leave this unanswered.

"Star," Ellen starts in a slow, determined voice. "I appreciate that your religion teaches you this view. I understand. Judaism has taught the same thing to generations of us who are observant. My older son, who's forty-five, is gay. He isn't XXY, by the way. Being gay isn't something that he chose. He didn't want to be gay. He's very religious, very observant, and he felt that homosexuality was a sin. That God forbids it, according to Torah. He prayed to be attracted to women, not to men. He even fell in love with and married a woman. They were married for seven years. But he finally admitted that he was gay, and he gave his wife freedom to get married again. It's only in the past year that he's been able to reconcile himself with his sexual orientation. Believe me, being gay is difficult. He would never try to influence anyone."

"Oh, I disagree with you," says Star. "Our church has held presentations on combatting gay lifestyles. And they tell us what to look for in men who are trying to attract others."

"No, I don't think that happens at all," says Jessica, the pregnant woman from North Carolina whom we met last evening. "It's well accepted that one is born gay. These men know it from childhood. You can't influence someone to become homosexual. And you also can't cure it with conversion therapy. By the way, my first OB, the one who told us our baby would likely be a criminal, informed us that there was also a good chance our boy would be gay. It was part of his rationale for telling us that the best thing to do was to have an abortion."

Another parent says that she is aware that a percentage of men with Klinefelter syndrome identify as gay, or bisexual, or transgender. It's still a small percentage. And, she says, it's a parent's job to love their child whatever the child's sexual orientation. No one at the table is ganging up on her, but I can tell that Star isn't taking this well.

Ellen looks around the table at the others and continues, "My son's a fine person. In fact, he'll be here tomorrow with his partner. His partner is one of the speakers, Dr. Eli Rubin, who is a pediatric urologist with a large practice of Klinefelter adolescents and young men. This is not something that I ever thought I would be confronted with. Everyone, take it from a mother. Please keep an open mind."

Just then, I see a tall young man wearing a yarmulke looking around the room as though he's trying to find someone. Ellen looks over at the same time.

"Oh, I'm sorry. I see someone that I have to talk with. Enjoyed meeting all of you," says Ellen as she stands up. "I'm sure that we'll all be having more of these discussions."

She hurries over to the young man and greets him. I conclude that this is Aaron Stein, the friend of Ben and Eli.

"My mother-in-law, Ellen Gold," I tell the people seated at the table. Then I realize that Star hadn't made the connection that Ellen is the mother of my brother-in-law who is gay.

Star looks at me with what I think is irritation, perhaps anger. "I knew that you have a brother-in-law who's gay. I didn't put two and two together that the woman sitting next to you is his mother. I wish you'd told me. Then I wouldn't have embarrassed myself."

"You don't need to be embarrassed," says one of the fathers softly. "We're all here to learn, having had this genetic condition dropped in our laps. We can't learn without discussions like this. There's no need to apologize. But it's beginning to make sense why some in the medical community may not want to touch Klinefelter syndrome and why we're warned to keep it quiet. Well, I intend to be proud of my son, whatever challenges or sexual issues he may have."

He chokes up as he finishes. I see tears in his eyes. And mine begin to pool.

"Star," I say. "This was a very private thing. It isn't something I would have remembered to tell you. But I agree with Ellen that no one chooses to be gay. You don't need to be embarrassed. We had to get accustomed to having a family member in a same-sex relationship. But we love his partner, and the depression and anxiety that Ben suffered for years is gone now that he can be himself."

The table is quiet. Most of us get up and leave because the afternoon sessions are starting.

"Ellen, I admire you for speaking up like that," I tell her on the drive home. "Star's been obsessed with this issue of XXY men who are open about being gay. I also told her some time ago that I have a brother-in-law who's gay, but I didn't introduce you today as being the mother of that man. She was irritated with me for not warning her before she spoke. Fortunately, the dad-to-be from North Carolina told her that there's no need to be embarrassed. I hope that made her more comfortable."

"I've started meeting with a group of parents of the chavurah members," Ellen replies. "We're mostly Conservative and Orthodox, but there are also Reform and unaffiliated families. We're proud of our kids, we support them, and we want Judaism to be accepting of them. They need to be able to fully participate in ritual. They shouldn't be condemned or shunned, and part of my efforts toward acceptance of them is to be honest and open when I need to. Like today."

We ride along in silence. I think that we're both overwhelmed by all the information we've been given during the day. There's an optional conference dinner this evening, but Ellen and I knew when we sent in our registrations that we'd want to have dinner with the boys. Sandra has had them all day, and she needs some time off.

The boys are waiting for us with Sandra when we arrive home. Sandra is being picked up for dinner by an old friend who lives in Boston. Ellen bustles about the kitchen getting dinner while I sit on the floor with Adam and Jake, playing animal dominoes. Jake and I are a team, although he can play this game quite competently with his brother, who's six years older. I look at my cheerful two-year-old. Concerns like sexual orientation or gender identity seem so remote. But between Ben's coming out to us and my experiences with Klinefelter syndrome and sexuality, I'll never think about these issues in the same way again.

Sunday is the final day of the conference, which ends early in the afternoon. We see Ben and Eli, along with Aaron, the BU student, outside the ballroom. Ellen introduces me to Aaron.

"Really nice to meet you, Rachel," says Aaron. "When I learned that Ben had a nephew with XXY, I'd only known about myself for a few months. I found out my sophomore year. I had developed bad chest pain and was admitted to the hospital for a pulmonary embolism. Then a few weeks after I got home, we got a phone call from the hospital to come in because they'd found an extra chromosome in a genetic test. As soon as the counselor described Klinefelter syndrome, my mom and I looked at each other and agreed that it explained everything—my learning disabilities, my poor coordination, having no beard.

"I was given a medical referral to Eli. He's been terrific, not just medically, getting me onto testosterone. When I told him that I'm both Orthodox and gay, Eli recommended the chavurah. It has changed my life!"

Eli excuses himself to get his presentation loaded. Ellen and I, Ben, and Aaron take seats in the large hotel ballroom. Lisa introduces Eli as a leader in the field of medical treatment for those with XXY. She gushes about his contribution to developing clinical guidelines and ends again by crying. The audience laughs as she apologizes for being so emotional.

Eli provides a presentation that explains in detail the impact of the extra chromosome on sexual development and on infertility, as well as how assisted reproduction techniques have allowed a few men to become biological fathers. At the conclusion of his presentation, he gets a standing ovation.

After the morning sessions, Ellen and I join another table of preschooler families. I discover talking with other parents of young kids that I am not the only one on overload. I'd been reluctant to get too involved in support groups, or too involved in making special needs part of our family life. But an advantage of having a community of support is that it keeps us from feeling alone. Sometimes I feel lonely, particularly when I'm in a group of Westchester County moms who are all discussing their kids' academic and sports accomplishments. And I think, secretly, that only one of my sons may fit into the competitive, high-achieving setting of suburban America.

The conference concludes with a panel of experts who presented during the conference, including Eli. Each speaker gives a summary of the state of clinical guidelines and research. There are questions for the panelists about how health professionals can be better educated about these disorders, how diagnoses can be made more quickly, and how research funding can be increased.

Near the scheduled end of the session, a parent walks up to the stage and hands one of the panelists a piece of paper. The panelist puts on her reading glasses and scans it, looking puzzled. She speaks into the microphone.

"This appears to be a petition. I'll read it. 'The undersigned parents of children with Klinefelter syndrome hereby petition KSA and the XXY researchers to end their focus on individuals who are either gay or transgender. Spotlighting individuals with sexual deviance damages the entire community. It scares families with prenatal diagnoses and will cause them to choose abortion. It causes us to be ashamed of the diagnosis. We respectfully request that no research be conducted into adults with XXY who live as gay men or transgender women. Also, that in the future we do not indulge these men by providing lifestyle rooms to talk about sexual orientation or gender identity.'" She stops reading and looks over at the other panelists.

Lisa leaves her seat in the audience to take the petition and read it, her brow furrowed. She motions for the mic, but Eli asks for it instead.

"Lisa, I think those of us on the panel, and some of the men themselves, can take this. There are several of us here who have medical practices with substantial numbers of adolescents and adult men with 47,XXY. We're all aware that there may be a somewhat greater incidence of gay or bisexual orientation than in the general population. We also know that gender dysphoria can be a concern in a small number of individuals. We do not know how much greater this is than in the general population, but all of us are clinicians first. We must listen to our patients' concerns. It's part of providing comprehensive medical care. Wishing this away, ignoring these clinical concerns, is not an option.

"I know that the adults have welcomed having their own discussion rooms at these conferences to talk about private concerns, away from the parents of preschool and school age children who are grappling with other issues. I'm glad that the board of KSA agreed on this. But it's a mistake to call this space the lifestyle room. This isn't a lifestyle. This isn't a choice. These questions are central to who these adults are."

A man in the audience stands up and says, in a loud voice, "But you need to understand, doctor. May I just say this?"

Eli yields the mic, and the man continues. "We're from Mississippi. The doctor told me and my wife that our baby was XXY and that there was a higher-than-average chance that he would be involved in criminal activity. So, that's bad enough. If you add being gay—this is the Bible Belt. We're pro-life but given the choice between abortion or having a gay child, most of us would terminate. And it's shameful. It's probably different up here in Boston, where I understand that Massachusetts allowed gay marriage as of last year. The doctor already told us not to say a word to anyone about his extra chromosome and maybe not even to tell our son."

Lisa takes the mic and speaks, "This organization has been life-changing for me in many ways, not only because of what it's done to help my son and others like him. I've learned so many things about how having an extra sex chromosome can affect lives. And I've had to change my viewpoint of differences in sexuality. I'm also a Christian, and my background is very conservative, very fundamentalist. Until I began to meet adults with XXY, I viewed homosexuality as sinful. I believed that being transgender was unnatural, that these people were making it up. But as I got to know these people individually and I learned their stories, I could not believe that the God who created this genetic variation would view the results of these differences as sinful. God means for all of us to have compassion for and to love and accept people with genetic differences. If those differences result in some people who identify as homosexual or transgender, then we are commanded by God to love them and embrace them as part of our community."

A group of men stand up and applaud. One by one, others in the audience stand and clap. Ellen, Ben, and I stand, along with about two-thirds of the room. Lisa motions for quiet, and most of us sit down.

"I hadn't planned to end the conference on this note, but the time that we've reserved for these rooms is ending. They're going to start coming in to clean the rooms to get ready for the next event. I'm glad that we've had this discussion. And I hope that we'll continue to address these issues.

"I especially want to thank our speakers for donating their time and expertise. We don't pay honoraria. I also want to thank the volunteers who helped to put on this wonderful conference. We'll be back in California for our conference next year. I hope that all of you will be able to join us. Don't forget to complete your evaluations and drop them in the boxes at the exits."

The audience applauds again, and Ellen and I get up to leave. I see Lisa go over to speak with the man who handed the petition in. I wonder if this issue will cause some sort of fracture in this small, newly organized advocacy group.

"This was the issue we were discussing in February, when we were down in Miami," I say to Eli. "One of the reasons that the medical profession seems to pay little attention to Klinefelter syndrome may be unease with infertility and with what seems to be a small but still significant portion of adults who identify as gay or transgender or intersex. This isn't the place right now, and I need get the kids back home, but I'd like to brainstorm with you about advocacy to destigmatize XXY. Maybe we could have a phone call later."

"It certainly looks as though this is going to present quite a bit of controversy before we can focus advocacy on these issues," responds Eli. "But I agree that it's truly unfair to this population. It's tough for families to face a multitude of developmental challenges if they're also being told that they shouldn't discuss the condition openly, shouldn't reveal the diagnosis to schools, for instance."

I'd love to hug both Ben and Eli before we leave, but I know better than to do that. Instead, Ellen and I wait until there's a break in the crowd that has gathered around them before we thank Eli for handling the petition so well and bid both men goodbye until our next family visit.

Ellen and I discuss this dilemma as we drive home from the conference. I remark about how little I'd ever considered issues of sexual orientation or gender identity—until Ben revealed that he is gay and our son was diagnosed with a chromosomal condition that has everything to do with fertility and may also affect him sexually.

CHAPTER NINETEEN

AUGUST 2005

We are at Jacob's evaluation, the last one he'll have at Building Blocks before he turns three and his program supervision transfers to the school district. His progress in speech and occupational therapy has been good. He's still sufficiently behind where he should be, however, that he'll continue to qualify for those services. The current concerns are his behavior and his social skills. He engages in lots of repetitive behavior, including hand flapping, and doing the same thing over and over, endlessly guiding his toy train around a circular track or flicking open and closed little doors on his activity center. He's become rigid about routines, throwing long tantrums if anyone leaves a step out of bedtime rituals or morning goodbyes. I am not surprised that the Building Blocks psychologist wants to recommend an evaluation for autism spectrum disorder. I'd anticipated this. After hearing about the number of boys with extra X or Y chromosomes who meet the criteria for ASD, I am realizing that Jacob may also require therapy to improve his behavioral and social skills. But Dave is hesitant.

"Rachel and I know that the diagnosis of autism has been expanded to include a much larger number of kids," he argues. "But given that autism is a serious neurological condition, it's associated with being dependent throughout life. Are we really helping these higher functioning kids by giving them this label? I'm reluctant to slap it on him, in addition to having a genetic disorder and speech delay. Why can't we just add behavior therapy?"

"You have that option," the psychologist tells us. "But if you do go that direction, everything will have to be private pay. The most effective therapy for maladaptive behaviors associated with autism is called ABA, or Applied Behavior Analysis. We aren't permitted to recommend ABA therapy as part of his preschool services unless Jacob has a formal diagnosis of ASD. So sorry to be throwing these acronyms around."

"What sort of costs are we looking at?" asks Dave.

"The hourly fee for ABA therapy starts at about sixty-five dollars for a therapist supervised by a board-certified behavior analyst. The supervisor would also have to be paid for an initial evaluation and for monthly oversight, so I'd add another hundred fifty per month for that service. If you contracted for eight hours per month of direct services and an hour of supervision each month, you're looking at privately paying around eight thousand dollars for the year. If you need the consultant to work with his preschool therapists, which we'd recommend for maximum benefit, probably ten thousand."

I look at Dave. We've had the discussion many times about the pros and cons of an ASD diagnosis. My point has been that a diagnosis opens up school district payment for the service. We cannot afford to pay privately with my greatly reduced hours now and no salary once the school year starts. Insurance companies consider ABA to be an educational, not a medical, service, so they will deny coverage.

"I have another question," says Dave. "If Jake is evaluated and gets an autism diagnosis, is he ever able to get rid of the label? I don't know that I want label this following him throughout childhood and into adulthood if he's only mildly affected."

The psychologist walks over to his desk and pulls a copy of an article from one of the piles. He hands Dave the copy, which has yellow highlighting on the front page. "You can keep this; I have a number of copies. We know from this research that just under twenty percent of kids diagnosed with ASD in childhood will move off the spectrum by age nineteen. If Jake does meet the criteria now, I can't guarantee that he'll be one of the kids who no longer meets criteria as an older teen or adult. But the diagnosis does allow you to get services that you can't get otherwise. School districts and colleges are now aware that autism doesn't mean someone whose behavior is totally out of control, who does head banging and self-injury and has little functional communication."

"I'm still not comfortable with yet another label," responds Dave. "But we're willing to get a referral to take him for evaluation. We can then judge, if he does get a diagnosis of ASD, whether to use that or not. We could think about not disclosing the diagnosis, even though it would be a stretch to pay for extra therapy privately. I just wonder if a kid can ever escape a diagnosis once it gets attached to him."

We continue to talk about a behavioral label but decide to see what Yale tells us once we finally get in for an evaluation. There's a twelve-week wait for the appointment, so we're not scheduled until November. And I am feeling somewhat overwhelmed with the issue of labels and with the fact that Jacob already has one, Klinefelter syndrome, that has so many negative connotations. Right now, all Dave and I can do is try to take the best direction to help Jacob achieve success in life.

The team recommends that instead of continuing home-based services in September, he attend therapeutic preschool five mornings a week. Building Blocks also has two mainstream daycare classes. When his special ed preschool class ends at eleven thirty, he can join the children in the mainstream class. I can pick him up at two. We will pay, of course, for his afternoon day care program. It's surprisingly affordable, although it needs to be fit into our increasingly stretched budget. This will certainly solve our problem of how to care for Jacob once Sandra leaves in a few weeks.

I'm saddened by the additional concerns regarding Jacob's behavior. Will having both Klinefelter syndrome and autism be too much for Jacob to overcome? What will the impact be on our family? How will Adam feel if we constantly give so much of our attention to his brother with special needs? And how will Jacob deal with having an older brother who appears to be academically gifted, reading and doing math at the sixth-grade level when he's only going into third grade? When we signed on to continue a pregnancy with a genetic anomaly, I didn't expect all these complications. Secretly, I sometimes wonder if we made the right decision. But I would never tell anyone of my doubts.

Sandra's daughter has a baby girl a week later. We prepared both boys for her departure. Now that her granddaughter has been born, they know that Mommy will be the one who takes care of them most of the time. I'm glad that I'll have this year to decompress, not to be so tightly scheduled as I was working full time. It may be especially helpful in getting Jacob through his terrible twos.

We decide that for a farewell lunch, we'll meet Sandra at the train and drive to a favorite park for a picnic. I take photos of the boys with her, their nanny for nearly three years. She's been their caregiver and their teacher, reading to them, pushing them on the swings, playing Candy Land and Sorry, building LEGO and DUPLO creations with them. Sandra and I tear up when we hug as she boards the train back to the city.

I'm still covering the administrative position in Neurology part-time. Dr. Weiss has offered me the position several times, even trying to sweeten the deal by telling me I can work shortened hours during the day and finish my work from home. The truth is that I'm no longer interested in medical school administration. I know that I want to pursue genetic counseling, or another type of counseling, even social work, that allows me to work directly with patients. Dr. Weiss follows my recommendation and offers the position to Beth. Rebecca, however, insists that Neurology allow Beth to stay at the faculty practice office for another two months while Rebecca hires a replacement for her. So, I will continue part-time in Neurology until mid-October.

Adam, as always, likes school and loves his third-grade teacher. He also gets special enrichment sessions to keep him engaged and give him challenges. He plays soccer each weekend, and he is a talented player! Dave and I are both surprised. It's a real pleasure to watch a little boy who can play goalie so well. Although I ran track and cross country, I was never very coordinated. Dave was never a competitive basketball player, although he loves it and still plays on a law school intramural team. Adam didn't inherit this ability from us.

After a first week during which Jacob sobs each time I put him on the minibus, our little boy adjusts well to spending each day at Building Blocks. He suddenly seems so grown up, going off to school each day with his little backpack and bringing home artwork for the refrigerator.

One afternoon, Karen phones me. She's no longer afraid to speak to me, even though Libby still reminds staff not to have any contact with me. Karen tells me that she'd like to come by my house after work with something she thinks I should see, although she won't even hint at what it is. I tell her that most afternoons are a little chaotic, but today will be good. Dave will be home late tonight, so I don't have to organize a complete family meal. This will be a good opportunity to have a glass of wine and catch up. I'm putting pasta on for the boys when Karen rings the doorbell. Adam runs to the door and opens it.

"Mommy, it's your friend Karen. Karen, please come in," he says like a little adult.

"You're really my friend now, Karen," I say. We hug.

Karen is carrying a large manila envelope.

"Come on into the kitchen and sit down. Would you like a glass of wine?" I ask. I choose some red wine from the rack. "How's cabernet?"

"That would be great," Karen answers.

Jacob wanders in holding a video.

"Mommy, Thomas video? Now video?"

Jacob is stringing three words together. His brother just watched a soccer video so I guess that a twenty-minute *Thomas the Tank Engine* episode will not warp them unduly.

"Okay. You can watch one story. Adam, take the soccer tape out and help Jacob put in the Thomas video. When that's done, your dinner will be ready."

I pour a glass of wine for each of us and sit down. Karen pulls papers out of the envelope.

"You aren't going to believe this, Rachel. These arrived in the mail yesterday from Noven Pharmaceuticals. They were addressed to Libby. I took them out and tried to match them to current contracts, but I have nothing on record for them. You remember how you wondered where those clinical trials had gone? The ones that were supposed to transfer from Central Florida and never did? Well, I think this may explain some of it.

"These are contracts for ten different trials. They include institutional review board papers and contract forms ostensibly signed by both the dean and the vice president for research at Hudson Valley. But these signatures don't match the real signatures of either the dean or the VP—or of the chair of the IRB, Diane Melnick."

Karen pulls out a signature example from another research contract. I can easily recognize that someone has done a bad job of copying the signatures.

"Also," adds Karen, "the contact information states that checks are to be directed to Hudson Valley Sponsored Research, LLC, at a PO Box in White Plains." She points out several titles on the contract pages. "So, these documents look like they're official medical center contracts, but they aren't. Libby and Dr. K seem to have set up a research organization with a similar name."

I'm speechless as I look at these documents. If they are what they seem to be, it's brazen fraud. Did these guys really think the hierarchy at Hudson Valley was all that stupid?

"In addition, there are some contracts here for consulting services." Karen raises her eyebrows at me and pushes more papers over to me. "Apparently, Libby and Dr. K both have private consulting contracts with Noven covering a five-year period. Seventy-five thousand per year for Libby, a total of three-hundred, seventy-five thousand dollars. For Dr. K, a quarter million per year, for a total of one million, two-hundred, fifty thousand dollars. Nice work if you can get it. They're in the second year of the five-year contract."

I'm looking at the details, looking for any sign that someone—maybe the dean—has authorized this or knows about it and looked the other way. Nothing obvious.

"I can't believe they thought they could get away with this. Of course, there's always the chance that one of the high mucky-mucks agreed to it. That's what makes me nervous about showing anyone these documents."

I can understand where Karen is coming from. And why she was so reluctant to tell me what this is about. Maybe it is sanctioned, and we just didn't know about it. But if it was all legal and approved by SUNY Central, there wouldn't have been any reason to have been secretive about it.

"Consulting income like this needs to be reported in their annual disclosure forms," I say, "as well as to NIH. I can tell you that they didn't report this. I saw their state forms. I'm not an attorney, but it looks like all sorts of regs have been broken here, if this is the sort of deception it looks like. This is a matter for the compliance office. I think they may be in hot water. Karen, you did a great job of recognizing this."

I get up to finish making dinner for the boys, trying to imagine how this can get to the proper office without identifying Karen.

"Would you like some cheese and crackers with the wine?

I put out crackers, brie, and some grapes. And pour each of us another ounce of wine. Then, I get the boys' pasta served up so it will cool before they eat.

Karen looks over at me "So, what should I do with this? I must tell you that I'm fearful of going to the dean's office or even to compliance. Dr. K is such hot shit in the medical school that my guess is they would want to shove this under the rug and fire me."

I think for a few seconds on the best strategy that protects Karen.

"I wonder if you shouldn't put the originals into an unused interoffice envelope so there's no "from" address filled in. Have it delivered to Libby, and she can wonder where it was sent from and where it's been seen. If you think it may jeopardize your employment to take it to compliance yourself, I'll do it for you. I'm ending my job in about six weeks, after Beth gets trained. I'm perfectly happy to request an early exit interview with both Dorothy and Cameron. Show them a set of copies and explain to them what they're looking at. I'll make sure that they know there are second copies. If they don't take this matter to the dean or to compliance, I will. That keeps you out of it, at least initially."

"Well, this would explain why Libby and Dr. K are so secretive," states Karen. "I've kept one copy for myself. You can have this set. Tomorrow, I'll put the originals in a new interoffice envelope and off it will go. I need to get to my mom's. She wants me to pin up a dress she's wearing to a wedding. They're always too long for her; she's four foot eleven."

Karen stands up and hugs me. "Really miss you. I've been looking for jobs in the medical center, but there aren't too many openings at my level. I keep hoping."

I walk Karen to the door.

"I'll let you know when I get time with Cameron and Dorothy. We may see fireworks. I'm not completely sure of the process, but we'll be finding out," I tell her. I wait until she's in her car, then close the door and return to the kitchen to feed the boys.

I give the boys their pasta. I've made carrots with butter and a little honey. Adam loves these carrots. Jacob rejects any unfamiliar food, especially vegetables. To increase the number of foods that Jacob will eat, I put three pieces of carrot on his plate and tell him that they have honey on them and Adam finds carrots yummy. Jacob scowls, his face crinkles up, and he throws not only his carrots on the floor, but also his pasta. Then he starts screaming, gets down from his chair, and proceeds to have a complete meltdown in the kitchen. I carry the flailing child into the sunroom and put him down on the rug.

He tantrums daily now. I tell Dave each time it happens, but he rarely experiences the full impact of it. Dave still gives me lots of pushback about a possible autism diagnosis. If he had to deal with the tantrums more often, I think he would also be looking for a solution. Now that I work only part-time, and soon will give up paid work entirely, it is inevitable that more of the housework and childcare falls on me. And we will also fall into more traditional gender roles—temporarily, I hope.

Jacob wails from the sunroom for more than fifteen minutes. I was advised by his therapists at Building Blocks to wait to give him attention again until he has been quiet for three minutes. His sobs are less frequent now. I want to start looking at the clock but Adam, who is now finished with dinner, is coloring a drawing he made of what looks like Thomas the Tank Engine, and tells me, "Mommy, I'm making a picture so Jake is not so sad. Let me take it to him."

Adam heads for the sunroom. Jacob sees him and sits up, changing his expression to a grin. Holding out the drawing, Adam says, "Here's Thomas that I made for you so you're not sad. But the carrots with honey are good. You only need to try two bites."

Adam holds Jake's hand as they walk toward the kitchen, with Jacob clutching the drawing in the other.

"So, Jake, my little guy, you're ready to have some dinner?" I serve up the plate again with his pasta and two bites of carrots with honey.

Jacob climbs into his chair and eats his whole dinner. He even asks for more carrots! Adam is a magician, redirecting his brother and putting him in a cooperative mood. But we can't rely on an eight-year-old to manage Jacob's behavior. We need better strategies. For now, however, I'm grateful to Adam. I hug him and tell him what a great big brother he is.

That evening, after the kids are in bed, I show the papers to Dave and explain the various regulations that I believe Libby and Dr. K have violated. He agrees with me that it looks suspicious, although he says that there is always the possibility that Dr. K got some waiver of SUNY regulations to set this up. Knowing the faculty contracts as well as Dave does, it seems unlikely.

CHAPTER TWENTY

SEPTEMBER 2005

After confirming that Karen sent the documents to
Libby by interoffice, I give them a few days to arrive then call Cameron's assistant to schedule an exit
interview with Cameron and Dorothy. I tell his assistant it's important that I speak with both as soon as
possible. She wants to know why, but I tell her that I
have some confidential information that both must
hear, the sooner the better. She pulls it together for the
next morning at eight. Dave arranges to get the boys
off to school.

Promptly at eight, I arrive in Cameron's outer office.
Dorothy is already there. I have copies of the contracts
and correspondence with me. I take a seat at Cameron's
small conference table and begin as soon as he sits down.

"When you arrived in my office this spring to tell
me I was being reassigned, I suspected that Dr. Katsaros and Libby were conducting some of the clinical trials independently, outside of sponsored programs. I also
suspected it was possible that both were receiving consulting income from pharmaceutical companies and that

this income was not being reported appropriately on disclosure forms.

"I didn't have any definitive proof at the time, but I've just received some documents that may show that. These records were mailed to a Psychiatry staff member and that staff member, understanding what these documents could mean, brought them to me. This is a matter that needs to be reported to the compliance office."

I show them the contracts and supporting documents for clinical trials and point out what appear to be falsified signatures for Hudson Valley officials. Also, the mailing address and payment instructions, Hudson Valley Sponsored Research, LLC, in White Plains. Altogether, the clinical trial funding that may be diverted totals more than about five million dollars. Then I show them the papers documenting Libby's and Dr. K's consulting fees.

"I've seen their disclosure forms, and so have you," I tell them. "And they didn't report these fees, even though they were effective last year."

Cameron is silent as he pages though the documents. Then he looks up at me.

"When did you receive these copies? And you need to tell us who gave them to you."

"I was given them last week on Wednesday. It's a current employee who recognized them as possible fraud, but she fears for her job and only wants to speak with the compliance officer. Because I'm already on my way out, I feel safe bringing them to you. But we both know what a favored recruit Dr. Katsaros was. We're both afraid that some here may try to look the other way, even though this looks quite suspicious.

"I know that the employee made copies. She then put the originals into an interoffice envelope and addressed them to Libby at the White Plains office, the one with all the special keypad locks on the doors."

"You don't need to worry about this being swept under the rug," Dorothy says, giving Cameron a knowing look. "We'll take this today to both the dean and Rick Mason over in compliance. I'm sure that you'll be hearing from him tomorrow, if not later today."

We talk more about the clinical trials office in downtown White Plains. Dorothy wasn't familiar with it as the centerpiece of Dr. K's recruitment. She wants to know why I didn't alert the dean's office to the missing clinical trials when I was first aware of this as Psychiatry administrator. I tell her that shortly after Libby arrived, I was excluded from seeing any of Dr. K's grant documents.

The next day, as expected, I receive a phone call from Rick Mason. He asks me to come to his office. I repeat the story I told yesterday, pointing out the likely falsified signatures as well as the contracts confirming the consulting payments already made to Libby and to Dr. K. This time, I also tell him Karen's name. I let him know of her fears that she has somehow jeopardized her job by alerting me about these documents. Rick quotes the state regulations that established his office and afforded protection to employees who report suspicious activity. Rick says that he will interview Karen. He tells me he's documenting our conversation and will be sending the materials to the attorney general for further action. He tells me to expect to be interviewed by the AG's office.

During the fall, the AG works quickly. Karen and I are interviewed, along with key employees in Psychiatry, the dean's office, and sponsored programs. Dr. K and Libby are suspended. Boxes of documents are removed from the clinical trials office. There are warrants issued to search Libby's apartment and Dr. K's condo, their phones, and computers. State auditors are dispatched to Hudson Valley to determine if there was additional wrongdoing with respect to Dr. K's recruitment incentives. Phillip Slater, a semi-retired Psychiatry professor who was one of the founders of the medical school, is appointed acting chair.

Local news reporters descend, trying to get statements about the financial improprieties, as they are referred to. The dean's office issues directives to all employees to refer any inquiries to the Department of Community Relations. But neither Dr. K nor Libby has many friendly colleagues, so enough faculty and staff are willing to speak on and off the record that much of the story makes it into local news. My name appears in some of the papers, notably the Westchester section of the *New York Times,* because some staff members give details to the papers about my reassignment on Dr. K's request. Reporters come to our house and ring the doorbell, but Dave tells them I have nothing to say and asks them to leave.

One evening, when Dave is out playing basketball, I'm in the midst of getting the kids to bed when Jacob has a meltdown after I wash his hair. He refuses to get into his pajamas and lies in the hallway, naked and wet, screaming and kicking the wall. The doorbell rings several times, but I ignore it. Then aggressive knocking at the kitchen door. Finally, I can hear tapping at the windows in the living room. I run downstairs, open the front door, and yell at two reporters to leave and stop disturbing us, telling them that I'll make a report of trespassing if they don't leave. Some curses are involved that I hope Adam doesn't hear.

I know I've lost it, because it never occurred to me to get their business cards and inform their editors of their unprofessional behavior. I simply go back upstairs and weep. It must make quite an impression on Jacob because he crawls over to me, still wet, and says, "Don't be sad." Then Adam comes out of his room and hugs me. I explain to my boys my frustration about the reporters who are just trying to tell everyone what a bad man the doctor at my work was.

"Jake, why don't we get your pj's on? Then you and Adam and I can go downstairs, and I'll make us all cocoa before bed. With marshmallows."

Dave arrives home an hour later. He promises to catch up once he has changed out of his sweat-soaked clothes and showered. I put some dinner together to microwave for him once he finishes. It's not his fault that he was out when both the tantrum and the door banging by intrusive, obnoxious reporters occurred. I've insisted through all this stress that we both keep up with going to the gym plus yoga (me) or playing basketball (Dave) and made a point of telling him this evening that he should leave. But I tell Dave about Jake's tantrum, and then losing it at the reporters.

I say, "I just need you to know that these meltdowns are happening almost every late afternoon or evening. Most of the time you aren't here, so I'm getting the brunt of it. Adam hears the screaming and reacts by escaping somewhere where he can't hear, but I can tell he's distressed about it."

Dave chews and gives me his "processing it" look, then says, "I'm not sure we have an alternative right now. I have the legal clinic on Mondays, a standing meeting on Tuesday, and my late office hours on Wednesday. Thursday, I play basketball. We need the acting dean of admissions salary bump to make up for losing your salary."

I know all this: the wrench thrown into my career by Dr. K, my decision to become a genetic counselor and leave the world of academic medicine administration, and the financial impact on our family while I get my second master's degree. I need to go upstairs to collect the laundry so we don't have stinky basketball clothes lending their odor to the master bedroom tonight.

But the bathroom is a mess. Sweaty clothes and wet towels left on the floor. The soap is on the floor of the shower softening in the water that drains slowly due to ancient plumbing. Is this all part of becoming a single-income family, with me taking on the role of housewife? I hang up the towels and grab the laundry bag to bring it downstairs. I'm on the verge of tears again. The phone rings downstairs. I hear Dave answer.

"Yes, this is David Gold. Were you by chance at our home this evening?" Pause. "May I have your contact information?" Pause. "What outlet did you say you work for?" Pause. "Well, Rachel is not giving interviews, and I caution you against returning to our house. Criminal trespassing is more serious when you both look into and tap on windows, which I understand you did this evening after ringing the doorbell multiple times and knocking on the back door. This over-the-top behavior upset my wife and children. I trust I'm clear about this." Pause. "Goodbye."

Dave now has the reporter's contact information. My guess is that he'll contact his publication. I feel better listening to him protecting us; I'm less inclined to confront him about the wet towels on the bathroom floor. I know he's taken on as much work as he has because he wants to get us through these next three years on one income. But I'll insist that we get some help with Jacob's behavior, and that may mean an autism diagnosis that Dave doesn't want.

CHAPTER TWENTY-ONE

OCTOBER 2005

Immediately following Rosh Hashanah, which we spend in Brookline, Dave and I are given a slightly earlier appointment at Yale. I've had Jake's teachers at Building Blocks complete detailed questionnaires. Dave and I also complete parent assessments. This reminds me of his first evaluation for early intervention services, but this time I expect not to be blindsided by the findings.

As of his third birthday, Jake's services will be authorized by the public schools rather than by the county early intervention office. I want the most current information on his functioning and needed services from one of the top child development clinics in the nation. Jacob's behavior often interferes with his being able to interact productively with all of us. His crying spells occur nearly every day now, usually in the afternoon. Dave has become more understanding of how serious this is. He tells me he's more willing to consider an autism diagnosis, if that is what Jacob has, to obtain specialized behavior therapy.

The day of our appointment arrives. The center has a waiting area for parents and a corner with child-sized furniture and books and toys. Some of the children waiting with their parents seem so obviously impaired with vacant looks on their faces, even unable to play or amuse themselves. Jacob, on the other hand, runs over to the play area and collects the toys that he wants. He sits down and plays on his own. We know that if he qualifies for a diagnosis of autism, it will be on the high-functioning end of the spectrum. A man with a folder appears in the waiting area.

"Jacob Gold?"

Dave points to Jacob in the play corner. The man walks over and observes him for a few minutes.

"Jacob," he says.

Jacob looks up, smiles, and goes back to arranging his vehicles.

"Jacob, I'm Dr. Leonard. Let's go back to my office. Mommy and Daddy will come with us."

Jacob stands up and reaches for the doctor's hand. We follow them down the hall. I find myself thinking that Jacob demonstrated that his receptive language is good; he made eye contact and smiled. He also reached out for the doctor's hand, a sure sign of appropriate social skills. So maybe he won't get a second diagnosis, ASD, to go with his XXY.

The morning follows a familiar pattern. Jacob has a structured set of tasks and interactions, called the ADOS, or Autism Diagnostic Observation Schedule,

administered by the psychologist and Dr. Wong, introduced to us as a fellow in child psychiatry. Then Dave
goes with Jacob for more evaluations by a speech therapist
while Dr. Leonard interviews me using the ADI-R, the
Autism Diagnostic Interview-Revised. I give him my collection of research articles on Klinefelter syndrome that
I've copied for the evaluation team. I also talk with him
about the recent family conference. After lunch, Jacob's
testing continues. We're scheduled to return in a week for
a meeting with Dr. Leonard to discuss their results.

When Dave and I return to Yale, we're greeted by Dr.
Wong, who meets us in the waiting area and brings us to
the room where the ADOS was conducted. She indicates
a small round table where we are to sit. The room is filled
with toys and child-sized furniture, reminding us that we
are here for concerns about a very young child. Dr. Leonard enters carrying a file and a videocassette, which he
pops into the player under the TV. Suddenly, Jacob appears on screen. I'd forgotten that the ADOS was recorded. Dr. Leonard pauses the recording with his remote,
and sits down, opens his folder, and pulls out copies of a
report that he hands around.

"Thank you for all the materials on Klinefelter syndrome. We're starting to see more children, particularly
boys, with X and Y chromosome aneuploidy. It certainly
seems to be a risk factor for autism, although generally
the diagnosis is either PDD-NOS or Asperger syndrome,
not classical autism. The children with forty-eight or

forty-nine chromosome variations are far more likely to meet the full criteria.

"Jacob, fortunately, has lots of strengths. He's a very sociable child, although he has a hard time sustaining those interactions. He tends to get distracted by objects. He also appears to have significant social anxiety, which may be contributing to his frequent meltdowns. In addition, moving from one activity to another is difficult for him. We observed that he often resists. You've probably noted how irritable he can become. His communication skills, not only his verbal abilities, are significantly behind where a child of three years should be. Keeping up with typically developing classmates is likely to be a challenge. I have some specific clips from the ADOS that I want to review with you so that you can see how Jacob performs in some of the domains where we have concerns."

Dr. Leonard goes on to review parts of the tape with us, illustrating why Jacob meets the criteria for PDD-NOS, or Pervasive Developmental Disorder-Not Otherwise Specified. The videotape shows me clearly how Jacob's behavior either meets norms for his age or deviates significantly. The good news, Dr. Wong emphasizes, is that intervention with behavioral therapy is often effective, especially with a child like Jacob who wants to please therapists. In fact, Yale is instituting a research program into behavioral methods training for parents. If we're interested in participating and are willing to follow a prescribed program at home, Dr. Wong will help us enroll Jacob.

"I'm still hesitant to give Jacob another label," states Dave. "But it's become clear to me that Rachel and I need to learn a better way to manage his behavior—his irritability. It's affecting family life. We're certainly interested in the research program. I'm just curious about how this diagnosis will affect him in the future. The schools seem to know almost nothing about Klinefelter syndrome, so the personnel don't have a preconceived notion of how Jake will act or perform academically. But will having a diagnosis of autism—even mild autism—lead teachers to expect that he can't interact well socially? Will they expect problematic behavior? Lower achievement in school?"

"We're also concerned about the effects of a label," replies Dr. Wong. "But we don't just label. We write a comprehensive assessment of how ASD manifests itself in a particular child so that the school understands the challenges that need to be addressed. Jake scores as having an IQ of 103, right in the middle of the pack. He's sociable, so he wants to interact with others, unlike what you see in classical autism. But he demonstrates a fair amount of anxiety, so developing social skills to give him confidence is important. It's likely that expressive language will be impacted, both verbal and written, so he may need specialized instruction to help him in these areas."

"Does your evaluation include detailed recommendations for interventions?" I ask. "Can we know specifically what you'll say? We're really doing this only because we think it may provide us with services to address his behavior."

"Absolutely," answers Dr. Leonard. "The key is using Applied Behavior Analysis, or ABA, to make his behavior less reactive. You'll learn not only to recognize situations that can result in a tantrum but also to modify the way that you structure those events. And we'll be recommending that the school initiate the same program and provide similar training for his teacher."

I reach for Dave's hand and give it squeeze. If we can get this to work, maybe family life will be easier for us. We won't have to feel that a screaming session is right around the corner. Dave and I continue the discussion about specific recommendations, and then meet briefly with Dr. Wong and her research assistant about the research program, signing consents and setting up an intake appointment.

It's a relief to have a plan for Jake and to start modifying his more rigid behaviors. We also have the good fortune to be in New York, where the schools provide significant resources for children with disabilities. From the family conference I learned that many states underfund such services so that Jacob's milder level of disability would not even be addressed.

My job for the coming week is completing the applications for the genetic counseling master's programs at Mt. Sinai in Manhattan and Sarah Lawrence in Bronxville. Sarah Lawrence is a much shorter commute than Mt. Sinai, but I'll be pleased to be accepted at either one. First, however, I need to find out if either program is interested in even interviewing me.

I know from conversations with the Attorney General's office that I will be a grand jury witness. The next day, I receive a summons. Although the investigation of Dr. K's fraudulent research activity has been open for weeks, neither Libby nor Dr. K has been indicted yet. Apparently, there are at least five pharmaceutical companies involved in clinical trial grants that were run through their private research corporation rather than through SUNY-Hudson Valley. I'm one of many employees being called to answer questions while the prosecutors try to unscramble all the activities so that they can determine what charges to file.

I'm not interested in the details of their fraud, or in the amount they were paying themselves. I could find out, I'm sure, by phoning my former colleagues. But the greed disgusts me. I'm also more than disappointed at Hudson Valley for being so enamored of Dr. K and his clinical trials machine that they chose to ignore warning signs when promised clinical trials did not transfer. The scandal has given Hudson Valley—and the Department of Psychiatry—a bad name. Of course, Hudson Valley will recover, but right now, it's in crisis.

Dave tells me that I'm certainly not a target of the investigation. But in his ultra-cautious, lawyerly manner, he insists that the grand jury and the AG know I have representation. One of his colleagues, George Maxwell, will serve as my attorney. George makes some inquiries with the AG's office to be certain that the defendants have not tried to finger me as the responsible party. He lets me know what I can expect and tells me not to discuss the case with anyone else.

Ten days later, I dress in a suit and heels, drive to the courthouse, and make my way through the metal detectors. In the seating area outside the courtroom, I recognize one of the research PhDs that Dr. K brought with him to New York from Florida, a young man named Eric Keefe. I ask how he is doing.

"Well, I still have a job. Oh, I forgot. I've been ordered not to talk with you. You're an obstructionist, according to our fearless ex-leader." Eric and I laugh. "You can imagine that the pharmaceutical companies want to salvage what they can of the resources they've already put into these phases of drug development, so we're doing what we can to continue."

"I'm glad that you were able to remain employed, Eric, especially since you relocated here from Florida."

"I know that you worked for a while in one of the other departments," says Eric. "Are you still at the medical center?"

"I could have been," I answer. "But I decided after this experience that I want to change careers. I'm in the process of applying to genetic counseling programs. I'm taking a leap of faith because the competition for admission to these programs is fierce. But I got an MPH from Michigan, and I have other experiences that I hope will help me gain admission. I have to say that one of the things that hurt most, even more than being summarily removed from Psychiatry, was having Libby tell my staff that they couldn't have any contact with me. Karen would defy that order occasionally, but the rest of them were scared and didn't."

The door to the courtroom opens. Alyce walks out with a court officer. She looks momentarily surprised when she sees me, then turns away and walks quickly toward the elevators.

Eric adds, "You know, Libby forbade us to speak with you from the very first. Initially, we were assured that you were a nasty, negative person who never wanted us at Hudson Valley. And we were sworn to report any phone calls or visits you made to the unit. But any time any of us had any contact with you, you were pleasant and cooperative—helpful, even."

I drop my voice. "So, did any of you have any hint of these machinations that landed them in such hot water?"

"Well, some things didn't add up." Eric replies. "The PO box, the fact that for some studies we got everything through Purchasing, while for others, Libby seemed able to buy them directly. Lots of things like that. Did you?"

"Yes, same thing," I say. "Stuff that didn't add up, secretiveness, Libby refusing to let me see any of Dr. K's financial reports, clinical trials that never transferred from Florida. But I guess this is discussing the case, which we can't do."

We talk about graduate school. He got his PhD from Ohio State and continues to be a fan of Buckeye football. Dave and I are great Michigan Wolverines fans. And we talk about our families. Then Eric is called into the grand jury by the officer, who apologizes to me that they are about half an hour behind schedule. I'm somewhat surprised to see my attorney walking up the corridor. I know that he can't go into the jury room with me. He takes a seat and tells me that grand jury witnesses often have their attorneys present outside, should they need to consult them. I wouldn't have known any of this on my own. Dave took really good care of me and made sure that George would be here, just in case.

When my time comes, I find that answering carefully prepared questions for a grand jury is not challenging. I know that I'm being asked to establish a record of facts for the grand jury to consider. Mostly, I identify documents and confirm the chronology of events from Dr. K's recruitment through my termination and on to the day that I took the contracts provided by Karen to the compliance office. Then it's over. The prosecutor thanks me, and the court officer escorts me out.

I brief George that everything went as he said it would and thank him for his support as we walk out to our cars. I know he didn't charge us, as a colleague of Dave's, but he made me feel more secure through this whole process.

On the way home, I reflect on the past three years. Never could I have predicted the direction our family's life would take: the prenatal diagnosis; becoming parents to a special needs toddler; my summary dismissal from Psychiatry; Dave's successful book; Ben's revelation about his sexuality; welcoming Eli into our family; Sarah's marital crisis and our mid-life changes in careers;

and testifying before a grand jury about the chair who changed my career trajectory forever.

I know that these events occur in families. It's called life. But having them so concentrated into just three short years makes it hard to process and explains why I feel as though we've been caught up in a whirlwind of life events. I'm just coping, reacting. I haven't had a chance to sit down and think about where I am in life and where I want to go in my career, in parenting, and in being Dave's wife. Do I want more? How else can I contribute? Clearly, I need to give myself more attention. I have the time to do that but will have to do so on a tight budget.

CHAPTER TWENTY-TWO

∽

NOVEMBER 2005

Jacob is three this week. His birthday coincides with the first night of Hanukkah. For a typically developing kid this would be great, but for Jacob, too much excitement with menorrah lighting and presents and a birthday cake can cause a meltdown. After his autism diagnosis, Building Blocks assigns a board-certified behavior analyst (BCBA) to work with us at home. She arrives twice a week for an hour, usually in the afternoons.

Melissa is a young woman whose career centers on helping families develop more adaptive behavior in their children. In Jacob's case, transitions, such as getting off the bus and coming inside the house or putting on pajamas and getting ready for bed, can result in tantrums. Melissa uses ABA to define troubling behavior and identify concrete events that trigger screaming or tantrums. She helps us to shape a replacement behavior, what we want Jacob to do instead of having a meltdown. When Jacob holds himself together, we reward him. If he melts down, we either ignore him or put him in time out. She helps us change how we interact with Jacob so that he

VIRGINIA ISAACS COVER

doesn't get overwhelmed with too much stimulus or too many choices. Dave and I are learning a new language. We also collect data on his behavior to determine whether our behavior modification strategies are effective for decreasing his outbursts.

We decide that instead of celebrating Jacob's birthday on the first night of Hanukkah, we'll do it several days early. I bring cupcakes to his preschool during the day. We plan to have cake at home and a few presents in the evening. Of course, Adam needs to be in on the plans so that he doesn't alert his brother to the slight shift in days.

This morning, Dave puts Jacob on his minibus while I walk Adam to school. Adam can walk by himself, but I tell him that I want to walk with him to talk about something.

As soon as we head down the steps to the sidewalk, Adam asks me, "Mommy, is this about a secret?"

"Well, it's sort of a secret from Jake," I tell him. "You know how Jake gets when too much excitement happens at once. Sometimes he starts crying, or he lies on the floor and screams. His real birthday is on Saturday, the first night of Hanukkah. But if we have both his birthday and Hanukkah the same night, he might get upset. Then it wouldn't be fun for any of us."

"Can I ask you something, Mommy?"

"Absolutely. What do you want to ask?"

"Does Jakey have a disability?"

"Yes, he does," I answer. "Why do you think he has a disability?"

"Well, when we were at Lake Tahoe with our cousins, I noticed that Noam talked lots more than Jake. And when they were running, Jake looked like he didn't know how to run, and he couldn't keep up with us, even with Noam. We're learning about disability in school. One of the kids in my class wears braces on his legs. His mom came to school to talk about his disability. But the teacher said some people have disabilities that don't show, but they still have them. Is Jakey's disability a secret?"

"No," I assure Adam. "We aren't keeping Jake's disability a secret. He was born with something called an extra chromosome. Chromosomes are tiny messages in your body that tell your body how to talk and walk and grow. He isn't sick, but these extra messages made him slower to talk than other children. Also, it's more difficult for him to run. It makes him super sensitive to noise and excitement, like birthdays and Hanukkah and presents. So, to keep him from having a meltdown, we're going to have his birthday cake and presents tonight instead of his real birthday, which is Saturday. And on Saturday, we can have the first night of Hanukkah. The secret is that he's too young to know his birthday is really on Saturday. You and Daddy and I aren't going to tell him."

"Okay, Mommy. I promise not to tell him. Mommy, I like that you're always home now when I get home. Is that mean man still at your work?"

We're getting close to the school now.

"No. The mean man did bad things. The university made him leave. But I decided not to go back there. I'm taking classes, starting in January, so that I can do a different job."

I give him a big hug. He doesn't want me to walk him all the way to the school door. After all, he's in third grade.

"Bye. Have a great day. See you this afternoon," I call out as he breaks into a run to join some friends.

On Sunday, the day after the first night of Hanukkah, there's another support group meeting in Brooklyn. I wonder if Star will be going, given her discomfort with having openly gay adults present. I phone her, and she tells me that she'll think about it. A few days later, she tells me that she'll go. She wants us to drive with a woman who has an adult son with XXY. We'll meet at our house.

On Sunday morning, Star arrives. Dave lets her in while I gather some mini bagels and spreads to bring as refreshments. A few minutes later, I see a gray-haired woman get out of her car and walk up the stairs to our front door. I open the door and realize that I know her face from the medical center, but I don't know her by name. Star introduces her as Christine Johnson. Christine tells me that she's a ward clerk who floats on all the inpatient units. That's why we have seen each other over the years. We both comment on the small world we live in and head to my van. As we enter the Bronx River Parkway headed toward the city, I tell Christine that I have a little boy who just turned three. Christine tells me that her son, James, is twenty-five. I ask if he lives in the area. Christine hedges.

"Christine," Star says. "We all reveal personal things at these meetings. You can tell Rachel."

Christine takes a deep breath before starting. "He's incarcerated right now in the Westchester County jail. He did some stupid things and was sentenced to one hundred eighty days. But I'm told by his attorney that he's been a model inmate. He'll probably be released early next week. I know that the myth is that males with Klinefelter syndrome are more likely to be criminals. I don't think that's true. I think they're just more likely to get caught and then sign anything they are asked to sign by the police, not realizing they have rights.

"You and Star are so lucky to have gotten the diagnosis when your boys are young. You can get special ed services, counseling, testosterone treatment at adolescence. I always knew something was not right with James."

"How did you know? What did you see that made you think that?" I ask.

"He was late talking. Very sensitive, always crying. He was behind in school from the start, but they passed him along year after year. When I complained that he couldn't read and needed extra resources, they would tell me that he had an IQ over one hundred and just didn't apply himself. They told me they couldn't provide special ed services to someone with a normal IQ. When he started getting C's and D's in junior high, they told me my divorce was the reason for his poor grades. I can tell you that wasn't the reason. My ex-husband and I had an amicable separation, and James spent time as much time with his dad as he did with me. We probably have a better relationship than lots of married couples!"

I tell her as I slow down to pay the bridge toll, "I've heard repeatedly at support groups and on the listservs that when parents and schools aren't aware of the extra X, they come up with all sorts of explanations for why children can't learn, or why they have severe emotional problems. Lots of times, the parents get blamed. Outrageous."

"So, in high school he went to live with his dad," Christine continues. "His dad works construction and had to be out of the house by six in the morning. Although Alan woke him to start getting ready, James went back to sleep. The only reason he made it through his sophomore and part of his junior year was that each morning I drove over, got him up, and dropped him at school before I went to work. But as soon as he was seventeen, he dropped out and went to work at a grocery store. That was fine for five years. Then he was pulled over for drunk driving, pled guilty, and lost his license."

Christine stops. Her voice is catching. She takes a tissue out of her handbag and dabs at her eyes. "That started his downward spiral. He had to take the bus to work, was late too many times, and lost his job. He took another job, but started hanging out with guys who weren't the best characters. They weren't even particularly nice to him, often standing him up on Friday nights. He was working at a liquor warehouse, and he allowed these so-called friends to take top-shelf booze and cases of beer. Lots of it. Apparently, they resold it. He was recorded on video handing it to them. The police tried to get him to name them for leniency, but James didn't want his supposed friends to get mad at him, so he took the rap himself and pled guilty to grand larceny."

"You know," observes Star. "I think these boys—these men—seem to be bullied a lot. I've seen it with Donny, being teased by neighbor kids. He just wants others to like him, and he'll do anything to be able to hang out with them. It scares me that his social skills aren't very strong and that he could do something bad just for acceptance."

"Yes, James was the same way in junior high and high school," says Christine. "He didn't have many friends. He wasn't into sports, and his grades weren't good. I wish I had known more back then. Anyway, back to James' trouble with the law.

"He was put on probation for a year, but he couldn't stay out of trouble. He was working, and he did get his license back. But he needed a car repair and didn't have enough money. He cashed a check for most of the money in his account at a check cashing place. And then twenty minutes later, he went to the bank and withdrew all the money supposedly in his account. The check he wrote was now bad. The check cashing company went after him. When the police interviewed him and asked if he knew that there would be no money when the check reached the bank, he told them he did know. So, he violated his probation and had a third charge. He pleaded guilty to knowingly passing a bad check and got six months."

"Christine," says Star. "One of the things I learned

at the Boston conference is that our guys mature more slowly than other young adults. How much do you think immaturity had to do with his problems?"

"I believe they were completely the result of being immature. He functions like a kid of fourteen. He doesn't really understand what he did—he has no concept of check kiting. And he thinks that wanting others to be his friend is a good reason to allow them to take the liquor. He doesn't understand that letting them take the bottles is the same as stealing.

"Anyway, we had no idea about his Klinefelter syndrome. After he was taken into custody to start his sentence, he had a physical. The doctor noticed that he doesn't have much body hair or much muscle, that his testicles are small, and that he has a history of learning disabilities. That doctor sent his blood work out. God bless that man, because the results came back with Klinefelter syndrome. The doctor called his attorney and said he should be on testosterone. And the attorney—my ex-husband insisted on hiring a private attorney—went to bat for James, got him proper medical treatment in jail, counseling, and even arranged for him to start his GED classes."

I don't know what to say. What an awful story!

"But he'll be out next week?" I ask.

"Yes," replies Christine. "And his attorney also set him up with a vocational program at a church in the Bronx for young ex-offenders. I'm keeping my fingers crossed and praying that he can get a fresh start. I thank his attorney, Ms. Higgins, for all her work with him. He's going to be living with his dad so that he's closer to the train to get to the program each day. And he has a girlfriend who didn't drop him when he was sent to jail."

"Christine, ever since you told me, I've been praying for James every day," says Star. "Looks like the good Lord is looking out for him. Maybe his second arrest was part of God's plan."

I cringe, but Christine just laughs.

"You know, I was brought up in the church and taught to view everything as God's plan, but I think that pediatricians and educators need to know the signs of Klinefelter syndrome. I think it's up to us to make sure other families don't have to go through this nightmare."

Star, changing the subject, asks, "Rachel, did you get another job or are you staying home?"

"For now, I'm staying home, which is a good thing. Jake has also been diagnosed with mild autism, and he's having lots of difficulty with the crying and sensitivity you talked about, Christine. We have an ABA therapist working on it with us, so it helps that I'm home to be as consistent as possible with handling his behavior."

"Donny's the reason that I never went back to work," says Star. "We could use the money, but I want him to adjust to school first. Even once he is in school, I don't want anything full-time. I'm thinking of working as a teacher's aide so that my hours will match his."

"I've decided to change careers," I add. "I'm applying to genetic counseling programs. They're quite competitive, so there are no guarantees. If I get in, I'll start next September. I lost any enthusiasm for medical administration after the whole Psychiatry thing. It was so awful and hurtful. It was about greed and huge sums of money. I'd rather feel I'm making a difference guiding people who have genetic abnormalities."

"Even the genetic counselor didn't have very much information on Klinefelter's," notes Star. "I'm glad you want to go into the profession. Maybe it will help XXY get the attention it needs. The schools haven't heard of it. I spend my life explaining XXY to teachers and to our relatives. Since there are no secrets here, my husband and I are in counseling, and the therapist we see had never heard of it. We're going to therapy because I believe Donny really needs special ed and speech and OT, and my husband thinks I'm babying him. He says Donny just needs a good kick in the rear."

Doesn't sound too supportive to me, but I keep my mouth shut.

I pull out my map to refresh my memory about the location of the church in Brooklyn. Soon, we're pulling into the street where St. Catherine's is located. I don't see any available on-street parking but just ahead of me a car pulls out. I gauge that my minivan will fit into the space, and I successfully manage to parallel park my aging Toyota Previa, a pod-like minivan so ugly that it's cute. We gather our things and walk into the meeting, depositing our donated refreshments on one of the cafeteria tables. Apparently, there are two topics: one on special education for school-age children and another discussion group on "adult issues." Christine heads to the far end of the cafeteria for the adult discussion while Star and I find a seat at the tables and chairs set up for the special education presentation.

An education advocate covers the Individualized Education Plan (IEP) process and 504 accommodations. I can see that there's huge variation in how school districts handle children with extra X and Y chromosomes. It really illustrates that schools aren't at all familiar with these genetic conditions. We learn the advantages of using the "other health impaired" category for kids with extra X or Y chromosomes, because it forces school districts to meet their multiple needs.

When I return home, I put my coat in the closet and walk over to Dave, who is reading the paper. Kissing him, I tell him, "You know, that meeting puts things in perspective. I'm so grateful to be in this school district. Other districts cut services when kids transition into preschool special ed, but we even have at-home ABA consulting. Our district didn't question any of the recommendations made by Building Blocks and Yale. I feel sort of guilty. Sometimes I look around the house at its funky kitchen and pink tile bathrooms, and I start to feel dissatisfied. Then I remember that we're lucky enough to live here. That you make enough money for us to live on for a few years so I can get a second master's degree. We're very, very fortunate."

Dave looks at me and wraps his arms around me. We just feel . . . grateful.

CHAPTER TWENTY-THREE

∾

JANUARY 2006

My free time decreases significantly in the new year. I register for introductory genetics, required for admission to either master's program. Each week there are two lectures and a lab. The lab is in the afternoon from two until five. Dave rearranges his work for that afternoon so he can pick up Jacob and be home for Adam.

I'm the oldest student in the class. Some of my fellow students ask me about myself during the labs. I tell them that I already have an MPH and that I've worked in research and academic administration. My goal now is to return for a master's in genetic counseling. Most of them are pre-med. I study as I always have: methodically. I know that I'm not brilliant, so I make up for it by writing and rewriting my notes, outlining chapters, going to all the lectures.

A letter arrives from Sarah Lawrence inviting me for an interview. I phone the admissions office and choose a date and time that doesn't interfere with classes or childcare. I get a needed haircut. On the morning of my interview, I put on one of my business suits, apply make-up, and wear a pair of high heels. They aren't very comfortable. Why did I put my feet through this discomfort for so many years? I think of Heather with her Birkenstocks. Maybe I'll wear flats; they are more my style.

Bronxville is only seven miles from home; it takes me no more than ten minutes to drive there. The campus is made up of a collection of Tudor mansions in a park-like setting on a curve of the Bronx River. I have experience as a student only at Wisconsin and Michigan, both Midwestern land-grant universities with large, imposing buildings in a combination of university Greek temple and nondescript, modern high-rise styles. It snowed last night, so there's a fresh coating on the campus lawns. Gorgeous. I could get used to this.

Sarah Lawrence is known for its small classes and tutorials. It also has the distinction of being one of the most expensive colleges in the nation. I always dreamed of going to a private liberal arts college. Until my family's financial reversals, I assumed that I would attend a college like Carleton, or Oberlin, or even Sarah Lawrence, but that wasn't a possibility by the time I graduated from high school. I breathe in the atmosphere. Perhaps this year, with the help of student loans and cashing in some of my retirement funds, I'll be here to study. I consult the map sent to me by admissions, locate Slatkin Hall, and find visitor parking. I touch up my hair and lipstick in the rear-view mirror and exit the car.

Entering the building, I follow the sign to the admissions office and open the door. No one is at the reception desk, but someone calls from down the hall, "I'll be right there. I'm back here, putting on some coffee. Please take a seat."

A slim woman with silver hair, a pink sweater set, and pearls enters the office and looks at something on her desk, then up at me. "You must be Rachel Gold. A student guide will be here in a few minutes. Now, I believe that you live nearby. Oh, yes, I see. Scarsdale. We usually have a few older students."

So, I'm now "older." We make small talk. "Yes, I told my eight-year-old that Mommy will be going back to school. He asked me if I'll be packing my lunch each morning or buying."

We're laughing as a young woman enters.

"Rachel? My name is Jessica Stokes. I'm your guide for the interview. We can go back to the conference room."

She leads me down a narrow corridor filled with filing cabinets and stacked boxes and into a small room. She motions toward a chair on one side of the table. I assume that this is the interviewee's chair and sit, placing my briefcase on the chair next to me. Two other women enter the room. I stand and shake hands with them as they introduce themselves as Anne Lomax, the program director, and Aviva Shapiro, the admissions director. I note that both women are also wearing pearls. Maybe a symbol of the program, or of Sarah Lawrence? We all sit down. Anne begins.

"We now do these in-person interviews because genetic counseling has become almost as competitive a program as medicine. But, in many ways, it requires more emphasis on interpersonal relations. You need to assist patients with critical decision-making regarding the most personal and intimate knowledge about the body. We want to make sure that candidates appreciate that in addition to mastering a highly technical discipline, they're aware that they'll be engaged in intense relationships with patients. We'd like to hear more about your background and what interests you about genetic counseling, particularly because this represents a career change for you. You already hold a master's degree in public health. How does genetic counseling fit into your career goals?"

The receptionist pops her head in. "May I get coffee or tea for anyone? Or a glass of water?"

I ask for a glass of water because I expect to be talking much of the morning. Then I tell them about being an undergraduate in economics at the University of Wisconsin. I explain that I took a job with a community mental health center as a worker in their medication compliance program, visiting chronic psychiatric patients living in the community and forming relationships with them. I then began working with public health studies of the clinical outcomes of various mental health initiatives. That's how I became interested in public health and decided to pursue it in grad school at Michigan.

After describing my graduate program, I tell them about our move from Ann Arbor to White Plains.

Without mentioning my removal by the new regime, I let them know that my interest had always been working with individuals and families, not doing administration. And then I tell them about our experience with a prenatal diagnosis. I pause to take a sip of water.

"That must have been terribly stressful," Aviva notes. "I'm assuming that this led you to explore genetic counseling?"

"I've thought this over, many times. Yes, being told that the child I carried has an extra chromosome was the most stressful event of my life—of my husband's life—particularly when we thought that we were testing for Down syndrome or lethal disorders. But the testing found this highly variable genetic condition, Klinefelter syndrome. I was impressed with the library research that our genetic counselor did for us to find the most recent articles and the way she supported us through our decision to continue the pregnancy. I've become fascinated with the genetics of X and Y chromosome variations and their impact on neurodevelopment."

I'd practiced some of these statements before the interview because I anticipated the questions. I didn't, however, anticipate how nervous I would feel answering the questions for real or how dry my mouth would become. I take another sip.

Aviva tells me that one of the advantages of students who have life experience outside of only undergraduate years is that they can appreciate the impact of genetic diagnosis on a family, across the lifespan. We continue our discussion on this theme. We then discuss the curriculum and field placements. Jessica takes me on a tour. I meet several other faculty members for brief chats that I know will be summarized, rating me as a potential student. I'm surprisingly relaxed during the process, as opposed to answering questions directed to me in the conference room. I know that I may have to repeat the interview at Mt. Sinai.

Ben and Eli arrive on the Friday afternoon following my first interview. They have plans with friends on Saturday evening, brunch Sunday morning, and a Broadway play later. They'll have Shabbat dinner with us and walk to shul at Young Israel, near our home, both Friday night and Saturday morning. If we stick with vegetarian food, they're perfectly happy. I've even invested in an inexpensive set of dishes, cutlery, and basic pots and pans to use when they visit. I have to say that this makes hosting Ben far easier.

My parents had a tradition of having all of us place our loose change in our tzedaka box on Friday afternoon before the beginning of Shabbat. My father gave the boys the family tzedaka box, and it now graces the dining room. We include it in our Friday night routine every week. Tonight, Adam puts in two dimes and takes the box over to Ben and Eli.

"It's important to give money to people who are poor," he tells Ben.

"Want money, Mommy," calls Jacob. "Money."

Jacob runs to the kitchen to get some coins from me for the box.

"Yes, it's very important to remember the poor, Adam," says Ben. "This is called a mitzvah. Have you learned about mitzvahs at Hebrew school?"

"I don't know," answers Adam. "I think they are the good things that we do."

Ben and Eli each pull out their wallets and slip dollar bills into the box. Adam and Jacob help me with lighting the Shabbat candles and the prayer for the candles. They say the blessing over the challah (that they helped me to braid and bake) with Ben and Eli. Ben has brought a Havdalah candle and spice box to teach the boys to mark the end of Shabbat at sundown on Saturday. Because the boys love candles, this should be a hit.

At lunch on Saturday, Eli tells us that he's reestablished contact with one of his sisters and his mother. "I had a phone conversation with my mother last month. I spoke initially with my sister, Chana, several months ago. She and I have always been close. She was the first person in my family that I spoke with when I wanted to go on to college and have a secular profession beyond the usual life of our community. She and her family continued to be supportive when I chose Yeshiva and then stayed in Israel for medical school. Her husband's a pharmacist. He managed to get a master's and to continue to work within the community at Maimonides Hospital."

"Chana's been the sibling most willing to live in both worlds, Hasidic and secular?" I ask.

"Yes. She's always worked at least part-time as a social worker, even while raising six children. She's amazing. Stayed within the community, married relatively early, and started having babies, but managed to complete college and graduate school at Touro. They lived with his parents while both completed their programs. She in no way rejected the community. In fact, she's held up by the Belzers as a model wife and mother."

"I've met Chana," Ben tells us. "She's quite successful at melding modern with traditional, as is her husband, Dov. They insist, for instance, that the kids be fluent in English even though they speak Yiddish at home. And that they attend yeshivas and day schools where academics are emphasized so they have the option of college. But go on, Eli."

"When I finally understood that I'm gay, and I'd reconciled with this, I confided in Chana. We discussed how to break the news to my parents and the rest of my siblings. Chana was with me when I told my parents. My father walked out almost immediately. My mother stayed and cried. She didn't understand why or how I could be so sure that this is my orientation or that I believe it's biological. I told her that I would remain discreet about it. After all, having someone in the family who is openly gay can affect the marriage prospects of siblings within Hasidic communities.

"I didn't want to do anything that would hurt my family, so I simply stayed away then. Occasionally I would meet Chana, and she did meet Ben. Six weeks ago, she phoned because my father, who's seventy-five, had a stroke. He had been in poor health even before that, largely confined to the house. I want to see him, but first I need to speak with my mother, if she'll see me."

"I've been thinking a lot about how we might do this," says Ben. "Would it be possible to have Eli meet his sister and mother here, in your house? With none of us around? It's a more comfortable setting than someplace public, like a kosher restaurant, even in Westchester."

"Absolutely," Dave answers. "We'd be happy to help you out with this. Eli, you're family to us. Please give us some possible dates. We'll let you know if we're free and can be away for a few hours to give you the run of the house."

This is the first we have heard that Eli may have some hope of a reconciliation—limited, perhaps, but still some breakthrough—so that he can have some resumption of a relationship with his parents.

Ben moves over on the sofa to sit next to Eli and puts his arm around his partner, silently acknowledging the pain Eli feels in being cut off from his family.

CHAPTER TWENTY-FOUR

FEBRUARY 2006

Karen phones to tell me that Libby and Dr. K have been indicted, charged with multiple counts of conspiracy, fraud, and obstruction of justice. They've been suspended since September. Now, Hudson Valley is moving to fire both. Karen warns me that reporters have already attempted to contact her, and she wants me to know they'll probably try to reach me. I regret not having an unlisted phone number. Not twenty minutes later, the phone rings. Fortunately, I'm out at class later and then have errands to do, so I won't be home for the doorbell ringing. Dave makes a trip to Radio Shack for two phones with Caller ID capability before coming home for the evening.

As I arrive home from the grocery store the next morning, a woman introduces herself as a reporter for the *New York Times* Westchester Edition. She hands me her card. It occurs to me that speaking with a reporter might allow me to comment on the negative influence of pharmaceutical companies at academic medical centers. I tell her that I'm not sure that I want to speak with the media, but I'll consider it. I believe that the sheer quantity of money involved in the Katsaros clinical trials blinded Hudson Valley to irregularities that seemed apparent early in his tenure.

I phone Dave to propose speaking with the *Times* reporter.

"I don't want to do any curbside interviews regarding Dr. K, but I think that there could be some benefit to having a sit down with the Westchester Edition *Times* reporter. The faculty and staff have all been warned that they're not authorized to speak to the media. I'm no longer an employee, so I'm not bound by anything. Our lives were totally upended by Dr. K. I think that if I want to state my opinions, I should be able to."

"You're free to do anything that you want to do," responds Dave. "Only realize that oftentimes the media will misinterpret things and what you meant to say doesn't appear in print. However, the *Times* is more likely to get it right than most other outlets, and this isn't a huge story, anyway. It's sort of regional. If you'd like to, go ahead."

"My concern," I tell him, "Is whether anyone from Sarah Lawrence or Mt. Sinai might see an article buried in a local section and view it negatively. Maybe I should continue to say no. I'm just not sure."

But in the end, I call the reporter and agree to speak with her at our house while the boys are in school. We talk the next day for about an hour. I explain some elements of how clinical trials are normally operated at Hudson Valley and confirm the amount of funding involved in all of

Dr. K's research projects that he committed to transfer to Hudson Valley but that went instead to a nonprofit organization he and Libby set up. Although it was nonprofit, it also paid them handsomely as officers and consultants. I tell her that, although I suspected something was amiss when two-thirds of his clinical trials failed to transfer to Hudson Valley, I had no evidence with which to go to the school's compliance office until I was shown the correspondence that went to my former assistant in error. We also discuss the very large sums of money available through pharmaceutical companies and the effect that money could have on hiring and other decisions.

The reporter then asks, "Are you aware that the dean of medicine has also resigned, effective immediately? Do you believe that he had any knowledge of Dr. Katsaros's private contract arrangements?"

"No, I didn't know. I'm not in regular contact with people from the medical center. As for whether the dean had any prior knowledge or suspicion of Dr. K's fraud, I can't really comment. I suspect he simply decided that he could no longer provide the leadership required, given the extent of the scandal involving his star recruit."

"I've also learned that both Dr. K and Libby are under investigation by the IRS for failure to report and pay taxes," she tells me. "I have to ask you if you harbor any bitterness toward either Dr. K or Hudson Valley for essentially demoting you?"

I need to think for a bit before I answer, but I decide that I no longer view the episode as a career tragedy.

"No, I look at this episode as a blessing in disguise. It made me realize that this sort of administrative position—where I serve at the whim of a department chair—isn't where I want to focus my career. I'm planning a return to graduate school, most likely in genetic counseling."

After she leaves, I phone my old boss, Jim Costa, at NIH. His assistant answers and puts me through to him. We've talked several times since he left for Washington. I know that he's aware of developments with his successor. But given that I may be quoted in the *Times*, I want to tell him myself about the interview.

"Jim, how are you?"

"Good to hear your voice, Rachel. Well, it sounds like justice is being served. I'm told that you and Karen blew the whistle just in time. Michael and that Libby person were in the process of breaking the contract with the county for the ambulatory centers. He also told Phil Slater that he intended to shut down Child Psychiatry except for covering the inpatient unit, because he thought they were a losing program. Better yet, Central Florida has now determined that he and Libby also ran some side clinical trials there. And I learned yesterday that the dean stepped down. Apparently, his idea of gaining world-class status tied to a clinical trials and imaging powerhouse backfired."

"I want to let you know," I tell him. "This morning I spoke with a reporter from the Westchester edition of the *New York Times*. I don't know if this will make it into the national edition, but you may see it. One of my points was that academic medical centers need to acknowledge that pharmaceutical money is enormously powerful. Medical schools need to put controls on these funds and have procedures in place so that faculty members attracted to the large amounts of money involved don't feel free to indulge their greed."

Jim and I speak for a while about Psychiatry. He thinks that although the department's reputation is temporarily sullied by the scandal, in several years few people will remember. He asks about my family, and I about his. I tell him that I have a good feeling about my application to the genetic counseling program at Sarah Lawrence. He assures me that his letter of recommendation was very strong and that both programs should accept me so that I have a choice. Jim's glad that I feel that my career path will be taking a direction more satisfying to me.

The next day, a well-written article appears in the *New York Times* reporting the facts that we discussed. I receive phone calls from other administrators and from Psychiatry faculty, as well as from Lynne Wexler. The article emphasizes my concerns about pharmaceutical firms and their outsized influence. Clearly, speaking with the media was the right thing to do. Dave brings home several copies of the article. We scan it and email PDFs to relatives and friends.

Ben phones that evening to speak with me about the *Times* article. We talk for a bit before he asks to speak with Dave. After Dave hangs up, he tells me about the call.

"They'd like to come next Saturday evening, arriving late. Eli's mother, sister, and brother-in-law would like to meet him at our house next Sunday. The kids have religious school, anyway, so we can give him the use of the house."

When Ben and Eli arrive, I have a late dinner of soup and fresh bread set out for them. I'm folding laundry, but Eli pulls out some materials that he wants me to see, so I pull up a chair at the dining table.

"The Boston area group's been meeting for about ten years," he tells me. "An area of increasing concern is the need to begin speaking more openly about Klinefelter syndrome, as well as XYY and Trisomy X, advocating for greater knowledge about the conditions. I'm helping them with brochures and with developing a continuing medical education program. We have one group member, a dad, who's a partner at a PR firm, and he created these materials for us, donating the design and the printing. He also will dedicate some effort to finding an alternative name for the organization, because it's now branched out to including the other X and Y chromosome conditions."

"Wow!" I tell him. "These look really professional."

I page through the graphics, brochures, and talking point kits. In addition, I see ads mocked up for inclusion in medical journals, and online and mailed marketing. This is exactly what we need.

"And this is all funded and ready to go?" I ask.

"Not exactly," replies Eli. "We're still looking for more funding for the CME program, and for lots of PR. I know that your previous department was pharm-free until the corrupt chair came in. I fear that much of our funding will have to come from pharmaceutical companies, but we'll do all the appropriate disclosures in the program. We're not there yet, but it's a start."

"Is this just for the Boston group or is there any possibility that New York could also use some of these materials?" I page through the brochures and the talking point sheets for lay advocates.

"I've mentioned to our working group that we could engage New York in the effort," says Eli. "That offers another large audience with potential access to additional funders. I have their permission to share this with you. The Boston group leader has spoken with Lisa of KSA, but I think that the national organization is not quite comfortable yet with acknowledging so candidly the sources of stigma."

Dave's entered the room. He asks, "You mean the dubious connection with criminality? The possible increased rate of homosexuality, the association with autism spectrum disorder, and other psychiatric disorders? How does this program approach these issues without scaring parents?"

"We're designing the CME program to cover only what's evidence-based," Eli answers. "And to focus on medical issues and some psychosocial issues. With respect to variations in expected sexual identity or sexual orientation, we don't have any numbers based on research. Only anecdotal observations that higher than expected numbers indicate sexual dysphoria or identify as gay or bisexual. It's very difficult to do that research because it's hard to get valid information. I'm handling the subject the way a urologist would cover any medical condition that I observe."

Looking through them, I observe that the materials are non-sensational, non–values laden. Very well done.

"This is a long-term project," Eli continues. "We'll start with getting it out into the medical community and among educators. We want families to begin feeling more comfortable disclosing the diagnosis to family and close friends. The PR firm can help us with placing well-written and researched articles, but destigmatizing Klinefelter syndrome won't happen overnight."

"Absolutely. I understand, and I agree. But first we need to give everyone permission to stop hiding it," I comment. "May I have these sample kits? I'd like to discuss this with the New York area leaders. I suspect they'll be interested in becoming involved. And I'm certainly interested, to the extent that I have time, in doing my part."

"Rachel," Ben adds. "you'll be in a good position as a genetic counselor."

"But I'm not in a program yet."

"I have every confidence that you will be in a few weeks," adds Eli. "And you'll provide lots of credibility for advocacy as a mom and as a professional."

Now, however, I need to get back to the laundry. Dave takes the folders up to the bedroom that serves as his study so that they don't get lost in the piles of stuff that seem to accumulate. I'll make a point of phoning the New York support leader the next day. Perhaps this issue can go on the agenda for the next meeting.

The next morning, Eli goes to a kosher grocery in Yonkers and returns with bagels, cream cheese, and salads for lunch. He intends to serve the food on paper plates with plastic cutlery. The rest of us leave as a minivan pulls into our street, driving slowly, looking for our address. I can see that the driver has on a black fedora and the two women with him are probably wearing sheitels, or wigs, that cover their hair, as ultra-Orthodox married women do. I know that these are Ben's mother, sister, and brother-in-law.

Adam has religious school and Jacob has his monthly Torah Tots class at the synagogue, so we'll be out for the morning. At the synagogue, we watch while a teacher leads the preschool class in songs and several short prayers. The class then works on some construction paper Ten Commandments "tablets" while teenage assistants help with the scissors, paste, and crayons. Afterward, there are cookies and juice for the children and coffee and bagels for the parents.

"I'm not a child development expert," Ben observes. "but Jacob doesn't seem to have any difficulty keeping up with his peers."

"Intellectually," I tell him. "He functions at a normal level. He has age-appropriate vocabulary, and he understands the rules of grammar as well as any three-year-old would. But his pragmatic speech is still well below where it should be. He has subtle difficulty in many interactions with other kids—getting their attention, pointing to objects that they're both playing with. You know that he's been diagnosed as having autism, although it's mild. You may have noticed that he has repetitive behaviors, like flapping his hands when he's excited."

"You have to hear about this behavior consultant we're using to help us reduce his tantrums," Dave adds. "She's terrific. Completely understands what sets him off and how to modify the way we do things so that we don't push his buttons. It's called Applied Behavior Analysis, or ABA. We need to keep detailed behavior charts, so we know how effective our strategies have been. I can quote the results exactly: Over the past seven weeks, Jake's number of tantrums around dinner and bedtime has decreased by sixty percent."

"Jacob is absolutely making progress," I tell Ben. "We're concerned for his future but optimistic that he's not going to be severely disabled, perhaps because he's had intervention so early in his life."

"That reminds me," adds Ben. "I want to discuss a related estate issue involving Mom. We can talk about it at lunch."

"You're right, Ben. I've been so focused on Jacob's immediate needs that I haven't thought a lot about what his needs may be in the future. It takes extra time for many of these young people to reach maturity and get established in careers. Many aren't able to support themselves until well into their late twenties, or even later. Some remain dependent throughout life."

"Yes, I am quite aware, and that's why I need to talk with you about establishing a supplemental needs trust," Ben replies.

Those were my thoughts, as well, although I didn't know the term for the appropriate trust.

Torah Tots and Hebrew school classes let out. We get into the van and drive Adam to the bowling alley for a friend's birthday party. Dave runs into the bowling alley with Adam, bringing his present for the birthday boy.

Ben calls Eli to ask how the visit is going. Eli tells him that they are all still there and that we should return home to meet them before they leave. I think it must have been a positive meeting if Eli wants to introduce us.

We arrive home in less than ten minutes. When Jacob goes to his toddler class and wears his yarmulke, he's reluctant to remove it afterward. He heads into the house, yarmulke slightly askew, held onto his head with a hair clip. Hearing Eli with his family conversing in Yiddish, Jacob runs into the dining room. I hear exclamations from Eli's family as Eli introduces Jacob.

Ben and I follow. Eli introduces me first, in English, and then Ben does the same in Yiddish. Their greetings are more than cordial. Eli's sister and brother-in-law are overtly friendly while his mother is more guarded. Chana thanks us as Eli brings their coats from the closet.

"We must meet again," Chana says. She looks at Eli with genuine affection. Her husband shakes Eli's hand, then Ben's and Dave's. Eli and his mother speak more in Yiddish, smiling and nodding. This may be reconciliation, but whether his mother will be able to win over Eli's father is uncertain.

After they leave, I give Jacob lunch while Eli debriefs Ben and Dave. Eli then tells us that he wants to go outside to walk off some of the tension from the morning, although he assures us that he will plan to see his family again in Brooklyn. God willing, he tells us, he will be able to see his father.

Dave makes up lunch for us from the generous leftovers of the morning's brunch. I jokingly tell Eli that he's a real Jewish mother, with his order of three times the amount of food than is needed. Jacob occupies himself assembling his Brio train all over the floor, around and under the table and chairs.

"I wanted to talk with you about the estate planning I'm doing with Mom," says Ben. "She needs to structure things so it can bypass probate. One of the areas that I'm familiarizing myself with is special needs planning. I'm not a trusts and estates expert, but I'm developing some knowledge in this area. I know it isn't certain how Jacob will function as a young adult, but if he's delayed in becoming independent, you may want to make it possible to access government benefits, such as SSI or Medicaid."

"Absolutely," states Dave. "From what we're hearing from other parents, it may take some time for him to become self-supporting."

"In almost all states, that assistance is Medicaid waiver-funded," continues Ben. "Eligibility requires keeping any assets in Jacob's own name at less than two thousand dollars. There's also the possibility that he could qualify for some income support through SSI, Supplemental Security Income. That also requires that his assets total less than two thousand dollars. So, while we all hope that Jacob doesn't need any special services, the common wisdom seems to be to hope for the best, but plan for the worst."

Dave and I listen carefully. We'd never really considered any of this, given that our concern right now is that he gains some control over his screaming fits.

Ben continues, "You can put funds aside to pay for education, tutoring, medical care, camp, and other things for Jacob, but they need to go into what's called a supplemental needs trust. That preserves his ability to qualify for these programs. I've done some research, and my recommendation is that you have one set up in New York, rather than Massachusetts. Mom's will is going to set up an educational trust for Adam so that he can't squander his funds on a Ferrari. For Jacob, it should be a supplemental needs trust, which would shelter his assets from disqualifying him for programs he may need."

"I play basketball with two trusts and estates guys," says Dave. "I can check with them. I assume it doesn't need to be funded immediately."

"No," answers Ben. "but keep it third-party, rather than providing the funding to Jacob, and then having to set up a first-party trust. My understanding is that a first-party trust for Medicaid eligibility is much more cumbersome."

Dave asks, "So, the term is 'supplemental needs.' What are the restrictions on expenditures?"

Ben replies, "Trust expenditures can't cover either food or housing. If they do, those expenditures will be considered income, and the SSI monthly award can be reduced up to one-third. 'Supplemental' refers to anything beyond basic room and board."

They continue discussing other provisions for Ellen's will and her plans to sell the Brookline house and look for a condo convenient to the T and shopping.

Eli returns from his walk. He takes off his jacket, gets a cup of coffee, and sits down with us. Ben reaches for his hand.

"So, how are you doing, Eli?" asks Dave. "I know it went well with Chana, but how did it go with your mother?"

"Good, I guess. She'll never accept what she views as a sinful choice, but I think that she may be ready to believe that this isn't a choice. It's who I am. How Hashem, how God, made me. I know that she's as proud of me as any Jewish mother can be. She understands my need to embrace science, medicine, rather than a life of learning, study, and prayer. But she's having a hard time with my sexuality."

We're all silent as we finish lunch. I reflect that I never considered the possibility of having a child with a disability. I also never thought that we would be dealing with supporting a same-sex couple in our family attempting to reconcile their sexuality with ultra-Orthodox Judaism.

"Father knew where Mother was going today. She told him, and he didn't forbid her to see me. I gave her the message that I love and respect him and that I want to make sure we don't wait too long to see each other. I can't be part of the Brooklyn Belzer community, but I think they're impressed that I'm not motivated by money and that I haven't abandoned an observant way of life, that I still pray three times a day, that I'm shomer Shabbat, or I keep the Sabbath, and am driven to perform mitzvahs. I hope that I'll be able to see him in a few weeks."

"Well," I say. "I think you've made extraordinary progress. I expect it may be some time before they can accept Ben, if they ever can. You're okay with that, Ben?"

"The priority is for Eli to be able to see his parents, given his father's poor health," Ben replies. "I'm not sure that I fit into any priority. I don't think it's important for them to accept me; it's much more important for Eli to be able to honor his parents. They don't need to accept me or my role in Eli's life. That may be a bridge too far."

Jacob walks over to his blankie and lies down with his thumb in his mouth.

"That's the sign," I say, going over to him and picking him up. He's tired and puts his head on my shoulder.

"All right, little guy. Let's go upstairs for a nap, okay? Dave, you'll have to pick up Adam at the birthday party in about twenty minutes. Eli, Ben, I usually lie down for a few minutes with Jake now that he's napping in the bottom bunk. I'll see you in a bit. Certainly, before you drive back to Boston."

Sometimes, however, I fall asleep when I lie down with Jacob. By the time that I wake up ninety minutes later, Ben and Eli have left to drive back to Boston. Dave tells me that they asked him not to wake me.

.

CHAPTER TWENTY-FIVE

MARCH 2006

My nephews' school in California is closed for spring break, so Sarah, Oren, and the boys arrive in New York City for the week. On Friday, there's a sleepover at the Museum of Natural History for the older boys and the fathers. Dave and Adam pack sleeping bags and pajamas and take the train into Manhattan to meet them. Planned activities for this night are flashlight tours of the exhibits, a visit to the planetarium, IMAX shows, and sleeping under the model of the blue whale hanging in the Hall of Ocean Life. We had to purchase tickets for our group four months ago because these overnights always sell out.

Sarah and Noam take the train in the opposite direction to Scarsdale for an overnight with Jacob and me. Sarah and I decide to have Chinese food delivered for dinner. We also treat the boys to a *Sesame Street* video before bedtime.

"How many credits are you taking this term? Are you missing classes this week?" I know that Sarah tried a full-time load in the fall term and wound up withdrawing from half her classes.

"Nine," Sarah answers. "It was a mistake to jump into full-time immediately. Oren and the boys expected me to devote myself entirely to their needs, even though I now have college classes. Some things they thought I should do could have been done by our nanny slash housekeeper slash chauffeur with a little bit of advance planning. They all had to get used to that. Camila is a gem, but I had to force the boys to have her run them to soccer or robot-making class."

"I think about this all the time," I tell her while setting out bowls, a pot of green tea, and cups. "Now that I haven't been working at all, I know that my boys, including the big one, are used to my being the point person for everything. The key will be to find a good caregiver and have her start well ahead of the fall term. I've applied to one of the programs for a live-in au pair. Some of our friends have used them successfully."

Sarah helps herself to lo mein and pours tea for both of us. "The week this all came to a head, when I decided to drop two classes, we had a family meeting. I laid down the law about planning ahead of time. On Sunday, they need to outline whatever's required for school and for activities for the next week. We have a big whiteboard now of Camila's duties. Oren enters the activities into a spreadsheet so that the adults all have the same schedule. Camila can bake cupcakes and take them to school. She can register them for whatever and pick up dry cleaning and shirts for Daddy. Mommy doesn't have to do everything."

"In order to get ready for an au pair, we have to do some work on the studio apartment above the garage," I tell Sarah. "It needs paint, carpeting, a new air conditioner, and probably replacement windows. We tested the little kitchenette unit, and it seems to work fine, although I had to give it a thorough cleaning. When we bought the house, we knew that this studio could be used for a live-in if we ever decided to have one. When will you be student teaching?"

"Oh, not until a year from January. I have some credits from Minnesota that I can apply toward the master's, but I still need eighteen more hours after this term. I'm also doing special ed certification and have a practicum in a class of first and second graders where most of the children have autism. I have to say that if Jake has a diagnosis of autism, it's mild compared with what I'm seeing daily. He has more speech at three years than many of them at six or seven."

"It's a spectrum disorder," I answer. "His type is called PDD-NOS. That means he meets many of the criteria, but not all, for a diagnosis of autism. If children with XXY have autism, it's usually mild, not the severe disorder you work with."

I start to tear up, although I try to stop. Sometimes it strikes me so clearly that Dave and I are in the process of accepting that Jacob isn't one of the kids with XXY who escapes learning disabilities or communication and social challenges. And when the realization hits, not often, it brings me to tears. Like now. Sarah sees my face and comes over to my chair. Kneeling, she wraps her arms around me, and I cry. I haven't done this before, and I'm surprised. Maybe it's because seeing Jake and Noam together makes it clear that Jake is delayed, despite the best therapy available anywhere.

"Take your time. Take your time. You and Dave are really dedicated. He's doing as well as he is because of you."

"I've never told anyone this, not even Dave," I say, trying to keep from crying. "But sometimes I wonder if we did the right thing by going ahead with the pregnancy. I expected some speech delay, some learning disability. I just never anticipated the behavioral stuff. Along with everything that happened at work, sometimes it just seemed like too much. Then, when I have those thoughts, I feel so guilty. Wonder what sort of mother I am?"

"Rachel, you're as good a mother as the rest of us. You're doing what you have to do with the hand you're dealt."

We're both quiet for a minute, contemplating the changes in our lives, changes that neither Sarah nor I asked for or wanted. I'm realizing that, although I never would have imagined the disruption and tumult of the last three years, perhaps my life might be richer for it. Is that possible? Is it possible to think that something so awful as having a child with a disability is not so dreadful after all? These thoughts have occurred to me recently. At first, I was surprised, but now, during these moments with Sarah, the feeling is more comfortable, more real.

Sarah stands up and pauses. "I have to admit that occasionally I've wondered if I brought on the affair with my insistence on trying for a girl. Did I subconsciously want to stir things up at home?"

"No, that's ridiculous. The affair was due completely to male assholedness. Is that even a word?" I ask.

We both smile. My tears have dried. I keep telling myself that we're very lucky to have known that he has an extra chromosome before he was born and to live in this state that provides generous funding for early intervention. We are able to afford a house—a modest one to be sure—in Scarsdale, with a terrific school district and a strong special ed program.

I concentrate on twirling my lo mein. "I don't think I've quite processed Ben's recommendation that we create a supplemental needs trust in case Jake needs to access services for adults with disabilities. It occurs to me that acceptance of a developmental disability is a long, incremental process for a parent, one I never thought I'd have to go through."

The *Sesame Street* video is coming to an end. I tell Sarah that we need to start the night-time routine that Jacob's behavior consultant wants us to stick with consistently, to control his evening tantrums. So far, I tell her, adhering to the routine has worked.

Jake knows the videotape routine. He then takes my hand and leads me upstairs. I have him take off his clothes. He runs to put them down the laundry chute, another thing that he loves. He puts on his jammies "by self" then brushes his teeth. I read him *Alexander and the Terrible, Horrible, No Good, Very Bad Day* and *Brown*

Bear, Brown Bear. I arrange his stuffed polar bear and Puff the Magic Dragon, always the same way. I cover him with the quilt Grandma Caroline made for him, then kiss him goodnight and turn off his overhead light, keeping on the Thomas the Tank Engine night light plugged into the wall. No tantrums. No tears. This behavior consultant is a genius!

Back downstairs, I tidy up the kitchen while Sarah gets Noam to bed in the guest room. Sarah and I love Irish coffee so I brew two cups of decaf. We had tea with dinner, saving our alcohol for this treat. As soon as Sarah comes into the kitchen, I pour in some whiskey from a rarely used bottle along with steamed milk. Settled in the living room once again with our mugs, I tell Sarah about the supplemental needs trust.

"I've had difficulty thinking about setting up this trust. Ben's been working with Ellen on her estate planning."

I tell Sarah why we must put any funds for Jacob in a trust so that he can retain eligibility for government programs, should he need them.

"The problem is that it requires us to acknowledge that there's a good chance that Jacob won't become independent and self-supporting at the expected age. We have to admit that he won't follow Adam's developmental trajectory and may have disabilities that continue into adulthood and are lifelong. I've been able to be optimistic and convince myself that he'll probably overcome these delays by elementary school, but they're more pervasive than merely speech delay. I need to be honest with myself."

We silently sip our coffee, cooler now that I've given Sarah the long explanation for why we need to set up the trust.

Sarah comments, "Well, you've been so on top of everything. I think that any disability he has is going to be minimized because you've dealt head-on with his delays. I've learned that a huge problem with parents who have a child with any level of disability is that it's painful to acknowledge developmental delays. Parents so often put off evaluation or intervention. I have to hand it to you and Dave. You haven't engaged in magical thinking that this will all disappear.

"I know genetic counseling is a competitive program. They'd be crazy not to admit you. You have a strong health policy background, and you also know what it's like to live with a genetic disorder where it's difficult to predict what will happen."

"I hope they see that in my application," I say. "I really do, especially when I'm spending so much time on this genetics course. I'll know in a few weeks. I'd take either Sarah Lawrence or Mt. Sinai, but that commute into and out of Manhattan would add an hour each way to my day. Sarah Lawrence is a ten-minute drive.

"Are you noticeably older than other students in your program?" I ask.

"There are several of us," responds Sarah. "The students are mostly younger, but there are a few who burned out of high tech and the insane hours of Silicon Valley. Most of them are women with children who want a career but also a life. But there is one guy. He sold his startup and then said, 'Now that I have money, what I really want to do is teach.'"

Sarah's fancy new cell phone, called a BlackBerry, rings. Sarah and Oren indulge themselves in the latest of technology. (Dave and I no longer share one cell phone, but we have basic phones that can't access the internet or do anything but make phone calls.) It's Oren calling from the museum. Sarah talks with him then with each of the three boys, and finally hands me the phone. I see Dave's face on the screen.

"So, how's the museum?" I ask.

Dave replies, "This is super cool. We're all in pajamas, having a type of scavenger hunt by flashlight through the darkened exhibit halls. You haven't lived until you go into a dark dinosaur hall with twenty-five kids, and they shine their flashlights up at T-rex and start screaming. Now we're having cocoa downstairs. I wonder if I'll get any sleep. Between these Army cots and four overexcited boys, I don't know. Adam wants to talk to you."

"Mommy, can we have a phone like this? Where I can see you? The dinosaurs are so scary at night! Also, the mammoth, and the elephants, and the bugs. Our beds are right by the polar bear and the bloody seal. But they're going to turn off the lights so we don't have to see the blood."

"Great, Adam. I'm so glad you're having a good time. Love you very much. Sleep well. I'll meet you and Daddy when you come back on the train tomorrow morning."

I have no idea how to end this call, so I hand the phone back to Sarah, who punches some buttons.

She asks, "How did you hear about this adventure? It sounds wonderful."

"The museum started doing them last year," I answer. "There was a write-up in the *Times,* and then I saw it again on local news. I thought that it would be a hit for your visit. Apparently, it is."

We talk late into the evening. Sarah tells me that she and Oren are no longer going to counseling. She is slowly getting her trust back, but it will never be the way it was before. Sarah doesn't regret staying in the marriage. She knows now that if it ever happens again, she will tell him to leave. She will have a career and her own life in addition to being Oren Robison's wife.

CHAPTER TWENTY-SIX

APRIL 2006

I'm reviewing for a midterm exam in my study when I hear the mail arrive through the slot in the door. Heading to the front entry, I see one large, thick white envelope. Turning it over, I see Sarah Lawrence as the return address, and I know it's an acceptance. I open it carefully and pull out the papers.

The letter asks for the form to be returned within ten days along with a check for the deposit. I take out my checkbook, write out the deposit, and complete the acceptance form. I should probably also send a letter to Mt. Sinai letting them know that I've been accepted at Sarah Lawrence and that they no longer need to consider me. But first, I call Dave's office. He isn't at his desk, but I leave a voice message for him. He calls later while I am out walking the letters to the post office. I also pick up a half-bottle of champagne to have with dinner and a chocolate cheesecake for a celebratory treat.

This is a late evening for Dave, so I feed the boys first and get them ready for bed. Dave opens the door as Jacob and I are going upstairs. He follows us up and gives me a kiss.

"Jake, Mommy is a very special and smart lady. She's also going to be attending school, like you and Adam do."

To me he says, "I can hardly wait to see the acceptance package. Is it in your study? Let me get the salad done for us; then I'll read to Adam."

We follow our bedtime routine with the two boys. After Adam is tucked in, Dave comes downstairs to the kitchen, kisses me again, and pulls out the champagne. He unscrews the wire, puts a dishtowel over the cork, and pops it over the sink. Then he pours the champagne into the flutes with a flourish.

"For my lovely and smart wife!" he toasts. We clink, and kiss again, and then take our champagne out to the sofa. Sitting there, we discuss the next step, which we conclude should be to redo the studio over the garage for an au pair. Of course, we will need to find the au pair and make sure that the arrangement works before my program starts in late August.

Over the next week, not only do I take my midterm, but I complete the application forms for the au pair. I also hire a contractor to replace the studio windows and the air conditioner, find a painter, and arrange for new carpeting to be installed.

Ben phones to tell us that he and Eli will be driving to Brooklyn to see Eli's father at Chana's home the next Sunday. Ben will drive with him there, but he won't go in to meet the father. They're wondering if it would be possible for them to stay overnight with us afterward. I tell Ben that, unfortunately, my parents will be visiting from Minneapolis that week, so the guest room is occupied.

My parents will be going with me to the Klinefelter support group meeting in Brooklyn on Sunday. Ben may also be interested in attending because an attorney will be discussing the Americans with Disabilities Act and its protections for individuals with XXY. The timing works out perfectly. We arrange to meet Ben at one thirty at the church where the group meets.

Star tells me that she doesn't want to attend the support group meetings anymore because of the openly gay men. She also tells me that she's part of a group of parents, the ones who circulated the petition at the Boston conference, who intend to form their own national organization. They view LGBTQ individuals as having deviant lifestyles. Christine, however, tells me that she wants to attend but needs a ride. I invite her to ride with my parents and me. She also tells me that we'll meet another family at the support group.

"Do you remember Madeline Baptiste, the nurse practitioner who heads infection control?"

"Yes, of course I remember her. We had to meet all those requirements for the ambulatory clinics, and we initially failed because of all the stuff we had stored in cabinets under sinks," I answer. I picture a tall, striking women in a white coat with a clipboard.

"Her son, who's in high school, was diagnosed about three months ago. The family will meet us at the church. That's another strong medical voice to add to our advocates."

Mum and Dad arrive on Thursday to visit White Plains relatives on their own. On Saturday evening, they want to babysit and give us a date night out, which is welcome. The last time that they were at our home, Mum noticed that my briefcase was very worn. In celebration of my admission to Sarah Lawrence, they present me with a beautiful Coach briefcase. I can't go on a placement, Mum tells me, with a briefcase that has one duct-taped handle, even if the tape has been discretely applied.

I show Dad the work on the studio above the garage. He recommends weather stripping the entry door and, finding that the eaves behind the dormers are not insulated, goes to Home Depot for work gloves, several rolls of insulation, and weather stripping, which he will install during the week. Dad can't sit around, especially when there is a handyman project that he could be doing. He also thinks that the plumbing needs some attention, so he buys various parts to upgrade the faucets.

On Sunday, Christine arrives at our house with a cake for the meeting. I joke with her about the flier requesting "healthy" refreshments and then introduce my parents. Before she arrived, I told them about her son and his incarceration for stupid crimes, stealing liquor and passing a bad check. We get into the van and set off.

"Christine, how is James doing? I know that last time he was set to get out early for good behavior. Don't worry, I told Mum and Dad that he had gotten himself in trouble for bad judgment. They know he isn't a bad kid, just very immature."

"He's doing really well," Christine answers. "His attorney referred him to a church-run job training program in the Bronx. He goes there Thursday through Sunday. They have counseling, culinary training, church and Bible study, and a work internship in their catering business. He's living with his father again because it's an easier commute from Yonkers, especially when he has catering jobs in the evening. Fingers crossed that this will take and he won't get into any more scrapes. And the best news is that he has a wonderful girlfriend. I've met her already. Last week, James told her about his Klinefelter syndrome and infertility. And she told him that she loves him anyway and that there are many ways to have children. I'm just so happy and so relieved that he seems to be getting his life in order."

"Wonderful, that's wonderful." I tell her. "I also need to let you know that we'll be meeting my brother-in-law at the support group. He's an attorney, so he's interested in the Americans with Disabilities Act and employment protections. The support group has a speaker on that topic today.

"Also, I don't know if Star told you: Ben is gay, and his partner was a keynote speaker at the conference, a pediatric urologist who has lots of XXY patients in his practice. It was one of the things that upset Star at the last conference. I hadn't told her ahead of time that Ben's partner would be speaking. When I introduced my mother-in-law, I didn't let Star know that Ellen was the mother of the gay brother-in-law. So, when Star began talking about how homosexuality was a choice, Ellen set her straight. I think that Star was embarrassed. She's been unhappy with me since."

"You know," Christine says quietly. "Star has many more problems than just that. Her husband isn't at all accepting of Donny's condition. He mocks the kid for acting what he calls 'girly.' He wants him to be more of a man. The kid is only five. Star's marriage sounds pretty rocky."

"Boy, it's hard enough being the parent of a child with special needs," I say, "without these complications and the pressure to keep it quiet. It drives me nuts. But I have some materials here that may help us move in a more positive direction. They were given to me by Eli, the urologist who's Ben's partner. The Boston group is trying to publicize XXY more widely to try to get rid of the stigma that keeps so many quiet about their diagnosis. I spoke with Julia Spencer—she's the family coordinator for New York—to let her know that if our group wants to be involved, we're welcome to use the materials Boston developed."

Mum hands Christine the tote bag holding the folders.

"By the way, Christine," Mum says. "We're not interested in what goes on in anyone else's bedroom. Rachel's told us that men with XXY may be slightly more likely to identify as gay, and some live as women. We are also aware of the controversy in the Klinefelter community about whether this is a true intersex condition or not."

"Mrs. Zimmerman," starts Christine.

"No, call me Caroline," says Mum.

"Okay, Caroline then. You have just the loveliest accent. Are you Irish?" asks Christine.

"Oh, yes, from Belfast. I married after World War II. War brides, they called us, although we married nearly three years after Victory in Europe Day."

"Ben's a great guy," Dad says. "I'm so sorry that he went through so much suffering, trying to be a good Orthodox Jew. You know, I grew up Orthodox, then I married Rachel's mother who was not Jewish at the time. Best thing I ever did. But I also know about being unwelcome once I violated Judaism's tenet against intermarriage. We also used to all be very negative toward homosexuals. I was until I discovered that I knew several men who were gay. I think many of us were like that."

"Ben's going to be in Brooklyn because his partner, the urologist, has been estranged from his parents for years," I tell Christine. "The partner, Eli, grew up Hasidic, ultra-Orthodox. When he finally told his parents that he was gay, they told him he wasn't welcome in their home anymore. His sister helped him arrange to begin seeing his father and mother again. Eli certainly isn't going to bring his partner, my brother-in-law. So, Ben will hang out with us for a few hours."

"I don't doubt that the New York group is going to want to help with this advocacy project," Christine observes. "I hesitate to say anything about Klinefelter syndrome because I know all the bad press about it. And the hell of it is that we knew nothing about this until James was fully involved in the court system and going to jail.

If James had been diagnosed as a kid, if pediatricians had been aware that he showed all the symptoms, maybe his problems with the law could have been prevented."

I tell Christine that Dad also grew up in White Plains, as did Christine. They talk about White Plains before urban renewal and reminisce about White Plains High School and Battle Hill Junior High, which both attended.

We are in the horrible traffic that can snarl the Cross Bronx Expressway. I sometimes think of having support group meetings in Westchester, but we probably need to continue to meet in a central location so that New York can have one unified group.

Christine introduces another topic. Speaking to my parents, she says, "You know that your daughter's regarded as a hero at the medical center. She blew the whistle on the crooks."

"No," I say quickly. "The hero is Karen, my former assistant. She's the one who saw the correspondence that wasn't supposed to come to her. She recognized that Libby and Dr. K were running clinical trials outside of sponsored programs and making lots of money doing that. She brought the evidence to me, and I took it to the compliance office. Without her brains and her courage—she was taking a chance—I could never have let the authorities know."

"I hear those two were sloppy," says Christine. "Eventually, someone would have turned them in. They certainly thought they were smarter than everyone else."

"That's probably true," I say. "I hear that they ran a similar operation in Florida for almost three years. But now, of course, not only are they in huge trouble with New York State, the IRS is after them. Apparently, they didn't declare much of that income."

"So, if your old department asked you to go back to your job," Mum asks, "would you take the offer? I know you decided to go to graduate school, but my guess was always that you would have stayed at your job if it hadn't become intolerable."

"I hadn't thought of changing careers," I say. "I was busy. I had a baby and a little boy. The baby was having some problems, so career change wasn't on my radar. But once I went through being forced out, I decided that I didn't want to be in a job so dependent on the whim of a department chair. That's when I began to think of other career directions."

"Well, I know a job offer is theoretical," says Dad. "But I would imagine it's going to be quite a financial sacrifice, you not working for two years and paying for a graduate degree at a fancy college. I know that you and Dave have no trouble putting food on the table, but I wish you didn't have to borrow retirement funds to pay tuition."

My parents are financially risk averse. I can't blame them, given the traumatic loss of job Dad suffered in middle age. Dad, however, was the sole breadwinner when that happened. Dave can support us for two years, although we won't be living the affluent Scarsdale lifestyle, or saving for college, or replacing our high mileage cars.

"Dad, we'll be fine. Sarah Lawrence has a one-hundred-dred percent placement rate for its graduates, and genetic counselors are in high demand. Also, genetics really interests me. Quite frankly, the details of the New York State budget process are arcane, not fascinating, and useful nowhere else on earth."

"We're not trying to convince you otherwise, honey," Mom offers. "We're just a little concerned. With Sarah and Oren, of course . . ."

"Look, Mom, I know Sarah and Oren have lots of money. Christine, these are my sister and her husband. He's a high-tech entrepreneur. They're quite comfortable financially. She's going back to finish her teaching degree.

"What Sarah's doing is wise," I continue. "No woman should ever depend completely on a husband for her security. Psychologically, Sarah needs and wants her own career."

Mum and Dad have no idea of the crisis behind Sarah's decision to complete her teaching certification, and they never will learn it from me.

We are finally on the street where the church and school are located.

We're now a large enough support group—almost forty households—that we've been given the church school lunchroom, with tables and benches that fold down from the wall. They must also use this as a gym because it smells slightly of old sneakers. I find Julia and give her the packet of advocacy materials. She tells me that their steering group is quite interested and that she will be asking me to say a few words later. Ben is already at a table and has saved space for us. I introduce him to Christine.

A family walks in, and I recognize Madeline, the nurse practitioner. Both the teenage boy and the father are dressed for golf. While they are signing in, Christine indicates that we should go over to greet them.

"Madeline, how are you? It's surprising what a small world this is," I tell her.

"It's so nice to see you, Rachel," says Madeline. "Christine told me that you'd be here. How are you doing after all the drama? Are you okay? I just can't believe what Dr. K did to you!"

"I am more than fine. In fact, the whole episode convinced me that I want to go back into a clinical specialty. Next September, I'll start in the master's program at Sarah Lawrence for genetic counseling."

A man interrupts us, addressing Madeline, "So sorry, but I want you to know that if your son would like to meet in one of the classrooms with other adolescents, we have a counselor leading a discussion group. What's your name, young man?"

"Aiden."

Madeline says softly to Aiden, "You hoped that you'd meet other boys with XXY. I think this is your opportunity. Why don't you go with them?"

Aiden quietly smiles and leaves with the man to locate the classroom.

"You know, we only found out a few months ago. Rachel, please meet my husband, Wesley. Rachel's the woman at the medical center who discovered the fraud."

"It's so nice to meet you," I say. "No, the fraud was discovered by my former assistant, but you may have heard that Dr. Katsaros had me demoted to keep me from discovering it, at least not right away."

Just then, the group's leader calls for all of us to sit down so that she can start the meeting. The speaker, a disability rights attorney, is interesting, although ADA is not especially applicable to my preschooler. But it's informative as well as disturbing to hear about workplace challenges that adults with Klinefelter syndrome have. Ben is quite engaged in the discussion.

After a Q and A session, Julia, the group leader, rises and speaks about the Boston group and their advocacy project. After our phone conversation, she had contacted the Boston group leader, as well as speaking with the volunteer who created the PR materials. She also discussed the CME program at length with Eli. She asks me to say a few words, which I do, although I am not sure I have anything to add. The reaction of attendees is overwhelmingly positive. And one father, who works in community relations in a large bank, tells us that he can help with fundraising.

I look over at Ben. During the talk, he gets a phone call and leaves the meeting room to speak in the hallway. Seeing Ben return, I stand up and walk over to him to ask if he has a report. He's not smiling.

"It didn't go well," Ben says. "It didn't go at all. After I dropped Eli off at Chana's, they waited for nearly half an hour. And then Eli's mother called to say that they wouldn't be coming. Not that his father would never see him. Just not today. Mr. Rubin's not ready."

"Oh, I am so sorry. How disappointing. Please give Eli my love. I know how much he hoped for this."

Ben nods, pulls out his keys, and turns to leave. I feel bad for him. I quietly tell my parents what happened. The meeting is ending, so I walk back over to Julia and several of the long-time support group members. We didn't really take a refreshment break during the meeting, so while we have drinks and some of the non-healthy refreshments (like Christine's Bundt cake) we continue the discussion about advocacy activities the group can undertake. One parent offers to spearhead this initiative, and five of us volunteer to meet with him. I'm suddenly feeling optimistic, empowered to address the most difficult aspect of Jacob's disability, the feeling that it is something to be hidden.

Madeline walks over and asks, "I know you're also in Scarsdale, not far from our house. Could I drive back with you rather than with Wes and Aiden? I really want to get up to speed on XXY. You and Christine have so much more information than even the pediatricians, particularly on the learning disability issues, like Aiden's dyslexia."

"No problem. We have a minivan, but my parents are also here and riding with us. If that's not a problem, we'll be happy to talk to you about what we know."

Madeline leaves to let her husband know the arrangement for transportation home.

Later, in the car, we discuss all the issues of learning disabilities, slower maturity, and possible lowered self-esteem. Madeline tells us that Aiden has certainly struggled with dyslexia, but that they're grateful, as we are, to be in the Scarsdale school district, which made numerous resources available to their son. Aiden is a quiet boy, but he's not particularly shy. And Madeline thinks that his healthy self-esteem is a product of golf.

"Wesley's the golf pro at the Bonnie Brae Country Club. He took Aiden out on the course from the age of three, and Aiden's on the high school golf team. He's a truly strong player. I'm so thankful to Wes for working with him to develop that talent. It's given Aiden something to be proud of while dealing with his learning challenges.

"The other thing that I'm grateful for is a new male pediatrician who joined the practice we've used since we moved here. We thought that puberty was progressing slowly, even as he got taller and taller. He's now six two, Wes's height. When he went in for his physical, having just turned fourteen, he saw this new doctor. I was asked to leave the room for part of the exam. They were in there for a while, and finally the doctor came out to tell me he had some concerns he wanted to discuss."

"You don't know how lucky you are!" exclaims Christine. "The doctor picked up on possible XXY?"

Madeline continues, "Yes. He told us what he suspected. Could be Klinefelter syndrome or could be some other anomaly that causes failure of puberty to progress. He wanted to send Aiden for genetic testing. Aiden seemed relieved. He'd become more and more reluctant to undress with other boys for gym class and golf. The results came back XXY. We got a referral to an endocrinologist, and he's already started on testosterone."

She tells us about her research to date: she signed up for keyword notifications and has already found the NIH study of boys with XXY. The family will be traveling to Washington, DC, for Aiden's initial evaluation and a brain MRI.

"I'm wondering," Christine asks, "if we could organize a more local support group? For Westchester County. I'd bet we would get attendees who won't drive to Brooklyn."

Madeline frowns, then says, "I think we need to keep the group as large as it is to have any power to help change things about the way Klinefelter syndrome is viewed. And from a personal standpoint, Aiden already deals with being one of only about thirty Black kids in his high school. He's surrounded by people who don't look like him. We try to balance it by attending a Black church in the Bronx and doing other activities where he isn't the only one. I thought it was positive that two other adolescent boys at the support group are also Black."

I add, "But we can all have lunch sometimes. Maybe Star will even come. I have a feeling that she badly needs other moms to talk with about XXY, even if she has a hard time at this point accepting the impact the genetic condition might have on sexuality."

CHAPTER TWENTY-SEVEN

MAY 2006

Monday is my parents' last day in White Plains be-fore they start the drive home. They plan to visit Aunt Margaret and Uncle Bud in Rockford, then spend a night in Beloit. They haven't been back to Beloit for years. It used to be too painful, but now there are few people left that they know. The manufacturing base has suffered with the relocation of factories to areas with lower labor costs, and now the downtown area has many empty storefronts. My guess is that it will be a sad visit.

I'm in the kitchen making appetizers with Mum while Dad, Dave, and the boys play Candy Land. Mind-numb-ing, but one of the few games a young child like Jacob can understand well enough to play. WNYC is on. Listening to "All Things Considered" on National Public Radio is one of Mum and Dad's retirement routines. They sched-ule themselves around being able to catch the program. The phone rings, and I pick it up. It's the acting chair of Psychiatry, appointed when Dr. K was suspended.

"Rachel, it's Phil Slater. How are you?"

"I'm fine," I tell him. "So, how are things in the department? Getting back to normal?"

"Well, I'll get right to the point," he says. "I've just come from a faculty meeting. We were meeting with the new acting dean, Dave Jackson, and with Cameron Ellis. We're struggling to get our clinical program back on track. Our residency program has suffered, our financial records and the budgeting process are in tatters, and we need to bring billing and operations back to the department from Rebecca and her faculty practice dictators. We all agree that you were treated abysmally and want to know if there's any way that we might ask you to return and help us. I'm authorized to tell you that we can offer you a salary that is forty percent higher than your previous salary. And if you want to return to the arrangement where you worked from home one day a week, we can do that."

I'm nearly speechless for a moment.

"Let me take this upstairs. I have a roomful of people here. Mum, could you hold this?" I hand Mum the receiver. "I'll run up to the bedroom to talk. Hang up as soon as I pick up there."

I go upstairs to our bedroom, close the door, and pick up the phone.

"Mum, I have it now. Thanks."

"Dr. Slater, I've been admitted to Sarah Lawrence's graduate program starting in September. It's something I've wanted to do for quite a while."

"That's known around the department," he answers. "We'd even consider having you for a year if you could defer admission. Or even on a part-time basis. My charge is to get Psychiatry into shape for a credible recruitment of a new chair. We do know that you want to move onto other things eventually."

"I need to give this some thought for a day or two," I tell him. "I don't know if any of you understand quite how traumatic my removal from Psychiatry was. I don't know if I would be freaked out walking back in the administrative offices."

"We can certainly provide daily psychotherapy to get you through this," he jokes.

"I need to get back to the kitchen. I have guests right now. Why don't I phone you on Wednesday? I need to discuss the options with my husband. We'll talk then."

"We do need you. You'd be a great help to all of us in recovering from this . . . episode, scandal, whatever. Okay, bye, Rachel."

I hang up and walk downstairs.

"Who called?" asks Dave.

I look at Mum and Dad.

"You know the theoretical you posed, Dad? What would I do if Psychiatry asked me back? Well, they just did. It was the acting chair. The faculty finished a meeting with the acting dean less than an hour ago. The acting chair told me the dean authorized him to ask me to return—at a forty percent increase in salary. And I can telecommute one day per week."

"Wonderful!" Dad cries. "I figured they would eventually come to their senses."

"Dad, I haven't accepted."

I tell Mum and Dad that full-time is off the table. I'd have to defer admission to Sarah Lawrence, and I don't want to do that. I will consider going back part-time, temporarily perhaps, to help get their records and their budget straightened out and rescue their clinical operations, but I don't want to abandon a career move to genetic counseling. Going through the experience of being demoted made me aware that I don't want to stay in a position where that could happen again when a new chair is appointed. Also, I'm not interested in being focused on budgets and human resources for the rest of my career. They aren't intrinsically interesting to me anymore.

"Did you discuss at all working temporarily with them until you start the genetics program in September?" Dave asks. "I think that makes the most sense."

To my parents, he says, "I've lived with Rachel through the last year, and I can understand completely that she doesn't ever want to be in that vulnerable position where a change in chair can suddenly upend your career and your life."

"I'm thinking that I'll propose a part-time, temporary option. But we can talk about this later. Right now, I want to get these kids fed. Dave, would you open the wine? Let me check on the things in the oven."

We return to the subject several times during the evening. Mum and Dad clearly thought that I only turned to genetic counseling because of being removed from Psychiatry. I assure them that if I had wanted to stay at

Hudson Valley, I could have had the job in Neurology. Putting things bluntly, I'm also bored with medical school administration.

It's true that as a genetic counselor, I'll probably never match the salary I was just offered. However, Dave and I have two salaries when I'm working. We have a lifestyle that's modest and probably always will be. I can afford to indulge my desire for a career where the work itself is interesting and personally satisfying.

But I also think about deferring admission to the master's program for a year to work in Psychiatry for eighteen months before leaving. Should I even ask Sarah Lawrence? What would be gained? A little more financial stability. More certainty about what sort of program—mainstream or self-contained special education—Jacob will enter when he is ready for kindergarten. How could things go wrong at home if I'm in a demanding graduate program? Can Dave and I continue to be consistent in providing Jacob's behavioral program? Or will the demands on my time interfere with his progress?

On the other hand, working as a part-time consultant for five months, just until I start at Sarah Lawrence, will give us a financial cushion and perhaps also provide me a sense of closure and erase any bitterness that I still feel when I'm honest with myself. I can recruit a replacement during that time. Dave and I discuss these considerations while getting ready for bed. Then we drop the matter so we can get a decent night's sleep.

On Tuesday morning, Mum and Dad's only reference to my decision is asking me to let them know later in the week what I decide. They walk with Adam to school to say goodbye. After they return, I help them bring their bags to their car. Jacob and I kiss them and wave goodbye as they drive away. The school van picks Jacob up for preschool. I gather my books and drive to my genetics class with the options circulating in my brain. After class, I phone Sarah Lawrence and speak with the admissions director to see if deferring for a year is even possible. It's possible, she tells me, but I'd have to make the request in writing immediately. I haven't decided that this is something I want to do, I tell her, but I'll inform her by noon tomorrow.

All afternoon, I weigh the options and ultimately reject deferring admission. Dave and I decide that I'll offer to consult until mid-August during the hours that the boys are in school or at day camp. It will mean not only working with Karen to keep administrative services operating, but also mentoring Alyce to take on some of the work while a new administrator is recruited. I determine that I can swallow my irritation at Alyce for aligning herself with Libby. I don't care. I also don't care if the department promotes her to the administrative position. I have no investment in Psychiatry anymore. If the department is willing to have me back on this basis, I can help them. If not, they're on their own.

After picking up the boys from their schools, I watch them play animal dominoes in the living room. Adam patiently explains the matching rules to Jacob. Jacob successfully places his matching dominoes on the floor. There's no sign of his disability. They're just two brothers playing a game. I realize now how far he's come in exercising self-regulation and learning to share a game with Adam. I feel totally freed by the decision and completely satisfied with the direction that my life is taking after the tumult of the last three years.

On Wednesday morning, after Dave has left for work and the boys for school, I phone Dr. Slater to give him my decision.

"I really don't want to defer admission, so this is what I can offer. I can work as a part-time consultant for the four months until the program begins. That will allow me to get you far along with recruitment of a new chair. I'll also have time to oversee Karen and Alyce in getting the finances and other records in order. They're both quite competent and knowledgeable."

He pauses. I am sure that he's disappointed I can't commit to more.

Then he answers, "As long as you can start tomorrow. Come in at nine, and we can discuss where we are and what the goals are for your time with us. Looking forward to seeing you."

We exchange some pleasantries and hang up.

The next day, I stop at the parking structure office to purchase a monthly card. I don't have keys to the office anymore, but Karen came in early to unlock. I walk in and she gets up to hug me. The weird thing is that I'll be moving back into my old office. Karen assures me that she's removed the few personal items that Libby brought in. I don't intend to decorate, but I do return with a framed photo of Dave and the boys and my trusty Rolodex, which I still use for contact information.

"Oh, it's so good to have you back!" Karen tells me. "Even if it's just for a few months. I think we're planning a morning coffee party later with some goodies."

"It's so strange to be here," I tell her, "after having been walked out with all my stuff in a cardboard box. Have you found hidden files or anything?"

Karen pulls out some drawers in one of what had been my file cabinet. She points me to some of the file labels that include Libby's handwriting on some and Karen's on others. "The group over in the clinical trials office has all the research information updated, and I've done what I can to make sure we have complete administrative files. You can see that I kept the documents she filed separate. Dr. K was a micromanager, but not very skilled at organization. I took his files and incorporated them here. The personnel stuff he kept in his office is now locked away in the file room. He really wrote some nasty stuff about faculty that I wouldn't want anyone else to see, although Dr. Slater has read through everything."

We walk to the coffee room where there's a big "welcome back" banner someone with graphics skills printed out. I also find plates of cookies and a pan of baklava made by the chief resident! Yummy! I hug several staff before I pour my coffee and update everyone on my plans for the future.

Back in my office, I look around. It all seems so unreal, to be sitting here after so many months. I know that I'll be working here for eighteen weeks. It won't be possible in that time to reverse everything that Dr. K did; I'll have to set priorities with Dr. Slater. Just then, his assistant appears in my door, smiling

"Are we ever happy to see you!" she exclaims. "Dr. Slater would like to meet with you in about ten minutes to draw up plans for getting the department back in shape. We'll also have Karen and Alyce in the meeting. There's a research meeting tomorrow at eleven down in the dean's office."

I spend a few minutes looking through Libby's files, or rather, her additions to my filing system. It appears that I should have little difficulty finding my way around documents. I glance through financial spreadsheets. No surprises there. Karen's left an unused diary opened to May, so I record today's meeting. She knows my preference for writing lists and gave me a pack of legal pads. I take a fresh pad, pick up a pen, and start my listing.

My cellphone buzzes and I see Dave's name. Answering it, I tell him, "This is just so, so surreal. Here I am at my old desk, prepping for a meeting later today to set priorities for reversing the actions of Dr. K and Libby."

"I just called to find out how the morning went," says Dave. "Also, I have the draft of the supplemental needs trust from Nelson. We can go over it tonight and then set up some time to sign it at his office."

I look at the photo of my boys, from Jake to Adam and back. I can't predict the life that either of them will have.

I do know that Dave and I will give them every opportunity to succeed and support them whatever their needs. I no longer view their differences as an issue. They are just my children. I am their mother.

"Honey, you still there?" asks Dave.

"Oh, yes. I was just looking at something and got distracted. My guess is that we could do this next Tuesday if that's convenient. Then I can be back home before Jake's bus comes. I'll be interested to see what the language contains. You'll have to interpret the legalese for me."

We talk about a few housekeeping things before ringing off. I resume looking at the photo of the boys. Acknowledging that Jake may need some extra help toward successful adulthood is just part of our parenting now. I don't see it as a tragedy anymore; it's just something that Dave and I figure into the rest of our lives. Would I wish any other life than the one I have now? I'm excited about starting on the path to a new career. Making Jake a part of our family was no mistake. I realize that I have no regrets.

I open a folder of printouts and other materials that Karen prepared for my first day and start reviewing familiar issues. I smile at how comfortable I am with the direction life has taken me.

ACKNOWLEDGMENTS

∽

Supplemental Needs, like so many novels, was a concept in my head for a number of years before I began sketching a story. Having written the guidebook *Living with Klinefelter Syndrome, Trisomy X and 47,XXY*, I knew that I could write a book that would make a difference in the lives of families and individuals with X and Y chromosome variations. I began also to believe that fiction accurately portraying sex chromosome aneuploidy (SCA) could help to publicize these conditions, particularly Klinefelter syndrome, around which there are harmful myths. I set out to describe the stress that expectant parents encounter when given a prenatal diagnosis of SCA and the impact on a family of a baby who begins to miss developmental milestones.

The early draft of chapters moved with my husband and me from Long Island to retirement near grandchildren who live just outside Washington, DC. Knowing that fiction is a new area for me, I enrolled in classes at the Writer's Center in Bethesda, Maryland, where instructors such as Kathryn Johnson helped me to develop the craft. The novel, however, didn't really begin to take shape until I began the Novel Year workshop, with Diane Zinna. The discipline of meeting every two weeks, submitting work, and writing critiques for each other allowed all of us to make progress. Even the diagnosis of a very early and tiny breast cancer, along with surgery and radiation, didn't stop me from completing initial drafts and a number of revisions.

No writer ever completes a manuscript and successfully publishes a book on her own. I am grateful for the feedback of my writing colleagues, including Bill Willburn, Erika Harrell, and Wendy Bessel Hahn, without whom the novel would be so much less authentic and descriptive. Early readings by members of the X and Y variations community provided valuable comments for addressing this special population. Many thanks to Carol Meerschault, Executive Director of AXYS; Erin Frith, Bill Mulkern, Myra Byrd, and the late Gary Glissman. A number of readers requested to remain anonymous because they have not shared the diagnosis publicly. I am also grateful to my good friends, Susan Firestone and Marge Ort, for reading a draft. My sister and brother, Patti Isaacs and Aaron Isaacs, both authors and more experienced with the world of publishing than I, shared comments and planning tips for success.

The team at Bold Story Press helped give *Supplemental Needs: A Novel* a professional character: Emily Barrosse, Nedah Rose, Julianna Scott Fein, JuLee Brand, and Sue Balcer. Thanks so much for your guidance and your patience with my phone calls and questions during editing and publication.

This novel is a work of fiction. There are some semi-autobiographical elements. But most of the characters and the storyline are completely fictional. The only characters that are based on real people are Caroline and Sam Zimmerman, Rachel's parents. For those fortunate to have known Florence and George Isaacs, you will recognize them and will remember Mom's interest in helping to resettle refugees, provide literacy lessons, and stock food pantries and Dad's drive to improve transportation systems and protest unnecessary wars. They gave me the compassion to understand and welcome those whose development or gender identity or sexuality differs from the norm. I think of them every day and am grateful that I grew up with them as parents.

Finally, to my husband, Al, and my sons, Josh and John, thanks for putting up with my time-consuming advocacy over the last thirty-plus years. It was really important to me to have X and Y chromosome variations accepted simply as developmental and genetic issues, not diagnoses that need to be hidden.

X AND Y CHROMOSOME VARIATION RESOURCES

Over the past thirty years, and especially with the expansion of the internet, support and resources for families and individuals who learn of a diagnosis of sex chromosome aneuploidy (SCA) have increased exponentially. Much of this is due to the advocacy and education organization AXYS, formerly Klinefelter Syndrome and Associates, which was founded in 1989. I had the honor to serve as a Board Member and as a support group leader in the New York Metropolitan area.

AXYS provides a helpline staffed by trained volunteers, as well as educational programs, regular family conferences, and an online library of research papers. The organization transformed diagnosis and treatment options and expanded research initiatives by establishing the AXYS Clinical and Research Consortium (ACRC) in 2015. There are now 17 specialized clinics throughout North America and Europe offering evaluations, state-of-the-art care, and research to benefit this population of children and adults. AXYS resources can be found at www.genetic.org.

Non-invasive prenatal testing has greatly increased the number of children diagnosed with these genetic conditions, giving them the option of earlier intervention and services for developmental and speech delays. At the same time, lack of awareness of the spectrum of symptoms by medical providers continues to prevent timely diagnosis. Healthcare and educational professionals rarely are trained in appropriate management of these common genetic conditions. Advocates for those with SCA continue to fight harmful myths that lead families to hide the diagnosis. More work continues to be needed.

There are two other initiatives that should be acknowledged: the GALAXY Registry and an online community, www.livingwithxxy.org, an organization created by a young man who has XXY. GALAXY is a registry of children and adults who have an SCA confirmed by genetic testing. It will provide longitudinal data regarding comorbid medical diagnoses, psychosocial development, educational attainment, and other important information describing the impact of extra X and Y chromosomes. The registry population can also be accessed for approved research studies.

Virginia (Ginnie) Isaacs Cover
March 6, 2024

ABOUT THE AUTHOR

Virginia (Ginnie) Isaacs Cover grew up in Minnesota. She holds a Master of Social Work from the University of Michigan and has worked throughout her career with children and adults with complex medical conditions and developmental disabilities. She is an advocate for those with disabilities and their families, and she has published a widely read guidebook for those affected by X and Y chromosome variations, *Living with Klinefelter Syndrome, Trisomy X, and 47,XYY*. Turning to fiction, she explores the impact of a prenatal diagnosis on a young family in *Supplemental Needs: A Novel*. Cover and her husband live in the Washington, DC, metro area.

BOOK CLUB QUESTIONS

The novel opens with Rachel and Dave receiving the news that their unborn child has a genetic abnormality. What might your reaction to such news have been? Did you identify with the reactions of Rachel and Dave?

1. Did any part of this book strike a particular emotion with you? What part and what emotion did it make you feel?

2. What were the central themes of this book? Did you have unanswered questions about any aspect of the story?

3. Did you learn anything new from this book about genetics, or disability, or Judaism?

4. With which character(s) did you most closely identify?

5. How do you feel that Rachel's character developed as she navigated both special needs parenting and a career crisis? Were you satisfied with her progression? Did you find anything about her responses to be frustrating?

6. Was there any part of the plot that frustrated you? Was it resolved by the novel's end?

7. Who would you recommend read this book? Why?

8. The Golds live in an affluent Westchester County suburb, but as state university employees, they aren't among the truly well-off and need to keep a close check on their finances. Was this a realistic portrayal?

9. How well is Rachel's and Dave's marriage holding up under the strain of Jacob's challenges and Rachel's demotion?

10. Did any of the story's settings seem particularly vivid to you? Which ones and why?

11. What role do you think Rachel and Dave play in helping Ben and Eli to feel accepted within the family? Does Ben's revealing his sexual identity have any impact on the parents' ability to accept Jacob's genetic condition?

12. Did any parts of the book offend you or make you feel uncomfortable? How did you react to those feelings?

ABOUT BOLD STORY PRESS

Bold Story Press is a curated, woman-owned hybrid publishing company with a mission of publishing well- written stories by women. If your book is chosen for publication, our team of expert editors and designers will work with you to publish a professionally edited and designed book. Every woman has a story to tell. If you have written yours and want to explore publishing with Bold Story Press, contact us at https://boldstorypress.com.

**BOLD
STORY
PRESS**

The Bold Story Press logo, designed by Grace Arsenault, was inspired by the nom de plume, or pen name, a sad necessity at one time for female authors who wanted to publish. The woman's face hidden in the quill is the profile of Virginia Woolf, who, in addition to being an early feminist writer, founded and ran her own publishing company, Hogarth Press.